# VESSELS OF HONOR

# VESSELS OF HONOR

VIRGINIA MYERS

THOMAS NELSON PUBLISHERS
Nashville • Atlanta • London • Vancouver

This is a work of fiction. Saint Polycarp Parish and the people and happenings in it are imaginary. They are not intended to represent any actual persons or any specific parish.



Published in Nashville, Tennessee, by Thomas Nelson, Inc., Publishers, and distributed in Canada by Word Communications, Ltd., Richmond, British Columbia.



**Library of Congress Cataloging-in-Publication Data**

Myers, Virginia, 1918—
Vessels of honor / Virginia Myers.
p. cm.
ISBN 0-7852-8004-9
1. Episcopal Church—United States—Clergy—Fiction. 2. Clergy—United States—Retirement—Fiction. I. Title.
PS3563.Y478V47 1994
813'.54—dc20 94-33184
CIP

Printed in the United States of America

1 2 3 4 5 6 — 00 99 98 97 96 95

## DEDICATION

TO

ELIZABETH HARDESTY

my cousin and friend, who had the good sense to advise me to write this book because I wanted to, whether I had a publisher for it or not. So I started writing it on faith, and before it was finished, I had found the publisher.


## ACKNOWLEDGMENTS

My heartfelt thanks to the following people who helped me with their expertise in writing this book.

Tyler Beatie, Marriage Family Child Counselor
Cathy House, Program Coordinator,
University Street Ministry
Thomas Pirie, Director, University Street Ministry
Peter Torelli, M.D.
The Rev. John Vruwink

If any error remains, it isn't because my advisors didn't have the right answers, it is because I didn't ask the right questions.

# CHAPTER 1

*Man, it is cold.* Mark Bascomb carefully stretched out his thin aching legs inside the dumpster. The church people's singing had wakened him. *It must be Sunday again.* Cautiously, he sat up, pushing aside the smelly trash that surrounded him. He paused, listening to the singing and organ music richly rolling out across the church parking lot to the alley.

*I gotta get outta here.* It was broad daylight now and the church parking lot would be filling up with people leaving the gray stone church. Going home. Probably to eat. His empty stomach ached at the thought and he eased the lid of the dumpster up to peer out, up and down the alley. Sunday was a long way from Tuesday. He better get out and hustle some money today. He wished he could find Henry.

On Tuesday and Friday nights the church people put a sign on their recreation hall door by the alley. It said FOOD PLACE, and street kids could go in for a free hot meal in a warm room. It was okay. No hassle. No preaching. They did it right.

He wondered who was on duty at the gas station on the corner. If it was the guy with the bleached hair, or the heavy guy with the pony tail, he could go into the men's room and relieve himself, wash up, and drink some water. Neither of them would run him off. He lifted the lid of the dumpster and climbed out, slowly, stiffly. *Cold.* And it wasn't even Thanksgiving yet.

Uh-oh, he hadn't been fast enough. Somebody was already

coming out of the church—an old guy in a black overcoat, skinny, with white hair. He was coming slowly toward the alley with his head bent down. Okay then, might as well hit him for some money.

"Got any spare change?" Mark asked without even thinking, he had said it so often. He blinked sudden wetness from his eyes. What a lousy way to live.

Irma Blalock sang with the rest of the choir, her soaring soprano clear and true. How odd that she could sing and sound the same as she always did. *Forty-five years old and pregnant.* The thought crashed into her mind again, along with Roger's stricken, outraged voice. *Good God, Irma. We can't have this child. We've just got the other two into college and I'm busting a gut paying for it. I'm only ten years from retirement.* His voice had skated upward, touching hysteria for a moment. She had ached with pity for him, for herself. It was her fault, all hers. They came together as husband and wife so seldom now that she had been off the pill for weeks. Too busy. Too careless. Then suddenly one night he had reached out to her. She could not have refused him. He was too unhappy. Now this. The hymn ended and she closed her book. Father Dunne was already by the front door to shake hands and beam as the parishioners left. He turned and began the closing words. He had a fine, ringing voice and he knew it.

"Let us now go forth into the world in peace . . ." This was his last Sunday at Saint Polly's. Thanks be to God. He didn't envy his successor, whoever he might be. Parish work was fine for those who had the stomach for it, but he was an educator. Well, he had stuck it out for five years. He should never have taken on parish work, but decent-paying teaching jobs in private schools were hard to find. Now God had granted him a small miracle and he had found a headmastership in a good old Eastern prep school. *Oh, thanks be to God.* Now, downstairs to the rec room where the ladies were giving him a little party-type sendoff. An hour or two at the most and then—*out of here.*

Malcolm Griswold sat silently in the polished wooden chair inside the altar rail, watching the other parishioners leave. Some would go home. Most would stay for the little bash downstairs for Father Dunne. The Vestry had already started their search for his replacement and the word from the bishop's office was that an elderly retired priest was coming to fill in for a few months. *Father, I have sinned . . . I hate my mother. I wish her dead. Yesterday I struck my mother. She didn't come to church today because her face is bruised. Today I read the lesson for I am a licensed lay reader in the Diocese but I wish my mother dead . . . Father, what is happening to me?* Better go downstairs now or people will wonder. "*No, Mom isn't here today, just wasn't feeling up to it. Thanks very much. I'll tell her you asked.*" Maybe he could talk to this fill-in priest, ask him to hear his confession, something, anything.

Natalie Pruitt pushed Peter's wheelchair up to the coffee end of the long table to get coffee for both of them. The rec room was filled with the milling crowd, talking, laughing, grouping and regrouping. She kept her smile fixed as she felt Peter's held-in anger.

"Everything looks so *good*," she said brightly. "What would you like, Pete? One of those brownies?"

"I'd like to go home, if it's not asking too much," and he added under his breath, "now that you have spotted your loverboy."

Her hand was unsteady as she handed him his cup. The coffee slopped over into the saucer. "Oops, sorry. Here, let me wipe it up with this napkin." How had she given herself away? She had tried not to even look at Evan. How had Peter found out? Evan wasn't going to wait forever. She must do something. Soon. She knew by the set of Peter's jaw that they were headed for another interminable quarrel. It would be just like last time.

*Okay, we both know I'm not the man you married. You've made your feelings very clear on that, but you can forget about a divorce. Whatever happened to 'in sickness and in health?' Tell me that, lady.*

*Pete, please. Lucy's crying. She can't stand it when we fight. Just let it rest, will you? I apologize for being a woman with a woman's desires. Where is Lucy? Where'd she go?* Then, when she had finally found their child, *Lucy, I've told you and told you not to crawl into cupboards. You're eleven years old. You know better. You could get locked in and we might never find you. Now stop crying. I'm sorry, baby, Mommie's sorry.*

Mark hesitated by the dumpster. The old guy was actually digging in his pocket. Mark took in the black suit, the backwards collar. *How come the priest had left first?* He usually left after, and out of the rec room door where they all stood around talking and drinking coffee and eating stuff they weren't hungry for. Besides, this wasn't either of the priests he usually saw.

"I'm sorry, it doesn't look as if I have much change," the old priest said, looking at the coins in his palm.

"S'okay," Mark shrugged and turned away. "Thanks, anyhow."

"Were you about to have lunch?" the old guy asked. "I think I'll stop for lunch now myself. Would you care to join me?"

Mark turned back to look at him. A nut case, maybe. What he wished he could tell the old guy was what he really wanted was enough money for one hit of crack. Just enough to keep going. On the other hand, he could get that later, maybe, and if the old guy was offering food, well, he had to eat.

"There's a burger place around the corner," Mark said cautiously. "That be okay?" Havin' lunch with a priest. How 'bout that? He better watch how he talked. No street talk.

"A burger place would do nicely, I think. You lead the way. I'm a stranger here."

"Stranger, huh? Yeah, well. Where you from?" Mark started walking down the alley. His legs felt stiff and creaky. He oughta put on some weight, get fit or something, stuff like that. Just as well to go slow though, considering the old guy wasn't too quick either. "It's just up this way." He'd have to talk the way Mom useda talk. No dirty words. What a pain, just to get a burger.

"I'm from Baltimore. I worked in Maryland most of my life, but after I retired from my last parish I came out here to Seattle."

They walked in silence the rest of the way to McDonalds, which was around the corner, facing the next street. Inside, they went to the counter and got in line.

"What would you like to eat?" the old priest asked.

"Quarter pounder? With cheese? And maybe fries? If that's not too much. And maybe a Coke?"

"No, that isn't too much," the old guy said. "You remind me a bit of my grandson, Timothy. That's why I asked you to lunch."

"No kidding."

"Yes. He's a fair boy like you are. Slender build. About your age, I would guess, if you are fourteen or so."

"That's close enough. My hair's lighter than this when it's clean, you know."

"I'll get our lunch if you want to go to the men's room. Wash up a bit?"

Mark grinned suddenly. "I stink, don't I? It's the dumpster. The restaurant guys, they come and hose it out, but the stink stays. You get our stuff and find a table. I'll make it as quick as I can."

"Okay." The old guy actually smiled a little. "What's your name, by the way?"

Oh, no. He wasn't about to give his name. Do that and the next thing happens is some social worker is trying to get you back to another lousy foster home.

"Mark McGillicuddy, what's yours?"

The old guy smiled again. "John Leffingwell. Father John Leffingwell."

"I already guessed the father part. Back in a minute."

When he came back the old man had found a table by the window and was looking out into the street. The food was arranged neatly. Mark felt a sudden surge of sickness. When was the last time he'd had some food?

"Sorry to be so long," he said, sliding into his seat. For a moment he resisted taking the burger out of its wrapper. Instead he nibbled on a fry. Spit filled his mouth. Food tasted good. "I'm sorry I was so long. But after I washed and stuff I picked up the paper towels off the floor. Some people got no class. Slobs. They just throw stuff around. I gotta policy, see. Whenever I get to use somebody's real john I always leave it neater than I found it. Fair's fair. *Hey,* you got the *big* fries and Coke. That's neat. Thanks a lot."

He began to wolf down the food. Maybe the old guy wouldn't notice that his hands weren't too steady. He'd get steady later. The food tasted terrific. He oughta eat more often. Get healthy. Maybe he wouldn't feel so sick all the time. But that was the lousy crack. Well, he hadda have it. He finished his food and arranged the trash neatly in a pile. The wrappings still smelled terrific of the burger and fries. More spit. He swallowed. "So you retired, huh? You like that, retirement and all?"

"I would have, I think. I had gotten rather tired of . . . what I had been doing." The old guy put down his Big Mac. He was looking out the window but he wasn't seeing anything, like he was way off in the galaxy, some place out there past Jupiter.

Mark sucked noisily through his straw. No more Coke. The sound of it brought the old guy back from outer space. Mark tore his gaze away from the uneaten Big Mac. The old guy had only taken a couple of bites. He was looking kinda funny, like he wasn't feeling too great, white-ish. He took a small bottle out of his pocket and unscrewed the cap. He shook a tiny white pill into his palm and put it into his mouth.

"Whatcha on?"

"I beg your pardon?"

"The pill. What is it?"

"Nitroglycerine. I have a . . . heart problem. Angina. When I feel an attack coming on I can use these."

"You're not going to have a heart attack, are you? You want me to call nine one one?"

The old man smiled. "I don't think so, Mark McGillicuddy. You needn't call yet. The drill is that I can take up to three of these, at five minute intervals. Then if I still don't get better, it would be time to get help. But we needn't worry. It's easing up nicely."

"What a relief. People getting sick kinda scares me. My mom . . ." He stopped himself and added, "You gonna finish your burger?"

"No. I think not."

"Can I have it?"

"Yes. Please help yourself."

Mark smiled. "You're sure polite. That's nice. Real nice." Mom woulda liked this old guy. He talked real classy. Sounded neat. He finished off the burger in seconds. "Thanks a lot."

"You're welcome. Would you like to finish the Coke?" The

priest pushed it across the table and Mark started sipping it. He was feeling real good now. Terrific to be full again.

"You still not feeling too great, right?" he asked.

"Not really. To tell the truth, Mark, I'm having a dread attack." The old man was looking out the window again and Mark quickly brought him back.

"A what?"

"Haven't you ever dreaded something?" The old man's voice sounded far away. Mark bent forward to hear better. "Really dreaded it? Dreaded it so much that it filled you with sickness? That's what people mean when they say 'sick with dread.'"

"Yeah, I guess," Mark said uncertainly. Well, he sure knew what dread was. And like all other stuff, dread came in different sizes. The old guy must be carrying a load of it. He wished he could help since the old guy had bought the food.

"Why you feeling this way? You know? Sometimes you feel in a kinda way and you don't know why. That can really kill ya."

"I do know why, Mark. It is because I couldn't retire just yet. I must work for a while longer. And . . . I'm not sure I can. I'm very tired . . . used up."

The old guy had that right. He sounded used up. He'd never thought of it that way before, but he could hear used up in the old guy's voice.

"Then why you doing it?"

"I must." The old man sighed gently and was quiet for a long time. "You see, someone in my family is very sick. And for the little time he has left I want him to be . . . comfortable. I need the money, you see."

"Man," Mark said softly. "*Dying*. That stinks."

"Yes, it does, rather."

Mark shook his head. "So. How long do you have to work? Forever?"

"No. Just a few months, actually. They are looking for a new priest here at Saint Polycarp's. I'm going to be the priest-in-charge while they look for the right man. Six or seven months, probably." His voice trailed off again.

Mark didn't know quite how to ask it. "Is that gonna be . . . uh . . . long enough? I mean . . ."

"Yes. The man who is dying will only last a few more weeks. So it will be time enough." The old man gave a kind of jerk, as if he had a little earthquake in his head.

"Well, then, when it's . . . over, why don't you just split? Tell 'em where to go. You won't need to work any more."

The priest smiled slightly. "Oh, I couldn't do that. Not if I'd promised to stay until they find someone. It wouldn't be ethical, you understand? It would be like . . . throwing paper towels on the men's room floor. I have a policy of keeping my word."

"Were you working there this morning? In the church? Saint Whatzits?"

"No. I just went to the service to sort of get the feel of it." The old guy was sweating now. His face looked slick in the light from the window.

"So how'd it feel?"

The priest sighed. "Like any other small parish, I suppose. I've served in four. More than forty years."

"Man. Forty years. That could make you tired, all right."

"Saint Polycarp's seems like all the others," he went on. He was looking far away again. "On the surface people gathering together in His Name. Beneath the surface—who knows? All sorts of things. I'm not sure I can help them anymore." Again he was quiet. "I suppose any incoming rector always hopes for a quiet parish, full of gentle, good people . . ." His voice trailed off and he was headed out toward Jupiter again.

"What you see ain't always what you get, right?"

"Right, Mark." The old man really looked sick now. Maybe he should pop some more of the little whites.

"Mark, do you know how to drive a car?"

Talk about changing the subject! "Drive a car! Of *course* I can drive a car. Is the Pope Catholic? *Anybody* can drive a car.

No offense about the Pope thing. It just slipped out." The old guy was sure shaky.

"No offense taken. Anyway, I'm a different kind of Catholic. You're right, what you said a moment ago. I don't feel at all well. I think I need a good rest. I haven't slept for a couple of nights. I'd like to go back to my hotel and sleep. I have to see the bishop tomorrow. I'll pay you five dollars if you will drive me to my hotel. I don't like to drive when I feel this way."

Mark felt his back stiffen. "Okay," he said cautiously, "where's your car?" It was ninety-nine to one that the old guy was being straight with him. Take a chance. Henry wasn't here to ask.

The car was an old blue VW beetle but you could tell someone had handed out plenty of TLC. Clean. Nice. Ran like a dream. Really a *neat* little car.

At the hotel Mark parked carefully where the old guy said to. He was looking sicker and sicker. Mark's hands caressed the steering wheel for a moment before he turned off the engine and handed the keys over. Sort of gray in the face, the old man was.

"Can you make it okay, Father? I can come with you if you want." Man. That was the last thing he should do, offer to go up to the old guy's room. On the other hand, the old guy looked as if he couldn't wrestle a flea, much less do anything else. He couldn't ask Henry. Henry wasn't there.

"Thank you, if you would be so kind." The old man pushed at the door handle, but Mark had to reach over and open it for him. *If you could be so kind.* Now that was polite. The old guy had class. Give him that.

There was a gagging sound. "You gonna throw up?" Mark asked in alarm.

It took Father Leffingwell a moment to answer. "I'm afraid so, but maybe we can make it to my room first. Shall we try?"

Of course they had to wait forever for the elevator, and the old guy was shaking now. And of course his room was on top of the hotel, but they did make it. Mark had to unlock the door. Once inside the old man staggered toward the bathroom, reaching into his pocket.

"Here, here's my billfold. Take five dollars," he gasped, tossing it over as he went in and shut the bathroom door. Mark winced at the deep retching noises. Sounded like the old guy's guts being torn out. He looked at the wallet in his hand. Man, the guy needs a keeper! You didn't just hand over your wallet and say, "Take five dollars." He could be out of here with every cent the old guy had. Wow. Except it wasn't his policy to rip off a guy who had paid for his eats. Besides, this wasn't exactly Executive Suites, so the old fool probably didn't have a whole lot. Would Henry *believe* this guy?

Finally, there was the sound of the toilet flushing. Then there was the sound of running water. A little later Father Leffingwell came slowly back into the room.

"Excuse me. I'm going to need to lie down for a while." He sounded weak and tired and very old. Used up.

"Yeah," Mark said. "Look, Father, you don't just hand over . . . Oh, forget it. You feel okay now?"

"Better, thank you. You didn't take your money?" He reached out a thin hand and Mark put the billfold in it. The old priest opened it slowly and took out a five-dollar bill and handed it to Mark. "Thank you, Mark. You've been very helpful." He lay down on the bed.

"Yeah, well."

"Shall I be seeing you again, perhaps? Are you often near the church?"

"I'm there every Tuesday and Friday, anyhow. To eat, you know. They, the church people, feed the street kids on those days."

"Oh, do they? That's very kind."

"So I'll probably be seeing you. And that's my dumpster. To sleep, you know. I mean, unless some bigger guy gets it first."

"I see. Thank you, Mark. The peace of the Lord be always with you."

"Yeah, well."

"The correct response is, 'And also with you.'"

"Okay. And also with you. Look, Father—uh—"

"Leffingwell."

"Right. Leffingwell. You take care, okay? And Father Leffingwell, maybe all the people at Saint Whatzits are nice. Maybe there won't be any underneath things. Maybe you'll really like working there for awhile."

"Maybe so, Mark."

"And if you don't, can't you . . . well, being a priest and all, you kind of have an inside track, sort of, with . . . God? Maybe you could just—uh—dump on Him? Maybe He could just, well, toughen you up, you know. So you could cut it okay. Could He do that? Toughen you up?"

"He has before." The old guy sounded thoughtful. "I've had my share of . . . bad times. And somehow I muddled through all right."

"Well, then."

The old man turned his head on the pillow and smiled. "Mark, I believe you are counseling me. Have you ever thought of becoming a priest yourself?"

"Oh, come on. Get real." Mark could feel his face warming. "I'm just talking basic brains here. You're a priest, pray a prayer."

"What an excellent idea. Thank you. I'll do that."

Mark went to the door and turned the knob. "Hey, Father Leffingwell, you know back at McDonalds when I said my name was McGillicuddy? That was a gag. It's not. It's Bascomb. With a *B* on both ends."

"Bascomb with a *B* on both ends. I'll remember that. The peace of the Lord be always with you, Mark Bascomb."

"Yeah. I mean, and also with you, right? I'll see ya."

Father Leffingwell lay on the bed thinking about the thin boy with the dirty blond hair and wary blue eyes. *And that's*

*my dumpster, to sleep, you know.* Dear God, suffer the little children. And what would Mark do with the five dollars? Buy crack, probably. That seemed to be the drug of choice these days with the young. Please, God, let Mark be a survivor. Not like Philip.

Unprepared for the sudden onslaught of grief, he started to cry. He sat up on the side of the bed and reached for the box of tissues on the bedside table. *My son, my son.* When the frenzy had passed, he sat for long minutes holding the wet balled-up tissues in his hands. There was an interval of blankness, during which he felt nothing, thought nothing. He did that rather often now. Fatigue? Very likely. Defeat? Oh, indeed yes.

What was his grandson, Timothy, doing now? He would be fourteen. Five years ago Serena had asked him not to send any more letters or gifts. Her anger and bitterness at Philip was unabated. She had married again. They were a family and Timothy was part of it. Best to forget the past. Serena, the lioness, protecting her cub. Losing contact with his grandson was one more blow, but he honored her wishes.

He'd better get some sleep this afternoon and tonight. He had to see the bishop tomorrow. His appointment was for eleven-thirty, which was too bad. It would probably run into the lunch hour and the bishop would invite him to lunch, thinking he was conferring an honor. Could one say to one's new bishop, "I really don't want to go to lunch with you. I think you are a fool. I think the whole House of Bishops is a trouble of fools. You are one of the spoilers." No, one couldn't say that to one's bishop. Not if one needed the job. He pushed aside the thought because it would lead his tired mind back to Philip. Thank God, Martha was long dead. She couldn't have stood this.

Think about the boy, Mark. What in the world had he said to the child to prompt him to offer advice on prayer? Perhaps it was the shock of learning about Philip. He was still in shock. He should have recognized it. He always had in his parishioners. That, and no sleep for two nights. He shouldn't have gone to the service this morning. He would learn about Saint Polycarp's in due course. He had pushed himself past his own breaking point, which he had always advised against in his counseling sessions.

"Pause," he would say. "Get some rest. If you exhaust yourself you won't be able to function." Good advice, Father Leffingwell, why don't you take it yourself?

Then he would bring out his handy old bromide with which he strengthened and reinforced all the bent and broken reeds in his care. "You are doing so many things right," he would say gently. Whether they were or weren't, it made them feel better, helped them to keep on keeping on. And sometimes, just the keeping on was part of the beginning of the cure.

Was there anything *he* had done right? Anything at all? Yes. Taking this last job was right. And why is that, Father Leffingwell? *Because it will keep Philip comfortable.* He was astonished at the savagery of this thought. Somehow he would stick it out, do the job. It was his last little gift to Philip. And how will you manage that, Father Leffingwell? Well, we're talking basic brains here. If you are an old man with a big job to do and you are exhausted, you will get some rest. First things first. One foot in front of the other.

He rose from the bed and dropped the damp tissues into the trash basket. He called the desk for a wakeup call the next morning at eight. He undressed and put on his pajamas. Then he carefully hung up his worn black suit in the closet. It would never do to wait upon the Right Reverend Bishop in a crumpled suit. Then he took one of the sleeping pills he should have taken the night before. Then he turned down the bed so it would be ready when sleep began to touch the edges of his mind. Then he sat down in a chair and tried to compose his thoughts.

He would need all the help God could give him to get through this. God had never failed him before. He began to pray.

# CHAPTER 2

Amelia Crawford, the bishop's secretary, a spare woman of a certain age, tapped on his office door and then went inside.

"He's here, Dick."

The bishop sighed and put down the microphone. He was dictating correspondence and was dressed in his customary in-office work outfit, faded jeans and a turtleneck top. It was a new top, though, rust colored. She had stopped hinting long ago that short beefy men didn't look good in turtlenecks. He wasn't even wearing his rug today and his bald spot in front had a nice shine to it. It appeared he wasn't making much effort for this old priest, Father Leffingwell.

"What's he like, Meeley?" It was a game they played, as Amelia's sizing-up-the-visitor skills were excellent. The bishop grinned. "In twenty-five words or less, please."

Amelia grinned back. Dick did have very nice teeth. "The primary word here would be *dignity*, I think. Very old school tie: he didn't sit down until I invited him to. Bit over average height, but thin. Silvery-white hair. Nice eyes, light blue or gray. Classic patrician features. Genteel poverty. Have I used up my twenty-five words yet?"

The bishop laughed. "Genteel poverty is new. Would you amplify that, please?"

"It means a bit shabby but meticulously groomed. Oh, yes, near-military bearing, and that's bearing, not posture. Like I said, dignity. Everyone's idea of the village vicar. I doubt if anyone has ever called him 'Johnny.'"

"Oh dear, I was afraid of this. The good guys at Saint Polly's aren't going to like this at all. Calvin Dunne was such a clever chameleon he could fit in anywhere. But . . . I have no choice. Send him in." He sighed deeply.

Amelia pulled a sympathetic face. Poor Dickie. He was on the spot. His father had called to tell him that an old friend was in Seattle and needed to work for a while longer, and when Daddy said "Jump," Dickie jumped. Daddy, unlike Father Genteel Poverty, had not been a parish priest all his life. He had taught in a posh prep school in the East, which would not have made him rich, but he had also written a baker's dozen of superlatively good textbooks which he kept revised and up-to-date. Daddy had amassed a tidy sum from royalties which Dickie wished to inherit. And Daddy, no dummy, knew how to use his negotiating position. In church circles, having a bishop for a son was an asset not to be wasted.

As John Leffingwell entered the office, the bishop bounced to his feet and held out his thick stubby hand. There was no bishop's ring, which wasn't surprising, nor was the casual mode of dress, nor the politically correct posters which adorned the office walls. Richard Jackson had sent him clippings over the years about his son's activities. He recognized the broad, attractive smile now. He'd seen it in a number of grainy news photos as Dick marched, protested, and waved placards on behalf of the latest trendy cause. He had always considered Dick Jackson the epitome of the term—used by other denominations—"flaky Episcopalian."

"I'm so glad to meet you at last," the bishop said with great heartiness as they shook hands. "I feel I've known you all my life—Dad mentions you so often. And you must call me Dick."

"Thank you. I'm John. Yes, your father and I went through seminary together. We were ordained the same day."

"Sit down then and we'll get acquainted while we go over the Saint Polly business."

A fragment of one of Richard's letters came to Father Leffingwell's mind.

*I didn't mean to imply I approve of Dick's mindset. I don't. But it's his life. Dick is ambitious and we both know there is no possibility of advancement in our church today without being part of the in-group, the liberal cabal. Not for the likes of you and me, John. And they are making such a hash of it. I've heard the term "post-Christian era" five times in the last month . . .*

"I think it's great that you two have kept in touch all these years, you in parish work and Dad in teaching." The bishop's voice was loud. Perhaps he was one of those who had a tendency to raise his voice when speaking to anyone over fifty.

"We managed pretty well. We're both good letter writers. That helped. And sometimes we attended general conventions at the same time. I appreciate your finding me temporary work here."

Bishop Jackson made a dismissive gesture. "No problem. It worked out well for us too." He paused slightly and Father Leffingwell braced himself. It was difficult when people mentioned Philip, but they all felt they had to. "I was so sorry to hear about your son."

"Thank you."

"Were you able to get him into the AIDS hospice?"

"Yes, I was. His insurance had run out for hospitalization and he really isn't up to managing by himself anymore. The social worker at the hospital was very helpful. The hospice is less expensive than the hospital."

"Will you be able to manage all right?"

"Yes, thank you. I have my pension, and a bit put by. That, and my salary from Saint Polycarp's should cover it." Then he added to change the subject. "I'm having trouble identifying

Saint Polycarp. I'm sure this is the only Episcopal church in the western world with that name. My books are all in storage in Baltimore so I haven't looked it up. I have a slight recollection that he's an obscure eastern saint. The city of Smyrna comes to mind."

"Right on target," the bishop said. "He was one of the early martyrs. The Romans were having one of their famous circuses, using Christians for the entertainment. That was in the amphitheater in Smyrna."

"Which Caesar was that? Which reign?"

"You got me. I don't know, but it was February 23, A.D. 156. The program for the day called for Christians to recant. Some did. Some didn't. Polycarp didn't. So they burned him at the stake. He was pretty old at the time, in his eighties, I think. And don't mistake me for a scholar. I just boned up on it when I went through the Saint Polly's file before you came."

"Can't help but wonder why they chose that saint for their church's name," Father Leffingwell murmured.

The bishop laughed. "They didn't. That was the whim of the wealthy man who donated the land on which to build the church. That was about sixty years ago, give or take. He was an atheist married to a very religious woman. His name was Clyde Gibson. I understand his daughter, Claire Gibson, is still a parishioner there. Spinster. Loads of money. Rules the Altar Guild with an iron hand. You'll meet her."

The bishop shuffled through papers on his desk and extracted from the pile a sheet from a yellow legal pad. "Cal Dunne, your predecessor, was in and gave me the latest rundown on staff there. I think you'll have plenty of backup. You have a young associate priest, Andrew Cullen. Now I'd appreciate it if you don't ask too much of him. He's a good celebrant and a rather good preacher, but his heart and soul are in his street ministry. This takes an enormous amount of his time, so go easy on him if you can.

"You have a deacon, Kimberly Fletcher, who can take most of the classes, confirmation instruction, and I think she looks after the Sunday school curriculum too. I will be ordaining her into the priesthood later this year. She is hoping to get the place at Saint Polycarp's, I think, but there's still a lot of resistance with some of the congregation to a woman priest.

"There is a secretary, Gloria Mason, but she works rather short hours, I believe—ten to three—but there is a good solid volunteer group at Saint Polly's to fill the gaps, mostly older women.

"And you have a sexton named Newton Crail working part-time. I think that's about it. There are slightly fewer than two hundred communicants at Saint Polly's now. People fall away."

"Not unique to Saint Polycarp's," Father Leffingwell couldn't resist saying. "The church has been losing membership for the last thirty years." Bite your tongue, old man. This well-meaning simpleton is giving you a job.

The bishop ignored his comment. "Oh, one other thing. Saint Polly's is one of the few congregations that has held on to the rectory. The vestry has been fighting for years about whether or not to sell it and simply offer the priest a housing allowance."

"That's usually preferable," Father Leffingwell commented.

"Yes, the good church ladies from time immemorial have considered the rectory part of the church. If the priest's family can arrange its own housing they get a lot more privacy. Anyhow, since it's a city church the rectory is miles from the church. It's eight rooms and, I believe, in fairly good condition. The neighborhood has run down, sorry to say. And the furnishings will be a mishmash of early rummage sale."

"Shall I be living there?" asked Father Leffingwell in surprise.

"They'd like you to. They don't want to leave it empty. And it would be an extra freebie for you, John, in addition to your stipend, if you don't mind."

"Not at all. I'd appreciate it. Is it ready now?"

"Yes, Mrs. Dunne moved their things out a couple of weeks before Cal left. And Amelia said that the church ladies have put back all the old furniture that Mrs. Dunne didn't use. Incidentally, your senior warden is Sarah Burris. She took care of it all. Cradle Episcopalian—been there forever. Real take-charge lady. If you need parish information, she's your source. And I think that about wraps it up, John."

"Thank you. That's a very thorough review." He reached out to take the brown envelope and yellow sheet the bishop held out to him.

"Addresses. Keys to the rectory. Church keys you'll get from the secretary. I understand you can start now?"

"Yes, of course."

"One other thing." For the first time the bishop seemed hesitant.

"What is it?"

"I'm going to run this past you and you can say yes or no as you wish. I wanted to invite you to lunch with me today, but I'm scheduled for a working lunch. I've been dialoguing very productively with the city's gay community and we're meeting again today. They are helping me with the church's study of human sexuality. Would you, or would you not, care to join us?"

A quick image of Philip's emaciated body and burning eyes came and went in his mind. "I would not, but thank you for the thought," he said steadily. He tried to push the image away. Think about something else, anything else. *My son, my son.*

The bishop stood up and spoke with fervent sincerity. "Now, listen, if you have *any* questions, *any* time at all, about *anything* at all, you give me a call. I am *always* available to my priests. We must keep communication lines open at all times."

Father Leffingwell rose. "That's very wise. Thank you. I'll be on my way now."

In the outer office he said a polite good-bye to the secretary. Smiling, she picked up a sheaf of papers and went into the bishop's office. As he left he could hear them laughing, sharing a joke. He wondered if he was it.

Downstairs in the building's garage, Father Leffingwell

unlocked the door of the old blue VW bug. Philip had said the car would last forever, and it was certainly going to outlast both of them. Philip had bought it secondhand in his third year of high school. A bright boy, Philip had always had several after-school jobs going and still managed to keep up his grade level. One of his small jobs had been tutoring the members of the football team to keep their grades up to passing. He could see the players now, big, raw, beefy boys entering manhood, hunkered around the rectory dining room table. He and Martha had marveled at Philip's patience. A gentle, thoughtful boy, Philip was never unkind to even the dullest and laziest. And somehow, he had pulled the whole team through.

He and Philip had shared a passion for motors and all things mechanical; together they had kept the bug in perfect running condition. He still did.

The rectory, when he reached it with his scanty luggage, was a squarish, one-story house of grimy fieldstone. It looked as strong as a fortress. It had a wide front porch with squat stone columns supporting the overhanging roof. The broad, heavy front door had been varnished many times. It contained an oval window of thick beveled glass with an etching of flowers around the edge. Martha would have said, "They don't make doors like this any more."

Inside it was dim and pleasant. Large square rooms with flat beamed ceilings. Sash windows. Lots of old-fashioned fringed rugs, some so worn it was difficult to see the whole pattern. The four bedrooms contained a mix-and-match of furniture. Why in the world had the ladies furnished all four bedrooms for him? And the ladies must certainly have had some help moving the massive sideboard into the dining room. The kitchen was huge, with a large, round oak table in the center. The cupboards had been painted so much some of the latches didn't catch. There was even an old-fashioned cooler with slatted shelves. Martha would have loved the ancient Wedgewood range with iron lift-off burner lids and a side trash incinerator. There was even a priest's study, the walls lined with empty bookshelves. He liked the living room best, with its two unmatched sofas and large easy chairs. In front of the fieldstone fireplace there were two aged rockers. Years and years and years ago someone had made seat and back pads for them of flowered fabric in warm autumnal shades. He tried to see the pattern without much success, a dim rose here, a bird's wing there. There was a feeling of sanctuary in the old-fashioned worn comfort of it.

There came a sound of jangling ringing. Was it the doorbell or the telephone? He had seen several phones. Going into the entry hall, he saw a shadow on the oval glass and went to open the door.

"Father Leffingwell? I'm Sarah Burris, one of the flock. I wasn't sure you'd have time to get in any food supplies so I got a few things for the fridge—courtesy of the ladies' discretionary fund." She was a short, trim woman with warm brown eyes and flyaway salt-and-pepper hair.

"How very kind of you. Come in." He stepped back and took the bag of groceries she handed over.

In the kitchen he watched as Mrs. Burris briskly put away her purchases. He tried to remember a little verse Martha had written about church women. Martha, always his ideal of the perfect preacher's wife, had lived life with humor and optimism. She'd been clever with words and her bits of nonsense doggerel always had a distinct rhythm, a definite beat. He strove to recall but couldn't find the opening line.

*Dah duh-da duh-da duh-da*
*Leave you in the lurch.*
*Nev-er under est-im-ate*
*The lay-dees of the church.*

He had kept a notebook of Martha's little verses, but it was stored back in Baltimore with the books, notes, old sermons, and all the other detritus of an aging parson's life.

"I must apologize for the dishes," Mrs. Burris was saying. "Something happened to the set we had before Father Dunne came, and went. They were rather nice, the one decent thing we had for the rectory, but they've just disappeared. We've filled in with some of that heavy white crockery stuff, pot-luck-supper kind. I hope that will do."

"Very nicely, I'm sure. I probably wouldn't have noticed. I'm only your visiting temp, anyway. I'll be long gone in a few months."

"There!" She shut the door of the ancient refrigerator. "At least you are set for a couple of days, until you get time to shop a bit. Is there anything else you need? Do you have any questions?"

"I did wonder," he said tentatively, "why you ladies furnished all four bedrooms."

She gave a quick laugh. "That's Claire Gibson. She has a number of absolutes, one of which is this rectory. Her late father donated the land for it as well as the church. She sees it as something of a shrine, not to be changed in any detail. I don't mean that in any derogatory way," she added quickly, color washing up into her face. "Claire's wonderful in her way. I don't know what we'd do without her."

"Of course," Father Leffingwell said kindly. He was familiar with the Claire Gibsons in the parishes.

When Mrs. Burris had gone he felt better for having met her. Not everything was bleak and sad. There was goodness abroad. Decent people were doing kind things. *Hang in there, old man, you'll make it yet.* He should get over to the church. It was well after two o'clock. He made a quick lunch from Mrs. Burris's donation of crackers, cheese, and an apple.

Going to the church he went through the alley, hoping to see the boy, Mark, but Mark wasn't there. A leggy girl in a McDonald's uniform was putting trash into Mark's dumpster.

Gloria Mason, the church secretary, had already gone when he arrived, and a pleasant middle-aged woman volunteer was answering the phone. Andrew Cullen, the associate priest, wasn't there either, but Deacon Kimberly Fletcher was. She went with him into the rector's office. She was an attractive brunette, probably about thirty. She wore a severe gray suit with a clerical collar. She had lovely hazel eyes full of apprehension, resentment, rebellion. Together, they started working out the schedules.

"Did the bishop mention to you that Andy doesn't take many of the services? He's pretty busy with the street ministry to the kids." Her voice was precise and clipped, her hands never quite still.

"Yes, he mentioned it. Will you give me a quick review of the duties, and we'll get down to business."

"Well, we have the two Sunday services at eight and ten o'clock, and once a month an Evening Prayer at five. There's a noon Wednesday Eucharist, mainly for downtown businessmen. We will offer services on both Thanksgiving Day and Christmas Day. And on Christmas Eve we have Lessons and Carols from ten to eleven.

"The city's clergy has a rota for hospital chaplaincy—you end up doing hospitals about five days a month. Then, let me see, we need to work out your office hours for Counseling and Reconciliation—or maybe you still call it Confession. And then, of course, you take the sick calls to give communion to parishioners . . ." Her voice rattled on.

*I can't do this. I'm so tired.* His mind closed against her words for an interval and he didn't hear her. He *must* reserve time for Philip. He had visited Philip this morning at the hospice.

"Do you mind if I come every day, Phil? I don't want to be a nuisance and hover."

Philip's skeletal hand had reached for his. "Oh, please do hover. I've missed you so much. I want to see you, talk to you."

" . . . really should be an Episcopal presence there and then there are the downtown luncheons, Rotary, Lions, and Kiwanis. Once a month for each. Now before Cal Dunne left and took this new job, he had made commitments for . . ." Kimberly Fletcher's relentless voice went on and on.

Philip's voice had been soft and breathy, with no strength behind it. His speech was now filled with pauses and sighs.

"Dad, if you can find a book of those old-fashioned poems I'd like to have it. Remember those rousing ballads? 'The

Highwayman,' 'The Charge of the Light Brigade,' and Poe's 'Bells?' I keep thinking of when I was eleven or twelve. I loved that stuff then . . ."

By sheer force of will he made himself shut Philip out and listen.

". . . and the Vestry meets the second Tuesday of each month at seven in the evening. They're working on next year's budget. Your long experience might be a help there. The Women's Group holds their working-lunch meeting the second Wednesday of each month. You don't attend because it conflicts with the Wednesday noon Eucharist, but you are expected to show up for about half an hour after the service.

"Now I don't know what you're going to do about this next item. There was an ugly upset this morning here in the office. Some of our pro-choice parishioners are deeply offended because the Episcopalians For Life group put up two pro-life posters in the rec room Sunday, clearly visible to everybody during the coffee hour.

"Then you officiate every fourth Monday at the Downtown Business Men's Prayer Breakfast and that starts at seven. And I do hope you can smooth over the ongoing dissention in the Membership Committee about how to recruit. There is also a sharp disagreement about the children's Sunday school curriculum.

"And Cal Dunne was scheduled for a viewer call-in program on 'Religion In America' to be broadcast on the local PBS. You would have some backup there as Rabbi Birnbaum and Monsignor Duncan are also on the panel. Andy says he can't possibly do it . . ."

It took them until six o'clock to work out the schedules. Kimberly Fletcher tried to hide it, but it came through loud and clear that she objected to having a conservative traditional priest foisted upon Saint Polycarp's.

He was glad to get back to the rectory, though it seemed very silent and empty. He turned on the old cabinet television. It took a while to warm up but the picture and sound were good. The weatherman was saying that a cold front was moving down from Alaska. He wasn't surprised. He had felt it outside. Then he noticed with a small spurt of pure joy that someone had laid a fire in the fireplace and he hadn't seen it before. All he had to do was ignite it. He did, and sat down in one of the old rockers to say his evening office. As always the familiar and beautiful words, the feel of the old leather book, had their effect. Somewhere ahead there was order, tranquility, and peace.

For his dinner, he heated some canned soup and drank it in front of the fire from one of the white crockery mugs. He would have to eat more sensibly from here on to keep up his energy. He thought about going to bed but couldn't bring himself to move just yet.

The next thing he knew a jangling bell was ringing and a glance at his watch showed eleven o'clock. Looking out the oval door glass he could discern a shadow. He groped for a porch light switch, found it, and saw a large man, hunched over from the cold. He opened the door.

"Yes?"

"I'm Andy," the man said impatiently, and it took a moment for him to recall the bishop's words, "You have a young Associate Priest, Andrew Cullen."

"Come in. I was sorry to have missed you at the church this afternoon. There's still some fire in the living room. You must be cold."

Andrew Cullen was not fat, just big, with thick, strong legs and massive shoulders. He wore the inevitable ragged jeans, topped by a once-white fisherman's sweater of heavy yarn—the kind tourists bring back from Ireland. No clerical collar. He had a shock of stiff black hair and angry dark eyes. He held his big hands out to the still-burning embers and shivered.

"Would you like some tea?" Father Leffingwell asked. "I think I recall having seen Mrs. Burris put a box of tea bags in the kitchen pantry. I'm a lifelong tea drinker."

"Yes. I would. Thanks." The *thanks* sounded grudging.

"I'm not sure what it is."

"Whatever. Anything. It'll be a change. Like most Seattle-ites, I swill coffee all day."

When Father Leffingwell opened the pantry door he silently blessed Mrs. Burris. Now, somewhere he had seen a gaudy tin tray. In one of the cupboards he found a collection of odd teacups and saucers. In one of the drawers was an infuser. *Ne-ver un-der-esti-mate the la-dies of the church.*

Back in front of the dying fire he and Andrew Cullen drank chamomile in chipped teacups. Some of the man's hostility diminished while they discussed the schedule. Apparently he was reassured at the division of labor.

"I'm sorry you had a rough day," Father Leffingwell said, offering a small olive branch.

"It's this cold front. It's going to last upwards to two or three weeks. I've been working like crazy, arranging some shelter for my street kids. This stuff tastes pretty good."

"Were you successful in arranging for shelters?"

"Partly, I guess. Not enough. But some. And then some of the kids don't like shelters and won't go near them." He sighed.

Father Leffingwell sipped his tea. "I met one of your street kids yesterday. In the alley behind the church."

"*You* did? Who? Did you get a name?"

"Mark—er—McGillicuddy." He wouldn't blow Mark's cover if the boy hadn't told anyone else his real name.

"Yeah. I know the kid." Andrew Cullen smiled and it briefly changed his rugged face. "I think . . . I thought he was going to be salvageable . . ." The smile was gone.

"You don't now?" Father Leffingwell felt a stab of dismay.

"He used to settle for begging. But I think he's started to hustle. That's usually the beginning of the end."

"You mean prostitution?" Father Leffingwell felt a little sick and put his cup down.

"That's right, Padre. There's a whole other world out there." Andrew moved and stretched out his right leg. "I have a fake knee," he explained. "I went to college on a football scholarship and I had a real career choice conflict—pro ball or the priesthood. This injury resolved my problem. And the insurance settlement paid my way through seminary. I'm glad I didn't need to make the decision myself."

Andrew accepted a refill and swirled the liquid around in the cup before drinking.

"Thanks for taking on such a big load." He sounded as if he wanted to add something else but couldn't get it out. The symptoms were clear to the older priest. Young man with a mission, desperate, frantic, shutting out everything else, resenting, blaming.

"Andrew," he said patiently, "don't try to save them all. You can't. Despite your every effort some will be lost. Don't let it tear you to pieces and impair your effectiveness with those who are left."

Andrew finished off his tea and gently placed the cup on its saucer. "Thanks for the counsel, but I'll do my thing and you do yours. You take care of the WASPS and I'll go out in the street and look after the real people, the ones who are hurting."

A flicker of anger crossed Father Leffingwell's mind. "It is your contention then that WASPS do not hurt?" *Bite your tongue, old man. It's only for a few months.*

"I stand corrected. But even you should concede that when WASPS do hurt they do it usually inside decent shelter with full stomachs."

Father Leffingwell had a good answer for that one too but he kept silent. He could sense retreat in Andrew Cullen also, and he made rather a business of putting the cups and saucers back onto the tin tray. Neither man could afford a confrontation. There was work to do.

When he saw Andrew out, a capricious cold wind was pushing fallen leaves this way and that on the wide porch, and great masses of black clouds were moving rapidly across the sky. He closed the door, shivering slightly. He and Andrew Cullen would never be friends, but they could co-exist, each in his own sphere, doing the work. He went back into the living room and was adjusting the fire screen when he thought of Mark Bascomb and the dumpster in the alley. Oh, dear God.

He stood silently for a long moment in the large empty rectory. Four bedrooms. They could divide the blankets. He went to get his overcoat.

The alley was deserted. It was bitterly cold now. Anyone with any sense was inside somewhere. The headlights from the car lit up the dumpster and he got out to rap softly on the metal side.

"Mark? Mark, are you in there?" When there was no answer, he lifted up the lid and peered inside. The metal was icy. Were his gloves back in Baltimore? There seemed to be nothing inside the dumpster but some trash and the odor of rotting food.

"Mark?" he said again uselessly.

He let down the lid and stood in the alley shivering. The wind whipped his hair this way and that. Had he packed his warm Astrakhan hat? Or was that back in Baltimore too? He got into the car and fumbled with the keys, his hands were so cold. He mustn't forget to set his travel alarm. It wouldn't do to be late tomorrow. He mustn't make any mistakes. He had to hang on for Philip's sake. He went back to the rectory, silently praying for Mark Bascomb with a *B* on both ends. And for Philip.

# Chapter 3

The warm knit-lined gloves and the Astrakhan hat were in the bottom of the larger suitcase. Father Leffingwell felt it was ridiculous to be so pleased about something so trivial. The hat, now fifteen years old, had been given to him by a friend who had traveled in Russia. Martha had liked it. She said the curly gray lamb's wool hat, worn with his black overcoat, made him look like a Russian diplomat. He didn't care how it looked; he just appreciated its warmth as he drove to church through the frozen morning. Everything glittered with frost, but it remained too dry for snow. He wondered if there would be a white Christmas. And if Philip would be alive to see it.

When he arrived at the church office no one else had, so he took a few minutes to go next door into the cold church to pray for guidance and strength.

By eight o'clock he had met the sexton, Newton Crail, and had been startled at the sheer homeliness of the little elderly man. Newton Crail had a very short body on bandy legs. Smiling, his heavy mouth revealed a mass of big crooked teeth, but his brown eyes were serene. He had barely escaped dwarfism, but somewhere along the way he had come to terms with his ugly face and misshapen body.

Newton came into the rector's office carrying a tray of cleaning materials and a push broom. "That thermos on your desk has fresh coffee in it, Father. I make the first office pot as soon as I come in every morning."

"Sit down then and have a cup with me," Father Leffingwell invited, and over cups of coffee they got acquainted.

"Was the water running all right in the rectory this morning, Father?"

"Yes, it was. Why?"

"Mrs. Burris had me go over yesterday and wrap the faucets and outside pipes in advance of the big freeze."

"How very kind of you, and I didn't even notice. Thank you very much."

In addition to the sexton's duties, Newton Crail had a small bookstore in the north end of the city. "It's called *Experienced Books,* my euphemism for 'second-hand.' Mostly I keep it open evenings. I have a lot of customers—my regulars—who like to drop in after work to browse and talk books."

"That reminds me. My son asked for a special book the other day. Maybe you have it." He explained Philip's request for the old-fashioned ballad poems.

"I'll take a look, Father. I'm sure I have it. The place is a wild clutter but I can usually put my hands on what I want. See you." And with a cheery wave of the push broom he went on about his work.

Father Leffingwell didn't meet the secretary, Gloria Mason, until eleven o'clock. Deacon Fletcher came in, tight-lipped with anger, to tell him that Gloria would be late again.

"I try to make allowances," she said, hard-eyed. "She is a single mother with two children and one of them is always getting sick or something. Her husband deserted her, and I've tried to counsel her to go after him for child support, but she won't have it. She persists in thinking he's sick.

"And I forgot to tell you yesterday that the acolytes are getting rebellious. You may have to talk to Ralph Chalmers. He's too hard on them. He wants them to wear regular shoes when they are serving. He says that Nikes look tacky under the hems of the cassocks. For my part, I think they should wear whatever they want to." And she hurried out.

When he met the secretary he was instantly moved to sympathy. She was grossly overweight, and dressed in what appeared to be layers upon layers of clothing, everything either too long or too short or hanging crookedly. She had recently been crying. More than forty years in dealing with the bereaved, the bedeviled, the bewildered, the befuddled, told him how near to her breaking point she was. Was Deacon Fletcher so insensitive she couldn't see it?

During his first Sunday Coffee Hour, he tried to make the rounds of as many of the parishioners as he could. Over the years he had become quite good at remembering names and faces. *It won't be hard to remember Natalie and Peter Pruitt,* he thought with dismay when he met them. Natalie with her too-bright smile, her incessant mindless talk, and Peter in his wheelchair, his face like a stone, but seething beneath the surface. Here was a volcano waiting to erupt. God help them. And he learned there was a child. God help the child. And he, as God's vicar, would have to do something. And probably soon. And he wasn't sure he could.

He was meticulous about doing everything he had agreed to do. He dropped in during choir practice Thursday nights. He took part in the Vestry meeting and the Altar Guild meeting.

He placated the pro-choice group by telling them to get some posters from Planned Parenthood and post them opposite the pro-life posters. The pro-life group was touchingly grateful that he had allowed their posters to remain.

He bribed the acolytes to wear regular shoes instead of running shoes when serving, by promising them the parking lot for a car wash in May to finance a trip to Disneyland in June.

As Advent began, he took both Sunday services as a matter of course. Andrew Cullen seemed to have vanished from the face of the planet. He didn't mind. Celebrating the masses and giving the sermons had always been the best part of his work. He had brought his own white linen albs and other vestments. Seeing them laid out with ritualistic precision by the Altar Guild women always made him newly aware of the order and discipline of the church in mankind's humble imitation of God's act in the beginning, the creation of order out of chaos.

He counseled two engaged couples about to be married. He counseled a set of new parents and the godparents on a coming infant baptism.

He sided with the two Sunday school teachers against Deacon Fletcher's recommendation of supplementary books for the primary children's lending library. *My Two Mommies* and *My Two Daddies*, promoting homosexual lifestyles, were rejected. Kimberly Fletcher told him angrily that she was deeply offended. He managed to refrain from telling her he could care less.

He visited Philip daily. He found a travelers' Scrabble game as Philip's Christmas present and gave it to him early. Neither of them mentioned why. The letters had small pegs to anchor them to the board so none would slide off. The travelers' game was ideal for someone lying in bed. The gift was a great success, and he and Philip played a number of games. Philip always won; he had an extensive vocabulary.

One day Philip said mildly, "Dad, when I go, leave the Scrabble set here, will you? Someone is always borrowing it, so it will have a good home."

Leaving the hospice, Father Leffingwell tried to be thankful that Philip was resigned to dying, ready to let go of his life, which had been such a promising life. He prayed that *he* could be willing to let *Philip* go when the time came.

On both a Tuesday and Friday evening he stopped in for a while when the FOOD PLACE sign was out. The rec room was filled with street kids, laughing, talking, jostling, and eating the quantities of food handed out by the church workers. The kids were a wild mix of genuinely desolate waifs who were hungry and youthful con artists. No Mark, though.

He averted a brewing battle between the Women's Group and the Food Place Group about the trash the street kids were leaving, like bits of used drug paraphernalia and empty liquor bottles. Someone had vomited in the restroom basin and hadn't bothered to clean it up. The Food Place people cooperated and told the kids to shape up, and they seemed to be trying.

The Fall Bazaar was a success and he made a pleasant ceremony of thanking the women as he accepted the check on behalf of the church. Their attractive tables of handicrafts, baked goods, and collectibles had paid off handsomely. There was a general air of a-job-well-done and many would benefit from it. Decent people doing good things always made him feel hopeful.

Sometime during his third week of tenure at Saint Polycarp's, it became known that his homosexual son was dying of AIDS in a hospice. Probably someone in the bishop's office spoke to someone in the parish. It really didn't matter. Philip was Philip, and he was paying dearly for his mistakes. The sexton, Newton Crail, told him.

"Just be aware of it, Father. Different people are reacting in different ways. And I did find a book for your son." He took a small fat volume from among his kit of cleaning materials. "It's got all the poems in it that you mentioned, except Poe's 'Bells,' and I Xeroxed that from another book and pasted it in."

Father Leffingwell was touched. "How very good of you. Philip will be pleased. How much do I owe you?"

Newton shrugged his broad shoulders. "Forget it. It's a gift. I practice random kindness." He grinned and ducked out of the office with a cheery wave of his dust cloth.

Lay reader Malcolm Griswold asked for an appointment, but didn't have much to say when he arrived. He rambled on about the lay readers' work, and Father Leffingwell quelled his impatience to get on to other things until he realized the man's inner struggle. There was something on Griswold's mind, but he wasn't able to state it in a face-to-face meeting. He felt a sense of relief when Griswold had gone, and was ashamed of himself. *You're not the priest you used to be, old man.*

When Father Leffingwell got back to the rectory after work, he was startled to find Claire Gibson waiting for him in one of the living room's big easy chairs. He had seen the light from outside and thought he had left it on by mistake. She rose when he came in. She was a tall, slim woman with auburn hair and small green eyes. She was about fifty.

"How did you get in, Miss Gibson? Did I leave the door unlocked?" he asked in dismay. Sometimes he was forgetful.

"No. I always keep a key to the rectory. My late father donated the land to the church, you know. I feel I have a responsibility."

When they got through the amenities she came to the point.

"I was sorry to hear about your son," she said stiffly.

"Thank you."

"May I ask if you plan to bring him here to the rectory?"

A spark of defensive anger crossed Father Leffingwell's mind. "Why do you ask that, Miss Gibson?"

"I'm afraid I'll have to be a bit blunt, Father. AIDS is a treacherous disease. I wouldn't want anyone with AIDS living in the rectory. You will only be here for a few months and then a new rector and his family will be living here. We wouldn't want to put anyone at risk, would we? I'm speaking for the Vestry now. I'm afraid I cannot permit you to bring your son here."

Father Leffingwell mentally went through Saint Francis' prayer for patience, which was his regular substitute for counting to ten. "Has the Vestry taken a vote on this burning issue?" He wasn't able to keep the sarcasm from his voice.

She stiffened. "No, but I shall certainly bring it to their attention if it becomes necessary."

He sighed. What difference did it make? "You needn't trouble yourself, Miss Gibson. My son will conveniently die in a very short time. He is in a hospice." His voice shook and he regretted his bitter cruelty too late to stop the words.

Her pale face reddened. "I'm sorry," she stammered. "I didn't know it was that . . . acute."

There was another labored little exchange between them and then she left. Before he could put away his hat and coat

Andrew Cullen was at the door in his ragged jeans and dirty white sweater.

"I was parked across the street," he said. "I waited for Battle Ax Gibson to leave. Two things, Padre. We've got two crises to settle somehow." The younger priest looked tired and strained.

"All right," Father Leffingwell said, "But why don't we light the fire and let me get some tea first. I think we're both beat tonight."

"Right. I'm asleep on my feet. I'll light the fire," he added, crouching his big frame down in front of the fireplace.

When both men were settled in front of the fireplace they watched the fire dart and dance as it took frantic hold of the kindling. It crackled and snapped loudly until it settled down.

"All right," he said. "Let's start with crisis one." He wished Andrew hadn't come tonight. The encounter with Claire Gibson had shaken him. He wanted peace.

"Both involve my kids, of course. I don't seem to be doing anything else these days." Father Leffingwell thought he detected a hint of apology in that. "Crisis one is that I've found Mark McGillicuddy. He's in juvy—juvenile hall."

"Oh dear. How bad is it?"

"Well, I think I've about got him out. I've been with the social workers, and the advocacy group for street kids, and the public defender. Child Protective Services is getting him into a foster home."

"Is that good or bad here?" Father Leffingwell's experience made him dubious about the foster home programs.

Andrew grinned. "Doesn't matter. I give it a couple of days before Mark splits again. He may or may not stay in Seattle. If he does, he'll come back here. But I'd like to stack the deck a little in favor of that. Would you go talk to him? I interviewed him at juvy twice and both times he asked about you. You seem to have made an impression on the kid."

"Really? I'm flattered. What did he say? But to answer your question, of course I'll talk to him. He and I got along fine."

Andrew laughed. "Actually, he was concerned about how

*you* are getting along. He asked me how you were 'cutting it,' his phrase, not mine."

Father Leffingwell had to smile, then asked, "What did the police pick him up for?"

"Grand theft, auto. He ripped off somebody's little blue Volkswagen and took a joy ride."

"I see."

"Incidentally, when you go to see him, ask for Mark Guthrie."

"Why?"

"Because the Juvenile Officer didn't buy McGillicuddy. I doubt if Guthrie is his real name either. Some of these kids come up with a new a.k.a. every day."

They talked of Mark for a while, and all the Marks, some of whom might be salvaged but most of whom were already lost, by their own choices made when they were too young to make choices at all.

"Are you ready for the second crisis?" Andrew asked. "Claire Gibson and I are going to lock horns again over use of the rec room on Thanksgiving Day."

"What's the problem?"

"Well, for the last two years Lady Bountiful Gibson has chaired the Singles' Thanksgiving Dinner at midday in the rec room. The Women's Group is coerced into providing enough turkeys to roast, and the singles who choose to come bring whatever they want to: vegetables, salads, pies, cakes, whatever. It's quite a bash. They usually have a crowd of fifteen to twenty. This is at high noon after the service.

"For two years now I've had the street kids in for Thanksgiving dinner with all the trimmings at five. Both years the soup hits the fan as soon as Claire finds out. She says it rushes the Singles too much clearing up, before the FOOD PLACE people come in."

"Is that true?"

"I don't think so. They've managed for both years. Cal Dunne always mediated a truce for me and my kids. Do you think you could? It would probably put you on Gibson's hit list," he warned.

"I think I'm already on it," Father Leffingwell said ruefully, and somehow he found himself telling the younger priest about Philip, and how he had been forbidden to bring Philip to the rectory.

Andrew's broad face was a study in concern. He said gently, "I'm really sorry. I didn't know."

Father Leffingwell felt better for having talked with Andrew. The younger man had depths of insight and sensitivity he had not suspected. He hoped someday Andrew would stop limiting himself to social work and experience the complete scope of his ministry.

After Andrew left, he settled for heated canned soup again for dinner, knowing it wasn't enough. He had intended to do a bit of housekeeping too, wondering if Miss Gibson had noticed the layer of dust on everything, but didn't have the energy. Most nights he fell exhausted into bed. Now and then he felt like the White Rabbit in *Alice In Wonderland*, running as fast as he could to stay in one place.

He didn't get time to visit Mark until late the following afternoon. Then he spent forty-five minutes in the bleak juvenile detention center, and spoke with three workers before he was told that Mark had already been placed in a foster home. Because he was a priest they gave him the address.

The foster home, when he found it, was in a shabby section of the city. It was a street full of small frame houses, most in some disrepair, set close together on small lots. There was a scatter of broken toys and other junk, cannibalized rusting cars, fast food trash, and drifts of unraked dead leaves. There appeared to be no foster mother or foster father there and the door was answered by Mark himself. There were other children. A small Hispanic girl with leg braces sat in front of the TV with the sound off, staring at it as if hypnotized. Somewhere in the house a radio was screaming out rock music.

Mark's face broke into a wide smile. "Hey, you came. Andy said you probably would. That's nice. Look, can we sit in your car? Can't hear yourself think in here." Mark was very clean, and dressed in obviously new jeans and T-shirt. He had on a wind-breaker. They went together to the little blue VW at the curb.

"I only like rock when I'm high," Mark said, shutting the car door. There were fading bruises all around his neck and he moved carefully, favoring his right side, as if there was pain in motion. "Other times I like real music, like they play at Saint Whatzits on Sunday."

"Are you all right?" Father Leffingwell asked, indicating the boy's neck.

"Oh that, yeah." Mark put up his thin hand and caressed the bruises gently. "They'll fade out."

"What happened? Did you get that in Juvenile Hall?"

"Where else?" Mark shrugged his bony shoulders. "Some bigger guy is always after you to drop your pants and . . . well, in juvy . . . fights happen." He had lost some weight and his young face looked gaunt. Heart aching, Father Leffingwell realized that the boy was probably censoring out the worst parts for his benefit.

"It should be better in the foster home, shouldn't it?" Father Leffingwell asked tentatively.

"Yeah, well."

"Mark, I'll put it to you straight. Father Cullen thinks you'll run away again. I wish—"

"Would you want to live in this place?" Mark's haunted blue eyes looked straight into his.

"Well, isn't it better than the street?" Father Leffingwell countered.

"No." The boy slid down in the seat and leaned his head back, his eyes half shut.

"But if you run away again, Mark, won't they find you? And next time maybe leave you in Juvenile Hall?"

"*If*," the boy said tiredly, shutting his eyes completely.

"What do you mean if?"

"*If* they find me, and that could take a while. No offense, Father Leffingwell, I know you are a smart old man but there is a whole lot you don't know yet. First, this Miz Ullman, this foster mom, she's gotta report me missing, see. *Then* the CPS starts looking. *But*, as soon as she reports me gone the payments stop, see. So she's gonna take her time. Then, say the CPS lady comes and does a spot check and I'm gone, this Miz Ullman can say I just dropped out of sight ten minutes ago. But maybe I'm already gone six months, and they been sending the payments regular, see. Everybody's got an angle." Mark sat up and turned carefully to look at him, and Father Leffingwell was touched at the boy's careful omission of the street kids' all-purpose words out of, he supposed, respect.

"Forget about me. I'm doing okay. How you been doing at Saint Whatzits?"

"Not too badly. It isn't as difficult as I had thought it might be."

"That's great. You had any more of those heart things? You know, with the little white pills?"

"Not a one."

"Terrific."

"You know, Mark, since you do like the church music, why don't you come over to the church on Christmas Eve? Starting at ten we'll have a beautiful program called 'Lessons and Carols.'"

"Lessons?" Mark looked doubtful.

"Not to study, just passages being read aloud, and in between there's Christmas music, church music."

"Could I hear it from my dumpster?"

Father Leffingwell sighed. "Probably, if that's as close as you'll come."

"Well, about church—I dunno. I wouldn't wanna come actually *in* it. The other kids would start calling me Holy Joe, like I got Jesus on the brain. I gotta take care of my reputation, you know."

They talked a while longer and before he left, Father Leffingwell gave Mark his address at the rectory and phone number. "Just in case," he said.

"Yeah, thanks. I hadda a lot of just-in-cases lately. I'll be seeing ya."

That evening, with a bit of time on his hands and not inclined for housekeeping, Father Leffingwell found Newton Crail's little book shop. He spent a pleasant hour browsing among the old books, bought two, and talked with Newton. He mentioned that Philip would have to miss the Lessons and Carols service, which he had always liked. Newton offered to tape it for him. Another random kindness. Newton was becoming a friend.

The secretary, Gloria Mason, came into his office on a Thursday, just as he was ready to leave for lunch.

"Father, Mrs. Blalock—Irma Blalock—one of the parishioners, wants to see you. I thought maybe you could take the time now. She's made two appointments in the last two weeks and cancelled both. Whatever it is, she's worked up her nerve again. Better see her before she chickens out the third time."

"Of course, Gloria. Ask her to come in."

A harried smile brightened Gloria's moon face a moment and she laid a small packet of tissues on his desk. "You may need these. You're out of tissues. I have to get you another box."

"Thank you," he said, putting them into his pocket. Gloria was a very good secretary when she showed up.

"Thank you for seeing me, Father," Irma Blalock said nervously when she came in. "It's been so hectic at my office. I've had to cancel twice, but I seized my lunch hour today."

"Good idea," Father Leffingwell said, standing up. He remembered having seen her at a couple of Coffee Hours, with a rather stocky husband at her side. Trim, with reddish blonde hair and blue-green eyes, she had retained a youthful prettiness into middle age.

"Please sit down. These days we snatch whatever time we can get. I'm the new kid on the block, but let me see if I can remember. You work . . ."

She plunged in, telling him about her job as a loan officer

at the bank. She had gone back to work after the children were old enough to leave alone, and she was doing pretty well.

The ice was broken and she rattled on. Soon she would get to the point. She told him about her two children, Clement and Diane. Diane was going to transfer to the university from community college. She'd brought her grade average up wonderfully well. And Clem was entering community college this spring quarter. When she ran out of chatter, she sat for a moment, her grip on her handbag tightening and loosening, and her eyes suddenly filled with tears.

He leaned forward. "How can I help?" he asked gently. "That's what I'm here for."

"What . . . what . . . is the church's stand on abortion?" She had to wet her lips to say it.

He kept his face impassive. What was the church's stand, indeed. On anything. For more than two decades the only decision the church seemed capable of making was to decide not to decide. Cringing away from taking any stand some pressure group didn't like. Inventing the new Gospel of Saint Convenience to keep everybody happy, thereby leaving the way open for renegade priests and bishops to make up their own rules.

"What is the situation, my dear? Who needs an abortion?"

"Me. I do." This surprised him, as he had assumed it was the daughter, Diane.

"Is there a reason you don't want this child? Can you tell me?"

"Well, it isn't a child yet, is it?"

"I'm afraid the jury's still out on that. Some believe that life begins at conception. Some don't."

"But you do, don't you?" she asked in a low voice. "And I'm . . . kind of leaning that way myself. But . . ." She started to cry, and her misery came pouring out. He hurt for her, and broke open the packet of tissues and put it into her hand. The situation came out in disjointed spurts; he got it in bits and pieces.

"I'm afraid to tell Diane . . . we halfway promised her a car

. . . and Clem . . . and Clem . . . and Roger is devastated . . . he's having such a rotten time . . . scared . . . he's so scared . . . can't keep up with the bright new guys with the bright new MBAs . . . his new boss is fifteen years younger . . . he brings work home . . . so you see I can't . . . can't . . . and he's losing his hair and he hates that . . . I'm so sorry for Roger . . ."

When the burst of anguish had spent itself her eyes still continued to seep tears and she mopped at them with a balled wet tissue. A little pile of wet tissues had accumulated on the edge of the desk. Father Leffingwell put them in the waste basket.

"How far along are you?"

"The doctor estimates six weeks."

"Then you and Roger have a little time to consider, time to explore all the options, if you want to."

A look of faint relief touched her flushed face.

He continued. "It's an important decision for both of you, and you want to make the right one. Would Roger be willing to come with you to see me?"

"Yes. I mean, I think so. But his mind is already pretty well made up."

"I understand that, and he deserves the chance to lay out his reasons. And to review the options so he'll have the whole picture. Why don't we pray together about it?" And after they had prayed, they talked, more easily now, for another half hour, and when she left her, "Thank you, thank you, Father," was fervent. Alone, he wondered why. He hadn't done anything yet to help her but listen. It was clear the poor woman wanted to carry the child to term and have it, but didn't have the courage to face down her family's opposition. He'd been in similar situations before; they could become bitter. It took strength and guts to prevail, and he had run out of both. He was a fraud; he wasn't doing his job. Where was God's vicar who had been so strong and dedicated in the beginning?

On Christmas Eve it was still cold and dry. The bitter chill hung like a pall over the city but the weather people warned that there would be no white Christmas. After Christmas, they said, there might be more moisture.

After the Christmas Eve service, which had seemed exceptionally beautiful, Father Leffingwell left the church at almost midnight. He was thinking about Andrew Cullen, who had read the lessons. He would be fine speaker if he ever decided to put his mind to it.

"That was neat music, Father Leffingwell!" And Mark was standing beside the little blue VW, waiting for him. He was shivering from cold. The jacket was gone, probably sold for crack.

"Mark, how good to see you. Did you hear the music from your dumpster?"

"Yeah. Can't you smell me?" He grinned his engaging grin.

"You've run away, haven't you?"

Mark shrugged. "Yeah, well."

"Look, it will be Christmas Day in a few minutes. Why don't we have another meal together? I was just going home to fix myself a late supper."

"You kidding?"

"Not at all. I dislike eating alone. And I'm a pretty good cook. I made a meat loaf yesterday. We could have meat loaf sandwiches."

"Man, I would like that!" The boy looked ecstatic. "I don't suppose . . ."

"Suppose what?"

"If I could wash up in your john?"

"Of course you can."

Mark took a long time in the big, old-fashioned bathroom at the rectory. When he came out, his skin was glowing and his wet hair hung down to his shoulders. He was enthusiastic about the bathroom.

"That john is really something! I *soaked*. I haven't soaked for a hundred years." He sniffed at his hands. "I smell like Comet now. I found a can on the shelf and scrubbed out the tub and sink for you."

"Why, thank you, Mark. Sit down. We'll just use the

kitchen table." Instead of sandwiches, he had decided to heat the meat loaf and steam some frozen vegetables. He had also made biscuits from a mix, and set out the mince pie Mrs. Burris had given him.

"Did you make all this?" Mark asked with something like awe.

"The pie was a gift. And the biscuits came from a box, but I did the meat loaf," he said, as Mark began wolfing down the food.

He was pleased. He had become a fairly good cook during Martha's last illness. Their kitchen in that place had been small and he had put her in a big comfortable chair drawn up to the kitchen door to coach him. They had enjoyed some rather good meals with that arrangement, but he had never quite made it with biscuits from scratch.

After eating, they sat in front of the fire for a while, and when the grinding from the old dishwasher stopped, Mark sprawled on the floor and listened to parts of the tape Newton had made for Philip. The boy lay in front of the fire, his eyes tranquil and dreaming.

When Father Leffingwell began to fall asleep he roused himself. "Would you like to stay the night, Mark? There are three guest bedrooms. You can take your choice."

Mark sat up. "How many you got?"

"Four."

"Four bedrooms," Mark said dreamily. "I don't mind if I do. You know it's safe with me. I wouldn't rip off anything from you."

"Yes. I know that, Mark."

"Yeah, well, I just thought I'd mention it."

On Christmas morning, before Father Leffingwell went to the church to take the Christmas Day service, he slipped a Christmas card with a five dollar bill in it under Mark's door. It was probably a mistake to give the boy money, but he didn't have anything else to use as a gift, and it seemed important that Mark get something for Christmas.

When he got back Mark was gone, but he had left a note.

*Dear F. Lefingwell*
*Thank you for the five and all.*
*and the nice card. I will keep it. See*
*you.*
*Your frend Mark*
*P.S. I warshed the sheets and stuff.*

And he had. They were folded and stacked on the back porch dryer. Driving down to spend a quiet Christmas afternoon with Philip, he prayed for Mark. The boy had an instinctive sense of decency. Ethics, after all he had been through, he must be salvaged. He would talk to Andrew about it.

There were sudden hurts and unexpected anguishes some days when he visited Philip as his son's condition worsened.

"I'm sorry about the odor, Dad. It's the infection. You got here a bit early today. The nurse doesn't come in until ten to change the dressings. I hate to be offensive . . ." Philip was embarrassed. Always a clean and fastidious man, he was learning to deal with the small unspeakable indignities of dying slowly, and he bore it with patience and quiet courage. Nor did he wish to abandon his life. He seemed to take deep pleasure in the very simplest of things as his life slipped away from him.

Philip died on a bright, cold, blustery day at the end of December. Entering the hospice that morning, Father Leffingwell had to walk through masses of wildly scurrying fallen leaves which rushed this way and that across his path. Now and then one whirled up from the pavement and went on a mad dance through the icy air, twirling and twisting. He tried to think of a quote about fallen leaves he had heard so he could tell Philip. What was it? *There is almost nothing with such a keen sense of fun as a fallen leaf.* That was close enough, but he couldn't recall who had said it.

As he went through the reception room a nurse put down a clipboard and hurried to him.

"We tried to reach you, Father, at your church and home, but you must have been en route. It's Philip. Come upstairs."

The doctor, a nurse, the hospice counselor, and a strange priest were in Philip's room. *Oh no, not yet. Not yet.* He put down the book he had brought and went to the foot of the bed. He took hold of the metal bedstead because he felt shaky. The other priest was speaking.

"Almighty God, look on this your servant, lying in great weakness, and comfort him with the promise . . ."

When the other priest finished, he went to the bedside and took hold of Philip's thin hand. It clasped his for a moment and then was lax. Too weak to open his eyes or speak, it was the best Philip could do in farewell. He was breathing softly at long intervals and then he wasn't breathing any more.

There was a time of blankness and Father Leffingwell was in the hall with the other priest and the counselor. The doctor and nurse needed to do something else with Philip. The door was shut.

He was somehow distanced from himself. He knew he was speaking to the other priest and counselor, saying the right things. Then after a while he was sitting on the stone bench outside the hospice. It had started to snow at last. The wind had died down. Large white flakes were floating languidly about him, coating the pavement and the tops of his shoes.

"Father Leffingwell?"

He looked up and it was the secretary, Gloria Mason, and at her side, Andrew Cullen. He stood up with great effort. "Yes?"

Gloria reached up a pudgy timid hand to brush some snow off his shoulder. "They called the church and we thought . . ."

"Yes. Thank you."

"Come on, Padre. We'll take you home," Andrew said. "You're coming in my car. Gloria will drive yours."

"Yes. Thank you. That's very kind."

# CHAPTER 4

The numbness began to leave Father Leffingwell as Andrew commenced reading the ancient service for the burial of the dead in the church on Monday afternoon. Andrew's strong young voice rang out through the small church.

"I am the resurrection and the life . . ."

Father Leffingwell made an effort to sit up straight despite the nagging ache in his back. Aching bones—the legacy of old age. He was seated off to the side by himself, in the pews set aside for the "family of the deceased." Well, that was appropriate. He was all the family Philip had left. He wondered again if he should tell Serena. She had been Philip's wife, had borne his son. His tired mind pushed it aside, to think about later.

So many people had come. How odd. None of them had known Philip. Even Bishop Jackson had come, sitting in the first row, resplendent in his purple vest, his heavy cross resting on his protruding middle, the clerical collar cutting into his thick neck. Father Leffingwell felt a rush of appreciation for the effort made.

And next to him—who was that? Oh yes, Mrs. Burris, but in a hat. She of the bags of groceries, and mince pie, and the collection of teas. The hat—in honor of Philip, perhaps—held down her flyaway salt-and-pepper hair so she looked different. How kind of them all to come. Many faces he didn't even recognize. But there was Newton Crail, hunched over because he couldn't sit up straight, broad, ungainly. *"I practice random kindness, Father."* And his coming today was another kindness, helping to mark Philip's passing. And behind him was Kimberly Fletcher, tense and taut. Next to her was Gloria, her round face blotched from crying. Why would Gloria weep for Philip? But of course, she wasn't. She was weeping for her own misery. She had approached him before the service.

"Father, Claire Gibson told me that she let some more ladies into your kitchen with her rectory key when you weren't there this morning. They brought some more things."

"Thank you, Gloria." For the last two days the ladies had been coming with their gifts of food and kindness, whispering quietly among themselves, putting their offerings away, changing things. Someone had vacuumed and dusted. And it seemed they were still coming with their platters of sliced ham, beef, pork, roast chicken, fried chicken, turkey, casseroles, vegetables, salads, pies, cakes, cookies. What in the world would he do with all that food? Perhaps it would feed Andrew's street kids.

Who was that? The man in the wheelchair with the burning eyes? He struggled for the name—Pruitt. Peter Pruitt. Father Leffingwell's heart sank, for he knew even without thinking about it that Peter Pruitt envied Philip his death. He couldn't keep his eyes off the coffin. Oh, dear God, how can I help him? He pushed the thought aside to think about later—sometime.

And who was the woman sitting beside that layreader? What's his name? Griswold. Malcolm Griswold. His mother, probably. Another woman who couldn't be still, moving constantly, smoothing her skirt, taking off her gloves, putting them back on, and beside her, Malcolm, becoming visibly more tense at her fidgeting.

Behind them a whole family of four, obviously together. Oh yes. *"Father, what is the church's position on abortion?"* Then the young girl must be the daughter, Diane. She resembled her mother somewhat, but a bit sulky around the mouth. *"We halfway promised Diane a car."*

A shiver went through Father Leffingwell, and he looked away from them, from all their faces revealing or concealing.

*Would the baby inside the woman die because the sulky girl wanted a car?*

*A car?*

He felt the now familiar cramping in his chest. It had persisted since Philip's death. Before coming today he had taken the precaution of dropping some of his pills loosely into his pocket. Now he could unobtrusively slide his hand into his pocket and, head bowed, slip a tablet into his mouth.

He tried to listen to what Andrew was saying over Philip's coffin. These were his flock, his people, for the time being anyway, and they expected something from him. He leaned back against the pew, unable to sit up straight any longer. With his head bowed, they would think he was praying. Perhaps he would. If he could. Later. Sometime. Andrew's vibrant voice came through.

"... our prayers on behalf of your servant, Philip, and grant him an entrance into the land of light and ..."

Later at the snowy gravesite he could hear in his mind Philip's weak breathy voice in the hospice.

*"I've already got a plot, Dad. Forgive my mentioning this, but we must. It's all here."* And his bony hand had held out an envelope. *"When Gideon died I knew I wasn't far behind so I bought two plots while I still had the money, one for him and one for me."*

" ... we commend to Almighty God our brother, Philip, and we commit his body to the ground, earth to earth ... "

Again Father Leffingwell was saying all the right things. They all meant well. There was goodness in all of them. They were trying to help him. The least he could do was go through the motions for them.

The funeral had been scheduled for 2:00 P.M. and he was back at the rectory by 5:00 P.M. It seemed like a sanctuary. He sat in the rocker in front of the fireplace, thinking that soon he would light the fire. The world was blanketed in silence, made more so by the snow which had even blown up onto the rectory porch. He looked down, and in his hand were his retirement home brochures. When had he picked them up? He hadn't had them at the funeral.

Idly, he opened the top one again. He knew them well by now. Here was a building of snug little apartments for the elderly. He gazed at a picture of the inside of one of the cozy apartments, occupied apparently by a man and woman with white hair and beaming smiles. The man, in an elegant sweater and slacks, held a putter. Father Leffingwell read on.

A nine-hole golf course and putting green. Well, that was nice for those who played golf. He turned a glossy page. A library in the main lodge offered a selection of books. Again, very nice. Landscaped grounds provided paved curving walkways for one's daily constitutional. The picture had been taken in mid-summer and masses of green shaded the paved curved walkways. There was a separate building for "assisted living." The phrase stuck in his mind. Wasn't all living assisted living, one way or another? Send for further information. No obligation, the brochure said. He had, some time ago, and found it far beyond his means.

The other one he could probably afford. Much less grand. It looked like a maximum security facility, smack in a congested area of Baltimore, but rent assistance was available if needed. And he might need that. The cost of the hospice had wiped out his savings and he would probably use all or most of his stipend from Saint Polycarp's to finish paying off the debt.

Unless, of course, the Vestry found a new Rector day after tomorrow. He had to smile. Not likely. They were still arguing about the qualifications they wanted the candidate to have. They had surveyed the congregation, but in the end the Vestry would make the decision.

He went on with the brochure. Yes, this was probably his future home. There was a community room and it didn't look too bad. It was near the cathedral. That was nice. And there was a large public park nearby. One could take walks there if done in broad daylight.

He leaned back in the rocker, remembering Martha, just

before her death. She had been far braver than he. He could hear his own voice. "*What am I going to do?*"

"*You're going to walk on through it,*" she had answered. "*There is always something better on the other side.*" Trust Martha for basic brains. She had been right. The last years—until he had learned about Philip—hadn't been too bad. He had had his work. God's work. It had been enough. There had been good times. Accomplishments.

He tossed the glossy brochure into the fireplace, continuing to hold the other one. He had better send in his application. There was probably a waiting list. It seemed so peaceful alone. He hoped no one would come, but even as he thought it, the doorbell rang. He glanced at his watch; it was almost seven.

The caller was only Andrew, still in his clericals. Somehow he looked bigger than he did in his old jeans and sweater.

"Come in," Father Leffingwell said. "It's freezing out there."

"I won't stay. I just wanted to tell you that I'm taking all of the services for the next few days. Kim and I just reworked the schedule at the office. She's going to handle all the office stuff for you."

"That's very kind." Father Leffingwell felt a sudden stinging in his eyes. *Andrew* taking *all* the services? Unbelievable. Andrew, the social worker, speaking the words of the liturgy day after day, handing out the wafers and the wine cup, standing at the pulpit and giving the sermons. He shook his head.

Andrew grinned. "Crazy, innit? Well, I gotta go. I'm starving. I didn't get lunch today and I'm going to get a burger."

"No! For Heaven's sake, stay and eat here. I've got a ton of food in the kitchen."

Light dawned in Andrew's dark eyes. "Ah, *yes*! The ladies!" In the kitchen he opened the refrigerator door and stood back in wonder. "Padre, you've got enough food here to feed a small nation."

"I know, and you'd better take some home with you. I'll never use it all."

"Don't think I won't. But can't you put some in the freezer part?" He opened the freezer door and added, "I see you already thought of that," and shut it. "Have you eaten? Can I fix you a sandwich?" He opened the bottom door again. "Is there such a thing as a ham-beef-pork-turkey-chicken sandwich with potato salad on top? Oh, what's this?" He pulled out a shallow casserole.

Father Leffingwell sat down at the kitchen table. He was rather glad that Andrew had come, after all. "I have no idea. I don't even know who brought it. It's a rather elegant looking dish, isn't it?"

Andrew sniffed it. "I know who brought it, and I know what it is. Claire Gibson and I maintain our state of war but I am willing to admit that she's the best cook in King County. This, Padre, is her *superb* eggplant parmesan. I've eaten it before. Did anyone happen to bring any garlic bread?"

"I wouldn't be surprised. Try the cooler."

They sat together at the kitchen table and shared the meal. Andrew devoured three-fourths of the casserole and half the loaf of garlic bread. Father Leffingwell did rather well too. He couldn't recall when he had last eaten. He must remember to compliment Claire Gibson when he next saw her.

After dinner, neither was sure that the elegant platter was dishwasher proof so Andrew, without his black jacket and with sleeves rolled up, washed it gently at the old soapstone sink.

Afterward they sat in front of the warm fire sipping their tea. "What is this? It's different from before," Andrew asked, peering into his cup.

"Darjeeling," Father Leffingwell answered and raised his cup. "God bless Mrs. Burris. She knows her teas."

Andrew raised his. "Amen."

They fell into a comfortable silence for a time. Was it possible that he and Andrew could be friends? That would be a help for the rest of the time he would spend here at Saint Polycarp's. It wasn't a good idea to prejudge people, and he had prejudged Andrew. Had he prejudged anyone else? He had so much unresolved anger at the way the church was going, and at the people who were taking it there. He had crossed swords with Kim Fletcher and "deeply offended" her, but she was willing to help him now if she could. And trendy Dickie Jackson had dressed like a Bishop for once. Perhaps he'd better think about this—sometime.

"It was good of Kim Fletcher to take on the office, but I'll be back soon. I have some letters to write, but I think probably day after tomorrow—I'll certainly take the Wednesday noon service."

"You don't need to. Think it over."

"Thank you, Andrew, from the bottom of my heart, but it will be easier if I work."

"I suppose so. Well, it's your call. Whatever. Kim was sympathetic because of your son. Her brother is gay, you know."

"No. I didn't know."

"They are very close. He's her twin, actually. She's very protective of him."

"I don't wonder." He wished now that he had been more protective of Philip. Another regret. Well, he would walk on through, doing what he could while he was here.

After Andrew had gone, Father Leffingwell remained in front of the glowing embers in the fireplace. He was thinking about putting the cups and saucers into the dishwasher when he drifted into a brief uneasy sleep. Almost immediately he awoke with a start, the fragment of an ugly dream clinging in his mind. He was in the church office and Mrs. Blalock was on the other side of the desk. She was crying. *"And we halfway promised Diane a car."*

Stiffly, he got up from the chair and picked up the tray, trying to quell the sudden rise of dread. *Walk on through, old man.*

# CHAPTER 5

Irma Blalock scraped the last of the wilted dinner salad from the bowl into the sink's disposal. She turned on the water and flipped the switch, listening vacantly to the hum as the waste was disposed of.

*What did they do with the fetus after an abortion?*

With a surge of anger at herself for thinking of it, she put the bowl into the dishwasher, slammed the door and turned it on to WASH ONLY. They would dry overnight. No point in wasting electricity drying them when she wasn't going to unload it until morning anyhow.

Dinner had been exceptionally good tonight. Seventeen-year-old Clem was working part-time, after school and weekends, in a restaurant, and had discovered a sudden interest in cooking. He had brought home a sauce recipe which was part tenderizer and part marinade for the London Broil. It had been delicious and tender enough to cut with a fork.

"You about through, Mom?" Clem stood in the kitchen doorway. "Do we really need a family summit meeting now? I got this neat video." He grinned engagingly and held it up for her to look at. "I want to watch it like day before yesterday." He was already taller than Roger, and since he resembled her side of the family he would probably mature into a tall, good-looking man like her father. She was secretly pleased at this.

"Well, just put the video on hold for a while, half an hour or so. Where are Diane and your father?"

"In the den, where you said to go. Your wish is our

command. You don't mind if I set the timer for half an hour, do you?"

She had to smile. "Don't get cocky, Chum. This is important family business. It concerns all of us. Got it?"

"Got it!" He gave a mock salute and ambled out of the kitchen.

The stupid video *would* come today. It was another of the interminable sports videos he was so crazy about. She had sent in the last payment on his Christmas gift subscription to *Sports Illustrated*, so this was probably about basketball, his current passion, seven-feet-tall men crashing into each other.

Irma went into the den rubbing hand lotion into her hands. She had nice hands and tried to keep them that way. She pushed a large ottoman closer to Roger and sat down next to his legs. He was in the recliner, leaning back. Diane and Clem were both sitting on the couch, Diane looking heartbreakingly beautiful, and Clem slouched forward, passing his video back and forth from hand to hand. They were both such beautiful children, with the reddish blond hair and blue-green eyes.

Roger straightened up. He looked tired, and somehow wilted. He used to shave twice a day but didn't any more.

"I guess I'm Chair, huh?"

Irma smiled and reached over to pat his thigh. They had always included the children in family decisions which affected them, and the kids had responded surprisingly well. Like when they made the decision to go ahead and get the small cottage on Camano Island and their sailboat, *Intrepid*, instead of moving up to a larger house in Seattle. They had stayed in this house and simply got a renovation loan to build on this den and another bathroom. The third bath had been a godsend in keeping down sibling fights.

Then when Clem had turned twelve they had decided Irma could go back to work to build up something for her and Roger's retirement. Both kids had cooperated well. Clem had been a responsible latchkey kid and Diane had been good about keeping tabs on him.

Now there was this. Roger began.

"Well, kids, I guess I'll give it to you straight. You both know the facts of life, some of them anyhow. We have a slight glitch in our perfect nuclear family setup here. And if we don't handle it wisely it could get sticky. I'm afraid your mother and I have been careless and irresponsible, for which I apologize to one and all."

Both young people were looking at him warily. "You haven't lost your job, have you, Dad?" Diane murmured.

"No. Not that, Pet." Involuntarily, he glanced over to the desk on which lay sprawled a stack of spreadsheets. "I guess there is only one way to say this, so I'll just put it bluntly. We've let your mother get pregnant. She's six weeks gone now and . . . I'm sorry. We're both sorry."

Both kids were stunned into silence. Diane was the first to break it. "Oh, *Daddy*," she wailed, covering her face with her hands.

"Wow!" Clem said, and his face immediately flamed red. At his age sex was never far from his thoughts, but the idea of parental sex embarrassed him acutely. He looked at the ceiling, the walls, at the video in his hands—any place but at his parents.

Roger cleared his throat. "Okay, we've had our moment of silence. Now let's discuss our options. A few days ago your mother went over to see Father Leffingwell at church . . ."

"Why?" Diane interrupted. "What's church got to do with it?"

Irma glanced at her daughter's worried face. "Well, honey, we *are* Christians. I just wanted to talk to him about the church's position on . . . on situations like this."

"I still don't see why," Diane persisted. "We aren't living in medieval times, Mom."

"Well, Sweetheart, without getting gushy about it, my faith means a lot to me. It's just *in* me. When Clem got hit on his bike by that car, the first thing I did was start to pray, even while I was dialing nine one one. Religion isn't something you have Monday through Thursday and toss aside on Friday when you have to make a tough decision, then put it back on for the weekend. Please understand."

"Yeah, I do, I guess." Diane's expressive eyes showed worry. "So what did Father Leffingwell say?"

"He said it was a pretty complex situation but there are a lot of options. He invited Roger and me back to discuss them. He's obviously had a lot of experience with this kind of thing. Then, you know, his son died and there was the funeral, so I let it slide." She turned to Roger. "Then the secretary said that Father Cullen said that Father Leffingwell would be back on Wednesday, so I made another appointment. Was that okay, Roj? You said you'd come."

"Wednesday? Oh, I don't know, Hon." He was biting the inside of his cheek. "What time on Wednesday?" A thin film of sweat had appeared on his forehead, and her heart sank. He was losing his nerve. And she knew instantly that Diane had sensed her father's reluctance. They were very close.

"Maybe we don't need his counseling on this, Mom," Diane said quickly. "We do live in the era of exploding information. We're saturated with information all the time. This family probably already knows enough to make the right decision without asking the village priest how to think."

Clem gave his sister a thumbs-up sign. "Not bad, Di. Maybe you're not stupid, after all."

She cast him a fleeting look of disgust and went on. "I've got a pack of stuff—leaflets and things—from my sex education class on this subject. Women can't be forced these days to bear unwanted children, and thank God for that."

"Well, Di, we haven't really decided yet if it is unwanted or not, have we?" Even to herself her voice sounded weak.

"Oh, Mom," Diane said almost laughing, "get real. It isn't even a baby yet. How long—Dad said six weeks. At six weeks it's a nothing, a blob, a hunk of bloody tissue . . ."

"Eee-yuk!" Clem yelled. "Knock it off, Di. I just ate. Unless you want me to gorp in your lap, and don't think I won't."

Diane turned on her brother. "Clem, either contribute or shut up! This is serious."

"I *am* contributing! I just gave you fair warning I was going to barf on your lap. That's *contributing*!"

"Cool it, both of you," Roger snapped. "Go ahead, Diane, what were you saying?" He passed his hands over his slick face, while Clem silently mouthed the words, "Go ahead, Diane."

Diane cleared her throat primly. "Well, first and foremost, it has to be Mom's decision. What Mom does with her own body is between her and her doctor, and nobody else's business. Right?"

"Right."

"Right." Roger and Clem both nodded.

"So then, I guess we just have to figure out the pros and cons. What would another child in the family, at this time, do to the . . . uh . . . quality of our family life."

"Lemme lay a little groundwork here, kids." Roger sat up straighter. "We're all aware that although I have a CPA after my name, your father peaked as a businessman at age twenty-five. Your father is not Seattle's answer to Donald Trump. I'll never get past middle management and I'll probably be lucky to hang on until my retirement. Which I should mention is just ten short years from *now*." This was a familiar refrain and he got the responses he expected.

"Oh, come on, Dad . . ."

"Daddy, money isn't everything . . ."

"Roger, you've done a lot better than most . . ."

"Well, hear me out now. Accounting was the wrong career for me, but I'm stuck with it. I'm a white-collar drudge. I don't like my work and I never have, but I've stuck it out. As you may recall, Plan A calls for me to retire at age sixty-five on the dot—and I'd rather not work a minute longer." He glanced around and saw they were all nodding.

"So, when I hit age sixty-five, your mother and I pack it in work wise. That's ten years from *now*. Hopefully both of you kids will be finished with college and launched into your own careers. Your mom and I sell this place and put the capital into a nice safe mutual fund and move over to the cottage on

Camano where we will live happily ever after, alternately sailing around the Sound in the *Intrepid*, or scraping the crud off the *Intrepid's* hull.

"To be perfectly honest with you, I can't see a third child in that picture. If there is one at that point, he or she will be ten years old. At that point I hope to God that he or she didn't inherit the same teeth-genes that Diane did, because Plan A does not include making another orthodontist rich. Have I laid out the picture for you?"

There was a glum silence for a time. Irma broke it. She had become increasingly tense during his speech. He had already made up his mind. "We did decide that it would be *my* decision," she reminded them firmly, and realized that none of them were looking at her.

"Of course, Mom," Diane said quickly. "Its just that we have to think of all the angles. I was reading the other day that the rise in child abuse relates directly to the birth of unwanted children—"

Roger interrupted her, seemingly to change sides for the moment, "Well, even with the worst possible scenario I can't see any child abuse in it. I doubt your mother and I would resort to child abuse even if we were scraping the bottom of the barrel."

"Idiot," Clem muttered.

"No, of course not. What was I thinking of!" Diane gave them an apologetic smile. "As parents you are more than civilized, I'll give you that." She reached over and patted her father's hand.

"There is this, though," Roger said thoughtfully. "You'd never guess it by looking at her, but your mother is forty-five years old. We don't know yet what special medical problems could arise in carrying a pregnancy to term at that age. We have to make ourselves aware of that. We'll have to talk to the OB guy about *risk*."

"Oh, good grief, yes," Diane agreed.

"Yeah, right!" Clem looked at his mother with suddenly

wide-eyed alarm. The video began to change hands more rapidly.

"I also intend to talk further about it with Father Leffingwell," Irma said. "Clem, put that stupid video down!"

Instantly, he shoved it down between the couch cushion and the arm rest, with the same stricken look he always got when she spoke to him angrily. Contrition flooded her. "I'm sorry, Baby. I'm not myself. You have no idea—none of you—what it means to be forty-five and . . ." She swallowed hard. She would *not* cry. She had to be the strong one. " . . . *pregnant*!" Then in spite of her every effort she did start to cry, gulping, strangling, trying to stop.

Instantly they all rallied around, all hugging one another in a tight little group.

"Oh, Mommie, Mommie, please . . ."

"Come on, Mom, don't cry . . ."

"Irma, Honey, it'll be okay. We'll work it out. We'll work it out . . ."

Father Leffingwell returned to work by taking the noon Eucharist on Wednesday. The pristine blanket of snow was beginning to sag and turn slushy around the edges. He had already become familiar with the sheets of what Seattle-ites called "black ice" beneath the white surface. In a city built upon many hills, black ice, in the years when Seattle had snow, was an insurance adjustor's nightmare. He had barely avoided some fender benders himself. Fortunately, the little car could slide into sudden unexpected places usually with room to spare.

Someone had left a white card—sympathy card probably—shoved under the front door. The melting snow had saturated it, and he put it on the sink to dry out before he left the rectory. He would open it when he came home.

After the noon service, as he was hanging up his white linen alb in the sacristy closet, he noticed Mrs. Burris.

"Thank you, Father, for the nice note you sent to the women's group. How are you doing?"

"Very well, thanks. And I'll thank you for the Darjeeling—it was you, wasn't it? And for the herbal teas."

"Mr. Burris's idea. He's a great believer in drinking herbal tea for stress." She gave him her warm smile.

"I don't usually see you here on Wednesdays—where's Claire Gibson. Doesn't she usually do Wednesdays?" He shut the closet door.

"Well, she is chairing the Search Committee for the new Rector—the Vestry finally hammered out the candidate requirements. The Church Deployment Office has suggested two candidates and the Committee has gone to interview them. One is in Boise and the other in Portland. They'll be back tomorrow. I really was glad to come to the Wednesday service, though."

"Why is that?" He watched as she took envelopes, cash, and some checks out of the alms basin and put them into a small lockbox.

"This." She tapped the lid of the box. "I don't know what you are doing, Father, but the Wednesday noon crowd is getting bigger. Haven't you noticed in the Registry?" She indicated the big red book in which priests entered each mass they celebrated.

"Not really, I guess."

"Well, more people are coming—lots of business people from the downtown area. We had forty-one people this noon. And we used to get between twenty and thirty. I think it's your sermons. You have such a clear no-nonsense way of looking at things."

"Thank you." He smiled at her earnestness. "Maybe you give me too much credit. Remember, it's January—people are full of New Year's resolutions to amend their lives. Give it until March—maybe it will drop back down by then."

There was a sound of pounding below, and Father Leffingwell went down to the rec room. Andrew was there, back in his jeans and T-shirt, nailing up a new NO SKATEBOARD-

ING sign for the unruly kids. This one said in big black letters DON'T EVEN *THINK* ABOUT SKATEBOARDING HERE. He stood back and looked at it with a troubled expression on his rugged face.

"Some creative types covered the other one with graffiti and there were two skateboarders in here last night. That can wreck the floors."

"There's some new graffiti on the stones in front too," Father Leffingwell commented.

"I know. I saw it. I'm going to try to get it off myself. Newton gave me some new solvent he found. Sandblasting costs so much. The Vestry keeps reminding me how much the kids cost—besides the food. Have you been up to the office yet?"

"No. I'm on my way now. Good luck with the graffiti."

"Wait up. I need to clue you in on something," Andrew began, but at that moment two police officers entered at the door off the alley. "Never mind," he said with a sigh. "I have to talk to these guys. But . . . try to avoid Kim, if you can. I'll get back to you."

In the church office, Father Leffingwell found Deacon Fletcher angry and upset. "Gloria isn't here?" he asked, and instantly realized his mistake. Kim's eyes were stormy.

"No," she snapped. "She called to say she would be in 'later' and only God knows when 'later' is. I'm getting pretty sick of being the acting secretary here. I *am* an ordained Deacon, you know. Sorry. I didn't mean to snap your head off." She was twisting her slender hands together, and swallowed hard, visibly striving for composure. "You've got a sick call to make this afternoon. I've got your God-Box ready and put it on your desk." He quelled a minor sense of irritation at her calling his portable mass kit a God-Box.

"I . . . need to talk to you." She sounded desperate.

Ignoring Andrew's warning, he indicated the open door of the rector's office. "Come on in, Kim."

"No. Not now. You . . . haven't had any lunch and you've

got that sick call . . . later. We'll need *time.*" Her eyes were bright with unshed tears.

"Kim," he said gently. "We can *make* time now. Come in." But she shook her head and hurried away.

Thoughtfully he picked up his case and left the office. At the rectory he had a quick snack and found that the sympathy card was dry enough to open. It was a rather simple elegant one, from Mark. There was a handwritten note on the back in Mark's labored handwriting.

*Dear F. Lefinwell*
*I woud of come to the funerel*
*bud didnt here of it in time.*
*Im sorry. Hope your OK.*
*Your frend*
*Mark*

Now where had the boy gotten the money for this expensive card? Or had he simply shoplifted it? He put the water-stained card back on the soapstone sinkboard. He must talk to Andrew about Mark. *Somebody* must help salvage that boy.

Hannah Griswold sat at her kitchen table, staring at the breakfast dishes still on the table before her. It was almost noon. She should get up, do something. Instead, she started to cry again and picked up the sodden balled-up paper napkin to blot away the seeping tears. It was her own fault that Malcolm got so aggravated.

At least he hadn't lost his temper so badly that he hit her this time. He had done that twice now, and it had frightened them both. Each time he had apologized so humbly afterward that she had forgiven him, of course. He had such a lot on his mind, poor boy. This time he had grasped her shoulders and shaken her, jolting her head back and forth, until her glasses flew off. After he had gone, she picked them up from the corner. Thanks be to God they hadn't broken. But to get angry about such a little thing. She couldn't understand it. She went through the scene again in her mind.

He had come out to breakfast looking so nice. Malcolm was a good-looking boy. He was always so clean, so neat, so well shaven. His skin glowed and he smelled faintly of soap and that nice shaving lotion he used.

"Mom, what's all this?" He stared at the breakfast table and her heart sank. The hot breakfast was a mistake, another mistake.

"Well, dear, I got a real buy at the grocery on those little sausages, so I thought I'd just give you a real he-man breakfast for a change—sausages, French toast, real maple syrup—the works."

"Mom," he said with heavy patience. "You know I'm not a great breakfast eater. I just can't take a lot of heavy food in the morning. Coffee, juice, and cold cereal—you shouldn't have gone to all this trouble."

"Now, don't be silly. It's no trouble at all. You're the only cub I've got, after all. Now sit down and eat up like a good boy." No. She shouldn't have said it like that. A flush of anger rose in his face.

"Mother, I don't want to hurt your feelings, but I just don't want this stuff—fried everything, loaded with cholesterol."

"Oh, Malcolm, I can't throw it out, dear. It's already cooked. That would be sheer waste, and you don't make enough money to just throw it out the window. Please eat it, Honey. You can go back to cornflakes tomorrow." Wrong again. She shouldn't have called him "Honey." He hated it when she did.

"I wish to God you didn't smother me so," he said angrily, sitting down, staring sullenly at the cooling food. When he picked up his fork his hand was unsteady. "What do you mean I don't make enough money—this junk cost a lot more than cornflakes."

"Malcolm, watch your tone. I *am* your mother. If you don't

want it, don't eat it. I'll get your cornflakes." Despite herself, her voice quavered.

He flung down the fork and stood up. "All right, start crying. Make me feel guilty. That's what you want, isn't it!"

Then he had said—what else had he said? She couldn't quite recall it, but he had said a lot of things, and maybe she had too. Anyhow, the next thing clear in her mind was that he was shaking her, his face an angry red, and her glasses flew off. And somehow ever since she had been sitting here doing nothing. She pushed aside the plate of congealing food and laid her head down on her arms. She was going to have to try to distance herself from him, give him some space. That's one thing he had said, something about not having any space. How did you distance yourself from your child? When your child was all you had left?

Father Leffingwell gave communion to a Mrs. Rhodes in a convalescent home, and lingered there for almost an hour. Mrs. Rhodes was an old-time parishioner of Saint Polycarp's, and she wanted to talk. It was the primary need of so many people who were old and lonely—talking, having someone—anyone—to just *listen* for a while. He wanted to leave, but he made himself stay. Would he be this way when he lived in the retirement home in Baltimore? Would he seize upon every caller? Listen to me. I exist. I am here. Hear me. Hear me. Would he too hastily fumble out family pictures? This is my wife, Martha. This is my son, Philip. This is my grandson, Timothy. Aren't they beautiful?

He left Mrs. Rhodes with a faint rosy glow of pleasure in her withered cheeks. It made him think of Mrs.—what's her name—Mrs. Griswold, the restless mother of the layreader, Malcolm. What was the problem there?

He stopped and used the phone booth at a convenience

store. Gloria had come into the office and looked up the Griswold's address for him.

As he went up the cement walkway to the Griswold front door he saw the living room curtains twitch back into place. Well, at least she was at home. He rang the bell and waited. Then he rang again. He had the odd certainty that she *was* at home, just on the other side of the door, waiting for him to leave, *willing* him to leave. After a third try, he went back to his car. Something was decidedly wrong here. Remember Malcolm Griswold had come to his office, rambling on about the layreaders when he obviously wanted to say something else. He must *make* an occasion to talk to one of them. He mustn't let this pass.

In the car, he had to sit and wait a few minutes because a sudden longing for Philip swept through him. There was so much they hadn't had time to say to each other. In a little while his composure returned and he drove back to the office, where he found Gloria typing the Sunday bulletin into her computer.

"Father, we have a de-ja-vu-all-over-again with Mrs. Blalock. Yesterday she wanted another appointment with you A.S.A.P. and when Andy said you'd be back today, I set it up. And guess what?"

"She just cancelled?"

"Bingo."

"Did she set up another appointment?"

"No. Said she'd have to call back later. Do you want me to include an item in the Sunday bulletin for, you know, Monday?"

It took him a moment to know that she meant: a graceful thank you from him to those who had attended Philip's funeral, and offered him their support.

"Yes. Thanks for thinking of it. I'll write something now. Give me five minutes." He could feel it closing protectively about him again, the regular routine. Work was so often the answer to so many things. Thank God for work.

That evening after he reached the rectory, Andrew rang the doorbell. "I didn't come over to cadge another meal," he said, his big shoulders hunched against the cold. "But I need to see you."

"Come in and eat anyhow. I was just about to fix something. What were the cops there for this afternoon? Something about the kids?"

"Always." Andrew sounded tired. "But it worked out okay. I managed to fix it." He followed Father Leffingwell into the kitchen and sat down at the table, resting his tousled black head on his hands.

"I found a nice carton of chili in the fridge," Father Leffingwell said. "I think that and some of that good cornbread, and some leftover cole slaw. That sound all right to you?"

"Sounds great, Padre."

"All right. It'll be a few minutes. Do you want tea or coffee?"

"Coffee, I think. I'm about to go to sleep."

"Fine. I'll make some." Father Leffingwell set about doing it, waiting for Andrew to speak about what was on his mind. Finally he did, the sound of sadness running through his voice.

"I really blew it with Kim today, Padre. And I'm so sorry, but . . ." He gave a deep sigh. "You remember I told you that her brother, Jonathan, was gay?"

"Yes." Father Leffingwell dumped the chili into a pan and set in on the old stove, adjusting the flame underneath it.

"Well, Jonathan's been living with this guy, Ross something-or-other, for about two years. Kim says it is a lifetime commitment. She's going to ask you to bless their union. There is a special gay liturgy for it, you know."

"Oh, no!" Father Leffingwell said in dismay. "I can't do that, Andrew! Why would she ask *me*? You're the liberal. Remember me, I'm the stodgy old conservative traditionalist."

After a long pause, Andrew answered him. "She *did* ask me. I turned her down." He hit the table softly with a big fist. "I *am* a liberal. I think my credentials as a bona fide liberal are in good order, it's just that . . . I try to be tolerant . . . and accepting . . . and, well, you know the drill, we must cherish our differences, celebrate our diversity, et cetera, et cetera, but

I guess gay is just too diverse for me. I was so naive for so long, but I ran into some of it in sports, the athletes . . . some of the most macho guys."

"Philip mentioned that once. He called it 'a cult of male worship, gone awry.'"

"I just can't stomach it. It's a real turnoff. I just don't *understand* it. Oh, I'm sorry. I forgot about your son."

Father Leffingwell sat down at the table across from Andrew. "I don't think anybody understands it. My son didn't. We talked about it some at the hospice. Philip referred to it as the 'riddle of homosexuality.'"

"It's a riddle, all right," Andrew said glumly. "Kim and I were pretty good friends—now I think we've parted company. Anyhow, I wanted to prepare you. She didn't ask today, I take it."

"No. Thanks be to God."

"Did your son ever figure out the riddle?"

"He thought he did," Father Leffingwell said slowly. "I don't know whether he was right or wrong, but it satisfied him. Philip was an engineer, a very good one. I don't know if I ever mentioned it. But even as a child he had a very analytical mind. He was good at seeking out answers when he was confounded. And his homosexuality did confound him. He struggled a long time. Alone. I have some of his books and papers on the subject. I mean to read them . . . sometime." He was remembering Philip, speaking slowly and thoughtfully in his bed at the hospice. They had been talking about a scientific paper supporting the idea that homosexuality was a genetic condition.

"Yes, I read about the report, Dad. It is a study of the brain formation in homosexual males, and how it differs just slightly from the brain mass in heterosexual males."

"You believe it to be natural condition, then?" He had asked, and Philip's answer surprised him.

"Not at all, when you consider 'nature' as a whole. Nature, all the total force and power of it, pushes every creature of every species toward reproduction, survival of that species.

Anything in any creature which turns that creature in the opposite direction can't be right, can it? Aren't we just looking at another example of birth defect? Nature has given us plenty of those, the autistic child, the blind puppy, the twisted tree." He smiled a wry apology. "These things happen."

He told Andrew what Philip had said, and Andrew answered slowly, "Maybe your Philip had the right answer. Sounds sensible." He paused a moment. "But don't try to sell it to Kim. She'd never buy the idea that Jonathan was anything but perfect."

Father Leffingwell sighed. "I suppose she believes that God made him that way—with all the difficulties the gay man has to face."

"I'm afraid so, but you and I know that's a load of," he paused, and added with a faint grin. "Sometimes I forget I'm a man of the cloth and can't speak as frankly as I used to in the locker room."

Father Leffingwell had to laugh. "I have Philip's books and papers in the back bedroom, if you want to go through them later. There is one book, rather new, about the sexual brain that he . . . had to put aside without finishing."

"Yes. I'd like to read it. I worry about Kim. I like her a lot and she's pretty brainy, but she's screwed up on a lot of things."

Father Leffingwell came back to this when they had finished eating and were sipping a last cup of coffee. "Forgive me if this is an intrusion, but you said you 'liked' Kim . . ."

Andrew grinned. "Do I lust after her? No more than one lusts after any pretty woman, ignores it, and moves along. If you are wondering about my personal life, Padre, I don't have much at the moment. I am—unfortunately—still legally married to my college sweetheart, and I haven't figured out what to do about that yet."

"You mean the marriage didn't work out?" Father Leffingwell asked. "Can't you . . ."

Andrew shook his head and got up from the table, picking up dishes to put into the dishwasher. "We married in my junior year, before my injury. Melanie didn't get what she thought she was getting, you see. She thought she was getting a pro ball player, which I would have been—several agents had approached me—pulling in millions of dollars a year. Rich. Famous. What she got was a combination parish priest and social worker, who sometimes has trouble making the rent. She's long gone."

"I'm so sorry."

Andrew looked somberly into the distance. "I'm not as sorry now as I was when she took off in a blaze of anger and frustration. I've gotten used to it. Have you finished with that cup?"

"Yes."

"You see, we were grandly suited in college, but later, after I'd had three years in seminary opening up my intellect, there was friction—boredom on both sides. I'm fairly bright, and I could skim through the college courses and, with some tutoring in the hard stuff, pass everything easily. But all my concentration was football, the game, the program. We thought of nothing else. We wanted nothing else. Athletes are separate from the other students and kept that way. We were like gladiators, a splendid collection of powerful male bodies, superbly trained, but not encouraged to think, and we seldom did. Then, when football was out of my life completely, I found I had a *mind*. Melly and I were still great in bed together, but that was it. Beyond that, we existed on different planes. I'm not saying Melanie is dumb; she's not. But she's never bothered to use the brain God gave her, and probably never will . . . I do wish her well." He sounded wistful.

"Where is she now? Here, let's not forget the chili pot." Father Leffingwell got up and handed Andrew the empty pan.

"I'm not sure. She was living with her family over in Bellevue for a while. She's sort of into acting, dancing, dabbling in this and that. She's been seeing someone lately, I know that, and don't really care very much, except that I always hope she's okay. I really don't know what I'm going to do—haven't figured it out yet. My work is such a hassle that I don't have any *time* to think. I will some day." There was a note of finality in his tone which told Father Leffingwell that the subject was closed for now.

In the back bedroom, they examined Philip's collection of books and papers accumulated in his search for understanding. Andrew borrowed two books. When he left, a mixture of rain and snow was falling, sure to melt away the icy slush remaining. As he closed the door, Father Leffingwell had an odd sense of well-being. He has always heard that one didn't make new friendships after middle age. But perhaps one did. It was a good thought.

He was preparing for bed when the doorbell rang again and he put on his robe to answer it. It was Mark. He stood shivering in the gleam of the porch light, his dirty blond hair was dripping. Against the cold, he was clutching about his shoulders what appeared to be half of a tattered army blanket. His face was bruised and scraped, one eye swollen shut. He was crying, and trying not to.

Father Leffingwell opened the door. "Good heavens, boy, what happened to you! Come in! Come in here!"

"I'm okay." Mark's voice was strangled. "It's just—some big jerk took my dumpster. Now I got no place. I got no *place*."

# CHAPTER 6

Inside, Father Leffingwell tried to take the smelly piece of blanket from around Mark's shoulders, but the boy's thin hand clutched it beneath his chin. His whole body was shaking.

"It's my blanket," he protested, his wet blue eyes filled with panic.

"I know it's your blanket," Father Leffingwell said gently. "We'll put it on the back porch so we can wash it tomorrow. You don't need it in here. It's quite warm." He kept his own voice steady with an effort. *Dear God.* From the looks of Mark's face, the boys had fought like two animals for the dirty cave of a dumpster. They were *human beings*, and it shouldn't be like this.

Mark's shaking hands let go of the blanket. "He tore off my shirt," he wailed. "The jerk tore off my shirt. Now I got no shirt!"

"I'll get you a shirt tomorrow," Father Leffingwell said. "Now, let's go into the bathroom and see about that scrape on your face. How did this happen?" He led the boy into the bathroom, with Mark mumbling curses and crying.

"I think I'll run a hot tub for you, let you soak a while," he said, and began cleaning the raw temple and cheek with disinfectant. The boy's bruises would be showing up tomorrow. Mark leaned against the side of the basin, his eyelids drooping as Father Leffingwell completed his first aid efforts. He didn't think the boy needed to see a doctor. The trembling had subsided.

"When you get washed up, would you like something to eat?"

"Oh, I dunno," Mark said dully. "I already threw up once tonight. I found this burger in the dumpster, all wrapped up neat, almost whole, and I ate it, but when . . ." He paused, a shudder running through his body, obviously remembering the intruder into his haven, the dirty fight, and his terrible loss.

"I'll make you some milk toast—that goes down easily," Father Leffingwell said. "My mother used to make it for me when I wasn't feeling too good." He began to run water into the bathtub, testing it for temperature. "I'll go get my old bathrobe for you to put on."

"Milk toast . . . what's that?"

"Just buttered toast in a bowl with hot milk poured over it. It's very good."

"Okay, I guess . . . can you make the water real hot? I just gotta get warm, see. . . ."

It was after eleven when Mark came into the kitchen wearing the old maroon-colored bathrobe. Father Leffingwell already had three slices of buttered toast in a soup bowl. He put aside his book and got the pan of simmering milk from the stove to pour into the bowl. The toast swelled richly in the hot milk and little globules of butter glistened on the surface.

"Try this." He pushed the bowl across the table as Mark sat down. Obediently, Mark started to eat, blowing on the spoonfuls to cool them. Obviously exhausted from his ordeal, his eyelids drooped.

"This is real good," he said once.

"Now, listen to me, Mark," Father Leffingwell said. "You're hurt and tired so I want you to sleep late tomorrow morning. You need it, but I have to go to work early, so I probably won't be here when you wake up, okay?"

"Yeah. Thanks . . . I'll clean up."

"No. Don't bother about that. You'll be feeling a bit better so you'll probably be hungry. Please eat whatever you want to, but rest here and take it easy all day, but don't leave yet."

Mark's eyes opened and he looked startled. "*Don't* leave?"

"That's right. Don't go. Please stay until I get home. I'll try to make it at noon, but sometimes I can't. Okay?"

"Yeah. Sure. Okay."

Father Leffingwell observed him for a time. The boy was half asleep. He hoped he would remember. *Please God, let Mark be here when I get home tomorrow.*

Before he left for the church the next morning, Father Leffingwell found an old flannel shirt, blue plaid, and left it hanging on Mark's doorknob. He left a note sticking out of the pocket saying he would get Mark a new shirt sometime today. Starting his car, he wondered if he could afford to get Mark a warm jacket, and if he did, would Mark wear it, or sell it. He must talk to Andrew—if he could *find* Andrew.

At the church office he was surprised to see Gloria seated at her desk, opening a pile of mail and sorting it into stacks. "Good morning, Gloria," he said, keeping the surprise out of his voice.

She glanced up and smiled. "Thanks for not acting stunned to see me here like Andy did," but she said it without malice. "I thought I'd better show up early today, no matter what. Kim was really ticked off yesterday, and I'm sorry."

"Well, we all do the best we can. Is Andrew still around?" That would be a bit of luck.

"Yeah, he's in the church doing something."

The 'something' Andrew was doing in the church was praying, so Father Leffingwell sat quietly in a back pew until he was finished. Instead of the old white sweater, Andrew was wearing an old navy pea jacket. When he crossed himself and rose from the rail, Father Leffingwell got up.

"Do you have a minute, Andrew?"

"Yes, of course," Andrew said, coming toward him. "How long have you been here?" There was a look of deep sadness in his eyes, quickly veiled.

"Just a couple of minutes. I need to talk to you before we both get to work. We've got to do something about Mark. Can you come over to the rectory this evening?"

"Mark? Mark McGillicuddy? What's he done?"

"More done-to than done," and Father Leffingwell told him about the previous night.

"Poor little devil," Andrew said somberly. "You know, of course, that the chance of rescuing any of these kids, really saving them from the street, is just about zip."

Father Leffingwell sighed, sensing the other's depression. "I know, but we have to try."

"What do you think I do twenty-four hours a day, Padre?"

"Well, first things first. I've told him to stay put at the rectory today because I want to have a talk with him tonight."

"Good luck."

"I know, but it's worth a try. During your rounds today could you stop into a boys' department of some store and pick up a new T-shirt for him? Here." He took out his billfold. "And maybe a jacket too. How much do boys' jackets cost these days? You know more about kids than I do."

Andrew took the two twenty-dollar bills and then handed them back. "Make it ten. I'll go out to Value Village."

"What's that?"

"A thrift store—good second-hand clothing. I can probably get the shirt and jacket for under ten dollars. He'll be just as happy with those." Andrew stood up. "I think Gloria wants to see you." He was looking over Father Leffingwell's shoulder. Father Leffingwell turned and saw Gloria coming toward them. Poor girl. She should try to lose some weight; she was killing herself.

"Kim's in your office, Father Leffingwell," she said, slightly out of breath. "She says she has to see you before you get into your day."

"Better you than me," Andrew muttered. "See you tonight, but maybe it will be late," and he took off.

"Thank you, Gloria. Tell her I'll be there in five minutes," and when Gloria left, he took Andrew's place at the altar rail. There was so much he had to do—and he couldn't do it alone.

Kim was waiting in the rector's office, standing in front of the tall bookcase, staring blankly at the spines of the books. She turned when she heard him come in.

"Sit down, Kim. What can I do for you?" He paused, waiting until she had seated herself before he went behind the desk.

She took one of the visitor's chairs. "Has Andy talked to you about this—I have a feeling he has." Her voice was hard, her eyes angry. Asked the direct question he could do nothing but answer truthfully.

"About your brother. Yes, Kim, he did."

"Well, that'll save some time, then," she said bitterly. "I wouldn't have asked you at all but you have—had, I mean—a gay son you obviously cared about. I thought maybe there was a fifty-fifty chance." She leaned forward, placing unsteady hands on the desk.

"My son, Philip, never asked me to 'bless' his arrangement with Gideon Fairfax," Father Leffingwell said gently.

"Are you saying you won't do it for us?" Her voice shook. "Father Leffingwell, we're not asking for anything out of the prayer book. It's an alternative liturgy, written by gays, and it is a beautiful service for exchanging vows." Her eyes pleaded with him.

"Vows for what, Kim?"

"Love. Faithfulness. Kindness. Consideration. All the things people vow when they love each other, and want to make a lifetime commitment."

"Kim, the way things are now—with the divorce rate with *hetero*sexuals at 50 percent, a 'lifetime' commitment is pretty much a daydream—"

"But you see," she interrupted eagerly, "they've been together for almost two years. They mean it. They *are* committed. The least the church could do is sanctify it, bless it."

"*I* can't, Kim. It goes against everything I believe, everything I vowed to uphold when I was ordained to the priesthood. I'm sorry."

She leaned back in the chair and when she took her hands off the desk she left two damp palmprints on the polished surface.

"I don't believe this. I can't *believe* that in this day and age you'd cling to those Neanderthal ideas. You're just writing off 10 percent of the human population—" She paused when he held up his hand to stop her.

"That 10 percent figure is one of the myths, Kim. The gays, like any other bedeviled group, cling to their myths. They have to, to cushion themselves against a hostile world."

"What do you mean, 'myth!' It's a matter of record that 10 percent of people on this planet are *gay*. That's fact!"

"No. It's not fact. That is a figure from the old flawed Kinsey report from the forties. It was repudiated long ago. And you can't lump all homosexual people together. Men and women are not interchangeable. The updated figure is less than four percent for men and slightly less than one percent for women. That's fact, Kim. And I can show you the documented survey data, if you wish."

She stared at him sullenly. "I don't believe you." And after a moment she went on, "Well, what difference does it make? We are talking about my brother, Jonathan, a good, responsible man, a Christian. And about his *very fine partner*, Ross Palmer. *They* are committed to each other. For *life*."

He couldn't repress a sigh. "Kim, this is hard for you. It's hard for me too. Believe me, I don't enjoy shooting down everything you say, but that 'lifetime commitment' doesn't wash either. The 'commitment' record for male gay couples is worse than that for heterosexual couples."

"I don't have to listen to this!" She stood up. "You're not going to help us, so that's that. Forget I asked!"

He stood up too. "I'm sorry."

At the door she turned around, uncertain, curious. "I suppose you have some sort of survey figure for commitment too?" Her voice was heavy with sarcasm.

"As a matter of fact, yes. And this is one taken by two gay psychologists, who didn't believe the straights' figures either. They found that the average time the male gay couple stays together is about five years. And during the five years, one or both of the partners has casual sex with other men. Is that commitment?"

She didn't answer, but turned and walked out the door, slamming it resoundingly behind her.

Slowly he sat down at the desk again, shaken, still feeling the force of her anger, near-hatred. Poor Kim. Poor Kim. Without realizing it he turned the page of the desk calendar, seeing it, and not seeing it. It was filled with Gloria's neat handwriting. Slowly it registered with him.

At nine o'clock he was to counsel a couple on their coming marriage. God help them. Tom Fugate PP and Marilee Johnson U. The *PP* and *U* were Gloria's symbols to let him know that Tom Fugate was a Polycarp parishioner but Marilee Johnson was unchurched. He'd have to mention a few things to them they might not want to hear. At ten-thirty the senior warden, Mrs. Burris, wanted to see him about something on the Vestry agenda. After Mrs. Burris, if she didn't stay too long, there was a short respite, but he had to leave by eleven-forty for the Kiwanis lunch at the Four Seasons. "Park in downstairs garage. They validate ticket," Gloria had written. So he couldn't go home to lunch. His heart sank. Would Mark stick it out all day at the rectory? Something else was also niggling at his mind. He reached over and pressed the intercom key.

"Gloria, Mrs. Blalock hasn't called back, has she?"

"Not yet, Father."

"Thanks."

It was so much, so many things. He reached for the bronze-colored carafe on his desk and poured himself a cup of strong coffee. God bless Newton Crail, coffee maker. The term "assisted living" came to his mind and he smiled.

It was after six o'clock when he reached the rectory. The mixture of rain and snow had washed away a lot of the slush. He was reassured as he opened the front door to hear the mutter of the television.

He found Mark, the blue plaid shirt hanging loosely on him, on the floor in front of the TV, watching the evening news, and eating something from a large bowl. There was an empty milk glass on the floor beside him.

He got up as quickly as his bruised body would let him, leaving the bowl on the floor. It looked something like beef stew—probably one of the ladies' gifts.

"Hi, Father. You said to eat anything." He sounded placating.

"Yes. That's fine. I'm glad you did, Let me look at that face." The bruised side of the boy's face was a vivid purple, and scabs had formed over the scraped skin. The swelling around his eye seemed to have diminished slightly.

"You wouldn't believe what I ate! I been eating all day! I can't seem to stop. I never saw so much stuff! Where'd you get so much stuff?"

"It was given to me by the ladies of the church when my son died." He kept his voice steady.

"Why'd they do that?"

"Oh, they just felt sorry about my son. And they are kindly people. They wanted to make my life a little easier, if they could."

Mark looked at him, puzzled. "Man," he said finally. "That was nice. Real nice." The way the boy was standing he could see out the front window. "You gonna get company. A lady."

Father Leffingwell went to the window. Claire Gibson was locking her car door. The committee had come back, then, from Boise and Portland. Suddenly he turned to Mark.

"Mark, don't ask questions, just do as I say. I'll explain later. Go into the bedroom, shut the door, and be very quiet. Can you do that?"

Mark caught his meaning instantly. "Sure." He started to bolt from the room, halted at the door, swung around, and with a lopsided grin on his swollen face, scooped up the bowl and milk glass from the floor and ran soundlessly down the hall. Father Leffingwell didn't even hear the bedroom door close.

He opened the front door as Claire Gibson came up the walk and invited her in. He could sense her controlled anger and frustration. Ah, too bad. What Mrs. Burris had talked to him about this morning then had been correct.

Once in and seated in the living room, she couldn't seem to begin.

"I can sense you are upset," he offered, trying to help. "Would you like a cup of chamomile tea?"

"Yes, please." She almost jerked the words out and he sought temporary refuge in the kitchen, hoping Mark was capable of absolute silence, but what fourteen-year-old boy was? Back in the living room he offered the tray to Claire and she took one of the chipped cups.

"Good heavens, Father, are these the best cups we've provided for you? I apologize."

"Don't worry about the dishes—they are dishwasher proof, after all."

She took a sip of tea. "I'll see that you get some proper teacups tomorrow." She took another sip, put the cup down, and leaned her head against the back of the chair. She looked older than her fifty-some years, despite the elegant clothes and grooming. And she was bone tired; exhaustion showed in the sudden relaxing of her slim, well-kept body.

"I don't know how to say this, Father, but . . . my church means a lot to me."

"I know it does," he said kindly. Insight told him that she was one of those women who had nothing of her own. She had always been somebody's sister, or somebody's daughter. She had never gone down into the mainstream to build a separate life.

"As you know, my father—my mother, really—practically created Saint Polycarp Parish . . ."

"So I have been told," he agreed. "It was a fine thing to do."

She sighed deeply. "I hate to see it all . . . slipping away."

"What happened in Boise and Portland? Did you see the two candidates?"

"Yes." She sat up, but with an effort. "But it's what happened before we left. It's the committee, the people on the committee. Ralph Prescott thinks and feels the same way I do about things, but he's too weak to ever contradict a majority.

And the other four are . . . let's just say they compete with one another to see who's the most politically correct."

"Oh, dear me." Mrs. Burris had been right, then.

"You see, the Vestry stacked the committee with liberals. Either of the two candidates we saw was worth an invitation to visit the parish and make the mandatory visits around, and the guest sermon—but I was voted down both times. The others wouldn't even give them a chance. I was just . . . routed."

He felt a quick sense of sympathy at her use of the old-fashioned word "routed." In a way they were kindred spirits, both outmoded and obsolete. It brought back his continuing sadness about the state of the church.

She gave a shaky sigh. "I think what those four really want is to get someone so shocking that the remaining traditionals in the parish will just bolt. A lot have already. I think what they really want is a woman priest or maybe a gay—Oh, I'm sorry."

"That's all right. Mrs. Burris was in to see me today. She thought something like this might be happening. She told me she thought the committee was lopsided."

"Oh," Claire said, looking rather pleased. "I didn't know Sarah Burris was really involved. She's such a peaceable person; she never takes a stand on anything."

"Well, a number of people are ready to take a stand and try to influence the Vestry, I gathered today. But to be realistic, she and I agreed that Saint Polycarp will probably never get another conservative priest. It seems the best we can hope for is a decent middle-of-the-roader."

"Well," Claire said slowly. "I could live with that. What do you think we should do?" Her tension seemed to have diminished.

"It'll take a bit more time, but Mrs. Burris and I both thought that, since the candidate has to come to the parish, visit around, preach and so on, that those in the congregation holding out for a middle-of-the-roader just drag their heels. Never let the liberals get any consensus. Always find so much fault with every candidate they present that we finally wear them down. It is bound to have an influence."

"Would you be willing to stay on a little longer if we need you?" She was looking at him imploringly and he realized that he had dug himself neatly into a hole. Oh, well. So be it.

"Of course, I could stay on for a while," he said, nodding. The retirement home in Baltimore would still be there when he was ready for it.

"You know," she said thoughtfully, "I'm Altar Guild on Wednesdays, and I've listened to you then as well as Sundays, and I wish . . . I just wish we could get someone like you. You are so . . . in tune with the . . . basics." She was biting her lip nervously and began to make leave-taking motions. "Thank you for seeing me in this impromptu way, but I just needed some backup." She stood up, and he did too.

At the door he said, "I'll help all I can. Just remember to stick it out. Sometimes the victor isn't the one who can fight the best battle, but the one who can hang on the longest."

When she had gone, he paused inside the front door for a moment. Today at the Kiwanis lunch he had encountered two men who had been Saint Polycarp parishioners but had dropped out of the church. Now they were both coming back to the Wednesday noon services.

Well, old man, maybe you're still God's vicar, after all.

He went back to Mark's bedroom and rapped on the door. It was opened instantly. "Everything okay?" the boy asked.

"Yes. I'm sorry about that, but this house belongs to the church and I'm the only one authorized to live here. I don't know how they would feel about houseguests."

"Like street kids, huh?" Mark grinned, and Father Leffingwell had to smile; street kids had their own wisdom.

"Come on in the kitchen. I want to put together a bite for supper. What would you like?" Father Leffingwell asked.

"Not me. I'm stuffed. I been eating all day. But I'll keep you company." Mark followed him into the kitchen.

After he had eaten and they were in front of the fireplace listening to the hum of the dishwasher, Father Leffingwell tried to open the subject of Mark's future. "Mark, we're pretty good friends, aren't we?" And as soon as he said it, he knew it was the wrong approach. He could see the boy tense, become wary.

"Yeah, I guess."

"Are you satisfied with your life as it is?"

Mark gave him a look of quickly veiled contempt. "You kidding?"

"Have you thought of doing anything about it?"

"You mean like robbing a bank?"

"Of course not. Please be serious. I mean something constructive. Something that might take a bit of effort. You're a very smart boy, Mark." Something in Mark's mulish look stopped him. There was an uneasy pause. Color had risen into Mark's face.

"Look, Father Leffingwell, we're pretty good friends, that's right. And you done a lot more for me than I done for you. But you can talk around and around it but I know where you're headed. You're leading up to 'Mark go back to school,' right? Well, no offense really, but that's not gonna happen. Ever. Got it?"

"Why on earth not?"

"Because I got my own action plan, see. I'm no dummy. I got goals. I know where I'm going. You're really great. I like you a lot, so I don't want you to worry about me. I'm gonna make it just fine. You'll see."

"Doing *what*?" Father Leffingwell couldn't keep the exasperation from his voice, and he saw Mark stiffen but he plunged on recklessly. "You can't do a single thing without an education. And you can't even begin without a high school diploma, or a G.E.D."

"Don't you even want to hear about my action plan?" The boy's voice was sullen, and then he added defensively, "All right, maybe right now—temporarily—I use a little when I can. But I don't deal, okay. I'm not so dumb that I want to get myself screwed up with the fuzz."

"Of course, I would like to hear your plan, Mark. What is it?"

Mark cleared his throat uneasily. He was all hunched over,

his thin fingers picking nervously at the worn carpet. "So okay. First step is I gotta stick it out on the street till I'm old enough to get a *real* job. In a *gas station*. I hang around gas stations a lot. I already know how to pump gas, of course. And I can charge batteries and test for antifreeze level and change oil and test for transmission fluid and *lots* of other stuff. Then, after I work in this station for a while I got enough money to buy my own station. I'm gonna be a *boss*." He glanced up, his eyes angry and rebellious. "And today I added a new piece to my plan, see. Wanna hear it?"

"Of course I do."

"Well, this house. I like this house. When I get my own station I'm gonna get me a house, just like this."

"Well, I must admit that most of it sounds like a very good plan, Mark. And I'm really relieved to know that you are being careful about getting involved in anything risky."

"What's wrong with it? What part don't you like?"

"I guess I'm afraid about your staying on the street until you get a job. Street living itself is pretty risky."

Mark was quiet for a time. "Okay," he conceded. "Sometimes I get into some hassles—like this time. But mostly I can handle it." His voice was so low it was difficult to hear.

"I'd like to get one thing clear between us, if we can," Father Leffingwell said. "I am your friend, even if I have made you a bit defensive at the moment. If there is any trouble when you're on the street, will you still come to me for help?"

"Yeah, I guess."

"And I would like you to stay on here until you are completely recovered from this present hassle. Will you do that? That's *my* job, you know, helping people, helping my friends."

"You're not mad at me because I'm not going to school? Ever?"

"No, no. Not mad. Maybe a little disappointed, but certainly not mad. Will you come to me, if you need to?"

"Yeah, well. Okay. *If*. But most things I can handle."

Father Leffingwell didn't press it any more and they watched a series of idiotic sitcoms selected by Mark from the TV guide.

Andrew came a little after ten with Mark's shirt and jacket. Instead of an ordinary T-shirt, he had bought a gray sweatshirt with long sleeves, and a blue down-filled jacket. Mark was elated. Especially with the sweatshirt. Not only was it wonderfully warm, but it had one of the traditional Seattle pictures on the front, an open black umbrella, surrounded with a circle of printing. The printing said: SEATTLE RAIN FESTIVAL. JANUARY 1 TO DECEMBER 31. Mark thought it was hilarious.

The two priests left Mark, in his new sweatshirt, in front of the TV and went into the study. They sat down in the sagging leather chairs.

"While I think of it," Andrew said, "lemme tell you this, Padre. I've been remiss about holding up my end here. From now on I intend to assist on Sunday and take a share of the other services. I've already told Gloria so she can get it all in the Sunday bulletins. No arguments, okay?"

"Well, it's up to you, Andrew. It would be a help."

"Done, then. How'd you come out talking to Mark?"

"I'm afraid I struck out, badly."

Andrew shook his head. "It's hard to reach them. Did you manage to retain his trust? Are you still friends?"

"I guess so. I backed off, although I wanted to shake some sense into him. Andrew, what is the matter with these kids? You've had more experience with them by far than I have."

"How much time have you got, Padre?" Andrew leaned back tiredly in the chair, causing it to creak.

"Do you know anything about Mark's background?"

"Some. But only what I've read in the CPS records and the juvy records. He's down as an 'abused' child, which may or may not be the case."

"What do you mean?"

"Well, these kids wise up fast. No runaway is going to admit to a social worker that he left home because he wouldn't or couldn't obey the house rules. They are all 'abused.'

And, to be fair, many are. Sometimes terribly. Sexual abuse. Violence. But some of them just cut out for trivial reasons and then they don't feel they can go back. With Mark, I don't know. He's a smart kid, and gutsy, but I just don't know."

After Andrew left, Father Leffingwell tried to read, but gave it up finally and went to bed. He was very troubled.

By Friday, the heavy rainfall during the night had washed away all of the remaining slushy snow. The city was gleaming with cleanliness. Seattle was one of the cleanest cities he had ever been in.

At Saint Polycarp's, Friday was the Rector's day off, to read, reflect, polish up his Sunday sermon, or whatever he wished to do. Actually, there was usually something left over that he had to attend to. At about ten o'clock, Gloria called apologetically from the church office. The pastor at First Baptist was down with the flu and couldn't do the hospital chaplaincy. Could Father Leffingwell fill in? So by ten-thirty he was driving the little bug up toward what the Seattle-ites called Pill Hill, where there was a cluster of medical facilities overlooking the beautiful Sound.

He didn't finish until almost three and, tired and hungry, he headed home. As soon as he entered the rectory front hall, he knew Mark was gone. The silence in the old house was palpable. He went to the back bedroom and found the bed neatly made. He hurried to the back porch, hoping that Mark had just gone out for a while, but when he saw the neat stack of laundered sheets, and his blue plaid shirt washed and folded beside them, he knew the boy had left. He wanted to cry. Mark had left a note, held to the front of the refrigerator with a magnet.

*Dear F. Lefinwell*
*Please dont be mad but I got to split. Thank you for all the food and stuff. If any bad happens I will tell you but it wont.*
*Your frend*
*Mark*

He sank down at the kitchen table, feeling a growing sense

of rage. Had the whole world gone mad? Philip was dead of AIDS. Mark, a fine and intelligent child, was intent on wasting himself on the streets and apparently nobody could do anything about it. Somewhere Irma Blalock was fighting a lone battle against family pressure to keep her unborn child. Something was very wrong inside the silent Griswold house. And that man with the burning eyes—what's his name—Pruitt? And the lovely young woman, Gloria, sick with a secret misery, was eating her way to an early death. And Kim, bitter and angry, trying to reshape her religion because she loved her impaired brother. And Claire Gibson, clinging to her half-life, and the church—his church—in the hands of clowns and fools.

Stiffly, he went into the study where his sermon lay half-finished on the desk. With shaking hands he crumpled it up and threw it violently into the wastebasket, and sat down to write another one. He was interrupted only once, when Claire Gibson rang the bell to bring him six exquisite teacups, saucers, and a matching pot.

He looked around the small church Sunday morning with a new awareness. It was a lovely church. The dark old wood of the pews was polished to a luster. From where he sat, as Andrew read the Gospel, he could see the delicate rose window above the altar. The strips of red carpeting in the aisles were immaculate, thanks to Newton Crail. The silver vessels on the altar were gleaming, thanks to the Altar Guild women. Order. Discipline. Reverence. The soaring voices of the choir seemed exceptionally beautiful. The congregation today seemed larger than usual. That was good.

*When two or more are gathered together in my Name . . .*

He sent up a silent prayer as he rose to mount the pulpit for his sermon. He must get their attention, wake them up, free them from their mindless drifting. Leaning forward, bracing one hand on each side of the lectern, he gazed out at their faces. Then he began.

"Today, my friends, I want us to start preparing together for the coming season of Lent, a time in our church year for reflection on amending our lives." He paused. They were all sitting there, listening politely, but were they really hearing?

"Toward this end I want us to start considering the large subject of *sin.*" Several people leaned forward in faint astonishment. He heard a startled gasp from someone in the choir. Episcopalians didn't talk about sin. Sin was for far-right fundamentalists. Turning his head slightly, he caught a sudden glint of amusement in Andrew's eyes, but he went on relentlessly.

"Our ancient church, in its wisdom, has thoughtfully sorted sin out for us into neat categories. Therefore, we have three sins of the body—sloth, gluttony, and lust. And we have four sins of the soul—anger, pride, envy, and greed. The seven *deadly* sins." Out of the corner of his eye he saw Andrew bow his head and hide a lower half of his face with his hand to conceal a grin.

"Every Sunday from now on into Lent we will study one sin. Today we will explore . . ."

He felt a defiant satisfaction and went on. Whether they liked it or not, Anglicans were too polite to get up and walk out. And by the time he left this parish—unless the bishop fired him tomorrow—these people would hear, and perhaps think about, a few things that hadn't been mentioned for a long time.

Maybe, just maybe—*please, God*—he could make a difference here.

# CHAPTER 7

Just before it was time to leave for the church office on Monday, Father Leffingwell dialed Andrew's number, and Andrew answered on the first ring.

"I was just about to call you, Padre. What's up?"

"Claire Gibson came to me with a problem and I just thought of something that might help. What's the name of the man on the search committee whose first name is Ralph? All I can come up with is Ralph Chalmers."

"No. Ralph Chalmers, I think, is in charge of the acolytes. Isn't there a Ralph Prescott?"

"Right. Prescott. Thanks. What were you going to call me about?"

"Just wanted to prepare you. Kim is annoyed about your sins sermons, so you may hear more about that. So are some of the more liberal members. On the other hand, I heard some very good comments too, so don't despair. I mention this in case you wanted some feedback."

"I do. Thanks, Andrew." It wasn't until after he had hung up that he wondered what Andrew himself had thought.

It was raining again and Father Leffingwell had trouble starting the car. Small wonder. As soon as he had heard about Philip, he had packed what he could in the front and driven across a continent to get here. The little old car had stood up well, but the telltale noises were warning him. The engine needed a complete tuneup, of course, and he'd probably find something else when he got into the job. Suddenly, he sat back.

Another good idea! Two good ideas in one hour. Not bad, old man.

He hurried back into the rectory and dialed Andrew's number, which Andrew didn't answer until the fourth ring.

"You caught me out in the hall. What can I do for you?"

"Today on you rounds, if you see Mark McGillicuddy, tell him that old Father Leffingwell has car trouble and is going to tune up the engine. He might be able to use some help if there is any heavy lifting."

Andrew laughed. "Gotcha. Okay. Can you really tune up an engine?"

"Yes. My son and I kept the beetle running like a Swiss timepiece. And I still do." In spite of himself, when he mentioned Philip his voice shook, but Andrew pretended not to notice.

"You got it. If I see Mark, I'll pass the word."

When he reached the church office he was surprised to see Gloria busily at her desk, sorting the stack of weekend mail.

"Good morning, Father," she said brightly. "I was in church yesterday. It's been years since I heard about the seven deadly sins. How come you started on sloth? This is all your stuff."

He took the stack of mail she handed him. "Have to start somewhere, and sloth seemed as good a place as any. Lots of grief is caused by simple laziness."

Gloria's round face, brightly hiding so much misery, became serious. "Yeah, I know. I could probably have a good friend in Kim if I could get my act together and get to work on time."

"You're on time today," he pointed out.

She smiled again. "I decided yesterday to conquer sloth, Father. Partly because I have no intention of conquering gluttony. When do you get to gluttony? I'll skip that one."

"Gluttony is next Sunday. Won't you come and just listen?"

"I guess so. I have to bring the kids to Sunday school anyhow." Her face flushed in embarrassment so he said nothing more. He knew that, with Gloria, tears were never far from the surface, regardless of the bright manner she put on for show.

He managed to track down Ralph Prescott of the search committee and set up a lunch date with him. Then he went through the rector's mail and dictated some replies. A little after ten Gloria buzzed his intercom.

"Father, Peter Pruitt, one of our parishioners, just called and wondered if you can see him this afternoon."

"Yes, if four o'clock won't be too late for him. I have a lunch date and two sick calls, but I should be back by four." He mentally braced himself. Would Peter Pruitt want a miracle? He prayed silently for a moment before going on with his work.

His lunch with Ralph Prescott went rather well. Prescott was a tall, lean man, with a hawkish face. He was a retired high school teacher and his manner seemed hesitant and somewhat timid. Father Leffingwell wondered how he had managed to control a classroom full of teenagers. But he found Prescott to be a thoughtful and intelligent man, deeply religious. As a traditional Christian, he hadn't been so much lukewarm about the search as hopeless. Now he promised to be more aggressive in backing Claire up on the committee.

Father Leffingwell made his two sick calls, and when they were completed it was only three o'clock, and he suddenly recalled Mrs. Griswold, and turned the little car into her street. He saw Mrs. Griswold before he stopped the car. She was on her front porch, clearing sodden wet leaves and trying to get them into a plastic bag. There was no way she could avoid him this time.

"Oh, good afternoon, Father," she said nervously as he came up the walk. "I was just getting rid of this mess."

"Here, let me help," Father Leffingwell said. "You need a couple more hands." And he held the bag while Mrs. Griswold pushed the wet leaves into it with her broom.

"Oh, you'll need to wash your hands," she said when the job was done. "Come inside, I'll make us some coffee."

"That would be wonderful," he said untruthfully, as he had just had two cups with lunch.

"What an immaculate house," he said when they were seated over fresh cups of coffee in the living room.

She looked around vaguely. "Yes, I . . . have to keep busy, you know. I've worked all my life and I . . . have to keep busy. I get so bored sometimes." Her face momentarily turned away and he thought he saw the shadow of an old bruise.

"I had a chance the other day to talk with your son, Malcolm, about the layreaders, you know," Father Leffingwell said.

"Oh, did you?" Her face brightened. Maybe he was mistaken. Maybe it hadn't been a bruise.

"Yes. It is so good of people to volunteer when they are working full-time too. I don't know what the church would do without people like Malcolm."

He had said the magic words. She began to talk about her son, her face glowing with pride, her speech pouring out in a nervous rush. Malcolm was her only child. She had been widowed when he was a few months old. She and her husband had both still been in college at the time and, of course, she had to quit and go to work, so she had never got her degree in Home Economics. But Malcolm had been worth it—he was such a wonderful son. They were so close. They had always been best friends. He was such a comfort to her.

"Why don't you go back and get your degree now?" Father Leffingwell asked when the flood slowed down a bit.

"Me? A degree? Oh, good heavens, at my age?" She gave a trill of artificial laughter, turning her head so that the light from the window showed the side of her face. There was indeed the yellowish tint of an old bruise. How had she gotten it? Perhaps she had fallen. He hoped that was all, but feared it wasn't. He had encountered elder abuse before.

"Well, if not a degree, then perhaps you might get into some of the Elderhostel programs. I understand they are quite interesting, and you said you like to keep busy."

"Elderhostel?"

"For retirees," Father Leffingwell explained. "Most colleges and universities participate. One- or two-week courses in a most fascinating array of subjects are offered. The elders live on campus. It makes a grand vacation and opens up the mind—"

"Two weeks!" She interrupted. "Malcolm would never stand for that. He couldn't possibly get along by himself for two weeks. Oh, Father Leffingwell, I'm afraid I'll pass up Elderhostel."

"Well, it was just a suggestion," he said easily. "You do make delicious coffee."

"Thank you, I . . . I'm a pretty good cook, but Malcolm is . . . a fussy eater. Always has been."

"What does Malcolm do?"

"He is so intelligent," she said in a new burst of enthusiasm. "He was planning on going into law but, somehow or other, you know the law schools are so crowded and he . . . he couldn't get in any school near here. That is, the only one who accepted his application was some place in Indiana. I was still working then so my moving to Indiana was out of the question, of course, so . . ." Her voice dwindled off and for a moment her eyes were haunted. "But what he did—he's so resourceful. He settled for the job he's got now. He's a paralegal in a very prestigious firm." She rattled off several names and Father Leffingwell nodded approvingly, although he had no idea how prestigious the firm was.

"What kind of work did you do, Mrs. Griswold?"

"I just took what I could get, Father. I had a six-month-old boy to raise to manhood, and I couldn't be choosy. I'd had two years of Home Ec. and I got a job as assistant housekeeper in the Marchant Hotel—it's downtown. It used to be one of the leading hotels in Seattle, but it's gone downhill a bit now. But I became head housekeeper there, running the whole show, for years and years. Then when Malcolm's income increased he insisted that I'd done my share . . ." She shrugged. "I wish . . . sometimes I wish . . ." Her voice trailed off again.

"Since you are a bit bored now, have you thought of doing some part-time jobs—just to keep busy, just to get out of the house?" He asked gently. It looked like a familiar pattern, the widowed mother and the only child.

"Doing what?" The mask slipped a moment and he saw naked desperation. "I'm sixty-three years old and the only thing I've ever done is housekeeping. Maybe on a pretty big scale, but still housekeeping."

"Actually, I may just have had a good idea. Why don't you do a bit of housekeeping now? Two-career families always need help. Working people—in fact, I'm not doing too well myself. I could offer you a small part-time housekeeping job at the rectory. I'm only here for a few months, so it would be temporary. You could test it out. I had no idea I'd be in a big, old-fashioned rectory. I had been thinking of a small studio apartment that I could keep up by myself . . ." He spread his hands.

"Oh, you poor thing," she said, smiling. "I've been in the rectory. I suppose Claire Gibson put everything back the way it was. All that furniture to dust."

"I believe she did."

"I wonder . . . I wonder . . ." Clearly the idea intrigued her.

"On my stipend I could probably pay a couple of dollars over minimum wage. I think I could afford two hours a couple of times a week. Why don't you think it over?" Father Leffingwell put down his coffee cup. "If you'd like to try it out you could set your own hours—I'm out all day. Part-time housekeeping jobs might not be a bad little sideline business."

They left it at that, and he headed back to the church for his appointment with Peter Pruitt. He felt rather pleased with himself. Three ideas in one day. Maybe the old man was ticking away on all cylinders, after all.

When he got back to the office Gloria was still there. "I thought you were supposed to leave at three," he said.

"Yeah. But I thought I'd stay today and catch up on some things. Don't worry," she said with a sudden smile. "I won't carry my battle with sloth too far and become a workaholic. And Mr. Pruitt is in your office. I gave him a cup of coffee."

"Did Mrs. Pruitt come with him?"

"No. He goes around by himself. He has a special van. Oh, and Andy said he needs to see you. He'll stop by the rectory tonight."

"Thanks."

Father Leffingwell hurried into the rector's office, apologizing for having kept the other man waiting. Seating himself behind his desk, he looked again at the devastated man in the wheelchair.

"No problem," Pruitt said. "I've been sitting here trying to think what I want to say to you—or what I want you to say to me." His voice was deep and steady. He was—had been—a big man, with muscular shoulders and chest. He had the remains of a rugged outdoor look. Father Leffingwell could imagine him hiking strongly up a mountain trail or hauling down a heavy canvas sail.

"My wife wants a divorce," he finally said bluntly. "And I've refused to go along. I may be old fashioned—or maybe just selfish—but to me marriage is forever. Am I wrong?"

"Biblically, no," Father Leffingwell said, regretting the sigh in his voice. "But if you are asking me how the church feels about divorce, I'm not sure I can tell you. There are so many changes today."

Pruitt gave a short, mirthless laugh. "I know what you mean. That little twit who calls herself a deacon has advised my wife to file for divorce, because I can no longer fulfill my nuptial responsibilities."

"Kim Fletcher?" Oh dear, was he going to have to battle Kim on this too?

"Yep. Little Deacon is part of the new wave in religion. If your vows start to bind, toss 'em out and make new ones. Well, I'm not going to, Natalie vowed in sickness and in health and—" His voice broke and it was a moment before he could go on. "Sorry. To hear my wife, you'd think that the only thing worthwhile in a marriage is the sex. It's important, I grant you, but . . . unfortunately my wife is a sexpot and I . . . won't be written off just because I . . ." His big fist clenched on the arm of his wheelchair.

"Peter, the need for sexual expression is a very potent force," Father Leffingwell said gently. "Are you asking your wife to be celibate? There are—" Warning signals clicked in his mind. How near was this man to his breaking point?

"Alternatives? Of course there are. I've offered, but she won't have it, thank you." Pruitt was shaking his head. "Natalie is something of a perfectionist, shall we say? She doesn't tolerate substitutes. She's something of a health nut too, a body-worshiper, if you will. Imperfections, in anything, repel her. When we first got married we lived in a rented house in west Seattle. The family next door had a little boy with Down's Syndrome. He was a sweet, affectionate kid. Everybody on the block loved him, but he made Natalie's skin crawl. We had a little dog once, Tuffy. He was hit by a car. One leg was so badly mangled the vet said he had to amputate, and rather than have Tuffy gimping around on three legs, Natalie had him put to sleep. She can't stand any impairment, and . . . God knows . . . I'm impaired."

"I understand where you're coming from, Peter. You feel furious and hopeless about your situation." He spoke carefully, knowing he couldn't take sides, if there was any hope of keeping them together.

"What about Lucy, your child?" He hated saying it, adding to the man's despair. He must get Pruitt's focus off his own fury. How much risk did his fury, his desperation, contain for himself, for others?

"Lucy? What about her?" Pruitt looked astonished. "How do you know Lucy?" He sounded puzzled.

"I make it my business to know all the Sunday school children. It's part of my job description." Father Leffingwell smiled to take out any sting.

Pruitt gave a wry smile. "Of course you do. I wasn't thinking. Well, what about Lucy?" He seemed less tense.

"I found her very withdrawn. It is clear that the family dissension is having an impact. I've made a point of talking to her."

Pruitt was shaking his head. "Withdrawn? No, I don't think so. Lucy has always been a quiet child. Shy. She's okay."

"She told me her grades were down. She's worried about it," Father Leffingwell persisted. The child was suffering and Pruitt must recognize it. Some of the street kids who ate in the rec room were no older than Lucy Pruitt. And in a marriage break-up, children often assumed guilt and simply ran away to escape it.

"Well, yes, her grades haven't been too good lately. But it's just a phase—kids go through phases . . ."

"She has bitten her fingernails down to the quick."

Pruitt was silent for a time. "You don't miss much, do you. Are you telling me to let my wife walk out on me?" A dull flush rose in Pruitt's face.

"No. I'm just telling you that there is more to this than whether or not your marriage survives. And that you may not win this one. If I read you right, you are accustomed to being a winner." There was a slight question in Father Leffingwell's tone.

"Yes. Pretty much all my life I've managed . . ."

"Win or lose, in this contest, your responsibility to your child doesn't end, Peter. If winning damages your daughter, it will be a hollow victory. I'll talk with your wife, if she'll let me, if you think it would help. Sometimes we can sort these things out."

"I'll talk to her, use whatever clout I've got left. Even with disability my income is still bigger than hers. Do you want to talk to her alone, or both of us together?"

"I think alone the first time, then perhaps both of you."

"Good. I'll have her call for an appointment." Both his hands balled into fists and Father Leffingwell could feel the held-in rage.

"Peter, can we pray about this?" He got up and walked around the desk, placing his hands on Pruitt's shoulders. Pruitt was looking up at him, his eyes sick.

"Sure," he said bleakly. "It can't do any harm, can it?"

Afterward, they talked about the man's disability. It had

been an on-site accident, the crane tipping over, the heavy metal head of it crashing down on him. There hadn't been time to get completely away.

"Just one second more and I'd have made it," he said, shaking his head. "And by now I'd have forgotten all about it."

He talked about his wife, Natalie. "She's having an affair," he said, and it took effort. "This jerk she works with, Evan Driscoll."

"That name sounds familiar."

"Oh, yes, he's one of your flock, Father. Divorced. Good-looking guy. He's the one who got Natalie her present job—probably to get her into his bed. Which he did. He's pushing her on the divorce idea." Pruitt's mouth twisted. "I can't wait for your sermon on lust, Father Leffingwell. Maybe when you get through the seven deadly sins you could do a series on the Ten Commandments and sock it to 'em when you get to adultery."

Peter Pruitt was obviously feeling better for having at least talked openly. He could make a joke—bitter humor was better than no humor at all.

Father Leffingwell walked Peter Pruitt out to his van, and after he had gone, went into the church to pray, but paused when he saw Claire Gibson. She was stooping to pick up some invisible fleck of something from the red carpet.

"Father Leffingwell, I was hoping to see you." She stood up and came toward him. Her face was flushed, and what Andrew had referred to as her "mean green eyes," that put a hex on him, were bright with pleased excitement.

"What can I do for you, Claire?"

"Ralph Prescott called me. He said you had talked to him. Father, I can't thank you enough. He's going to talk to the other committee members and try to get them to reverse their decision on Chester Bledsoe, the man in Boise."

"That is good news indeed. I am glad. Maybe Saint Polycarp will get someone suitable to everyone."

"Yes," she said, looking around the small church, at the

beautiful rose window above the dark wood of the altar. She ran one hand over the carved end of the pew they stood next to. There was something loving, almost sensual, in her touch. "When my mother died, my father replaced the old pews—they were rather ordinary—with these, in her memory."

"How kind of him. I didn't know." Poor soul. He wanted to say, "This is not the church, Claire. This is just the building. The church is the *people*," but he didn't.

"Yes." Her face changed, became angry. "There was a brass plaque, commemorating the gift."

"What do you mean 'was?'" As soon as he said it, he dreaded the answer.

"One of Father Cullen's street urchins stole it."

"What?"

"They are such destructive little vandals. There are several commemorative plaques in various places—this church is sixty years old, after all."

"I'm so sorry," he said lamely. Andrew was right. In anger, Claire did seem to have mean eyes. "Couldn't we replace it? Really, we should. Your father went to great expense, I'm sure." He placed his own hand on the back of the pew. He wondered what kind of wood it was. Probably something terribly expensive.

"It wouldn't be the same," she said bitterly, her pleasure about the search committee extinguished by this old anger. He must work a line into his sermon on anger; about the change anger effects in the person who surrenders to it.

"Did you speak to Father Cullen about it?" he asked, knowing she undoubtedly had.

"Probably a hundred times," she said grimly. "He promised to try to find it." Her tone implied that this would never happen and, having seen the unruly teens in the rec room, Father Leffingwell silently agreed with her. Those kids were outsiders, wild cards, having abandoned—or been abandoned by—the world of rules and laws. The words of an old song he had heard went through his mind. *Freedom's just another word for nuthin' left to lose,* and when there was nothing left to lose, and a shiny brass plaque appealed to you for a split second, why not take it?

"Well, I mustn't keep you," she said briskly. "I just wanted to thank you for talking to Ralph Prescott."

When she had gone he knelt at the rail and began to pray—always first for Philip and Martha, then for Peter Pruitt and all the others.

When he finished it was dusk outside and he went from the church into the adjoining building. Everybody was gone so he went into the rector's office to tidy up the desk. But as he left he noticed a light under Kim Fletcher's door. He knew he should talk to her, but was too tired. It had been a long day. He wanted to make peace with her, but on the other hand she shouldn't be counseling parishioners he was working with. He wondered if she had any training in counseling beyond the few courses offered in seminary.

The decision was taken from him when she opened her office door, snapping off the light as she did so. She faced him a moment and then said a cool, "Good evening. I thought I was the last one to leave."

"I'm just leaving too. Do you think we could talk tomorrow a bit, Kim?"

"Yes, of course. I'd like to talk with you too. Several things. What time do you plan to get here?"

"Usually at eight, but I could come in earlier if you like. What's your morning schedule?"

"Eight will be fine for me," she said briskly. "Good night." There had been nothing openly discourteous in her manner but he felt dismissed, written off. The angry, upset young woman who had walked out of his office last week was no longer angry and upset. There was an air of complete confidence about her, and he wondered what had changed.

He had just finished putting his dinner dishes in the dishwasher when Andrew rang the doorbell and soon they were seated in front of the fireplace. No fire this evening, as a burn ban had been issued. Whenever air pollution reached a certain level, fires were banned until it cleared, unless the fireplace was the only source of heat. The rectory basement had an old oil furnace, which Newton Crail had kept in working order for decades. He rather missed the open fire.

"I was talking with Claire Gibson today," Father Leffingwell said, "were you able to locate that commemorative plaque?"

"Ah. The sacred plaque surfaces again, does it. That woman has the memory of an elephant."

"Well, her father did donate the pews, Andrew, and you must admit it must have cost him a packet."

"I'm sure it did. I can't think of the name, but the wood is something that only grows in Brazil or some place, and is supposed to be the hardest wood on the planet."

"Must have cost another packet to carve it, then."

"I tried to find the plaque, but when the kids feel threatened, they close ranks. And if you must know, that's not the only one. I think we've lost three, in addition to other stuff. I'm sorry . . ."

"Let it go, then. If it's gone, it's gone."

"I stopped by to give you some more feedback on your fight against sin, and good luck with it."

"Okay. Let's have it. Is it all bad?"

"Surprisingly, no. For one thing, you're a good preacher. You never sound judgmental, just reasonable. It's very persuasive. There's some uneasiness with the very-liberal crowd, but one person said to me today—no names—but he said it couldn't do too much harm, since there were only seven deadly sins."

"On the other hand," Father Leffingwell murmured, "it was suggested to me today that I start on the Ten Commandments."

Andrew gave a shout of laughter. After a moment he said, "What I came over to tell you is that the bishop and Kim are trying to arrive at a date for her ordination."

"What's the problem?"

"He offered to do it in the cathedral, but she wants it at Saint Polycarp's. I can't imagine why."

"I can," Father Leffingwell said slowly. "I'm recalling something the bishop said to me in our interview when I first got here. He said she wanted to apply for the rectorship here at Saint Polycarp's."

"You're kidding. She can't be serious. An ordinand one day and running a whole parish the next? I don't think Dick Jackson would go along with that."

"On the contrary. I think it's just the kind of thing he would do. I know Dick's father well. We were in seminary together. Dick has made his career on being more politically correct than anyone else. If enough of the congregation went along, he would back her in a minute to keep his credentials in order with the radical feminists."

"She hasn't the experience. And . . . she's so set in her ideas that I think she'd lose half the parish in six months."

"We'll just have to wait and see how it comes out. Have you made your peace with Kim?"

"Not yet. We're still in the icy-polite stage." He was frowning. "She can't do it, Padre. I'd . . . hate to see her try and make a hash of it. She'd never get over it. Despite the brittle exterior, Kim is . . . vulnerable. How's the search committee coming along?"

They talked about the search for a while, and then Andrew came back to Kim. "What are you going to do about it?" he asked.

"Do? I suppose we'll arrange the church schedule to accommodate it. There is nothing else I can do. I'm just the temp. In a few months I'll be gone from here. I don't have any right to . . ." A kind of pall settled over the two men.

"I'll be . . . sorry when you go," Andrew said.

"In a way, I will be too."

After Father Leffingwell had shut the door behind Andrew, he stood in the hallway, looking blankly at the old carved Victorian side table pushed against the wall.

He would be sorry. How odd.

# CHAPTER 8

Irma Blalock swallowed two aspirin tablets and then wondered if she should have. Did aspirin affect the fetus? In her other pregnancies she had been so careful about what she put into her body. Had she used aspirin then? She tried to think but her head was pounding.

"You okay?" Roger asked, standing at the bathroom door. He was dressed for work, his worn briefcase in his hand.

"Pretty good. I just lost my breakfast again. And I can't seem to shake this headache, but the aspirin will take care of it."

"Are you going to work today?"

She shook her head and regretted it. "No. I think I'll call in sick. There's only one thing on my desk that can't wait and I can ask Eva to take care of it." Remembering Eva, her co-worker, made her uneasy. She had taken off three days already this month. She'd forgotten about the morning nausea.

"Maybe you could go in a little later," Roger said worriedly. "You don't want to take off too much time. It looks bad on your record."

"I won't be fired, Roger," she said with an edge to her voice. "My job is secure." She was sorry as soon as she said it, for he seemed to shrink inside his clothes.

"Okay. I'm sorry. Take it easy today, then . . . And don't worry too much about Diane's explosions. She doesn't mean half what she says. She's still a kid, an adolescent."

"She's nineteen: That's young adult in my book. And in one breath she says a woman should be in control of her own body, and in the next *she* tells *me* what to do with *my* body. It's not her body. It's *my* decision."

"Well, we did let her think she'd get a car if she got her grades up, and she made three point five, Irma. And all she wants is that little Ford Escort—not anything really expensive."

"And the insurance, Roger? At nineteen, we'll be paying a small fortune."

"Yeah, there's that . . ." His voice dwindled off, and she turned away. She couldn't look at the defeat in his eyes. He was tired, and it showed. He seemed tired all the time now.

After he had gone she went into his study and sat in his big recliner, tilting it back, staring vacantly at the ceiling. It was raining outside and the room was dim but she didn't want the lights on. The headache began to fade. She'd have to make up her mind soon. She sat up suddenly, another gust of anger sweeping through her.

How dared that little devil, Diane, bring in Deacon Fletcher without asking! Without any warning! Suddenly, right after dinner last night, there she was at the door in her neat gray suit, and her white clerical collar. So kind. So patient. So reasonable. And in her gentle, quiet voice she had convinced Roger—not that he had been hard to convince. And probably convinced Clem too. Clem had sat there uncomfortable but listening politely. And Diane had, of course, already convinced herself. Irma sat back tiredly in the chair.

Maybe they were all right and she was wrong. Deacon—please call me Kim—Fletcher had sounded so *sensible*. There hadn't been any agreement yet on when life actually began. The fetus was just another part of a woman's body, like tonsils, like appendix. Of course, the fetus was alive, but so is an egg. So is sperm. But it isn't a person—just a potential person.

And never had Kim Fletcher used the word *abortion*. She had always said "terminate the pregnancy." As Kim Fletcher's gentle voice droned on and on, Irma had begun to feel more and more isolated. Roger was listening intently, and Diane kept nodding brightly, and tossing in a word now and then.

"See, Mom?" or "I told you that, Mom." or "They brought that up in sexual education class, Mom."

And Clem, darling Clem, sat silent as a sphinx, but taking in every quietly spoken sensible word.

"I think any reasonable person can admit that life begins at birth," Kim had said, smiling her charming smile. She spread her graceful hands. "We don't celebrate conception days, do we? We celebrate birthdays. The church doesn't hold funerals for miscarriages, do they? They hold a funeral for the deaths of *people*."

Irma wiped angry tears away with her hands. She hadn't even realized she was crying. What had Father Leffingwell said? He'd said there were options. That Roger should know all the facts, so they could make the right decision. She dug into the pocket of her bathrobe for a tissue and wiped her eyes. Roger would never go with her now to see Father Leffingwell. Deacon Fletcher had come. Deacon Fletcher had spoken. She represented the church, didn't she? So it was all settled. Everybody else had decided what she should do.

*No way!*

Still crying, she picked up the phone on Roger's desk. Maybe Father Leffingwell made house calls, too.

Father Leffingwell reached the rector's office at a quarter to eight and, amazingly, Gloria was already there.

"Still working on sloth," she said, taking off her coat and hanging it in the office closet. Her eyes seemed puffy and he wondered if she had been crying. He wondered how best to reach out to her.

"You seem to be winning the battle," he said.

"I'm trying, anyhow," she said, moving her bulk toward the desk. "I'll just get these messages off the machine and bring them in," she added, gesturing to the flashing buttons on the answering machine.

He went into the rector's office. What was he going to say to Kim? He tried to recall just what it was that Dick Jackson had said her duties were. After a few minutes, Gloria came in with a stack of little pink message slips.

"I put Claire Gibson's on top. She said urgent."

"All right. Thanks." He picked up his phone.

When he reached Claire, she was almost exuberant. "I don't know what you said to Ralph Prescott," she said, "but you certainly stiffened his spine. He has talked to every member of the committee."

"Wonderful. He promised he'd get to work on it."

"They've agreed to invite Chester Bledsoe to come for interviews and a guest sermon."

"Chester Bledsoe?"

"Yes, the man from Boise. He's the solid middle-of-the-roader we talked about."

"Splendid. I hope it works out."

"There's another side to the coin, of course. There's always a hidden agenda when you deal with Greg Talbott. We—Ralph and I—had to agree to invite someone we haven't seen yet. And no telling what sort of freak he might be. But he's a friend of a friend of Greg Talbott's."

After they hung up, Father Leffingwell had to laugh. Claire was probably right. Greg Talbott was the driving force behind the ultra-liberal group at Saint Polycarp's. It would be interesting to meet his candidate. He was reading the rest of the slips when Mrs. Burris put her head in the door.

"You're here very early this morning," he said.

"My day to polish the brass, but I wanted to talk to you for a moment first," she replied. "I know you're busy so I'll make it quick. Is there any chance that you could take a confirmation class?"

"I . . . haven't been taking confirmation classes here," he said, his mind running quickly over his crowded schedule. The thought of taking on an evening class in addition seemed appalling. "Isn't Kim doing confirmation preparation?"

"That's the problem, Father." Mrs. Burris came all the way

into the office and shut the door. "Blanche Morgan has complained to me about Monica—that's her daughter. She's been in Kim's class. Blanche is rather traditional . . ." She let it rest there.

*Oh, dear, what in the world was Kim teaching in confirmation class?*

"And then," Mrs. Burris resumed, "last year, two of the adult confirmands dropped out in mid-session. They were new to the church and inclined to be traditional, go-by-the-book Christians. The parish is kind of split down the middle—I'm sure you have realized that by now. And I was thinking, Father, if the church is going to be so—I think the current buzz word is 'inclusive'—why can't we include traditionals. Although I am sure that's not what the new breed meant."

"I take your point," Father Leffingwell said slowly, wondering how in the world he could include a series of evening classes.

"I think that couple would come back if . . ."

"All right," he said. "Can you get me their names and addresses? I'll get in touch with them. Should I get in touch with Mrs. Morgan too?" He was thinking that if he was taking on a class he might as well announce it at the Wednesday and Sunday services. Perhaps more people were interested.

Mrs. Burris, very pleased, left and Kim was already waiting in the outer office. He hurried to invite her in. He wished he could make peace with her but they were poles apart.

Seated in front of his desk, she began briskly. "I suppose you already know this," she said, "since the church grapevine is never out of order."

"About your ordination? Yes. Congratulations, Kim."

"Thank you. I completed all the seminary work last year and I've been working here at Saint Polycarp's for over a year now. Dick said any time we could arrange it."

"I understand he suggested Saint Mark's Cathedral."

"Yes. But I'd rather it be here at Saint Polycarp's. That is, if we can work it in." Her nervous hands betrayed the bland expression on her attractive face.

"Of course, you can have it here, Kim," he said. "Were you thinking of before or after Lent?"

"Before." Her tone was very firm.

"I'm sorry," he heard himself saying just as firmly. "I just remembered. My series of seven connected sermons takes us right up to Lent. I would rather not break into the series." He felt a little angry and chided himself. She had wanted to break up his series, and he couldn't let her. He should have, he thought, he mustn't get too attached to this parish and its problems, because he would be leaving it soon.

"All right," she was saying. "If that's the way it is, Dick is committed the first Sunday after Easter. Let it be the second Sunday, then." She was angry, and trying to hide it.

As she got up to leave he raised his hand. "Can you wait a moment? I'd like to talk a bit."

"Of course." She sat down again.

"Why don't we start with a cup of coffee," he said, getting up for another mug, and pouring from the carafe of fresh coffee Newton had left on the desk minutes ago.

"Thanks," she said, her eyes wary.

"I was interested in your background, Kim. Have you had any training in counseling beyond what is offered in seminary?" He might as well come out with it.

"Well, I had good clinical pastoral courses—excellent courses—"

"I agree. But, Kim, it doesn't go far enough. The seminary training doesn't equip a pastor for counseling beyond hospital chaplaincy and bereavement and very little else. There isn't time in seminary, with all the other subjects, to get into personal problems involving marriage, sexuality, depression, and all the other things which require long-term counseling."

A dull flush rose in her face and her jaw set. "And I suppose you have a separate degree in counseling?"

"Yes, I have." He was remembering that it had taken him four years of part-time study in addition to his parish work. And Martha had paid for it from a small legacy she received.

Kim took a cautious sip of coffee. "Well, many times it isn't counseling, per se. Sometimes parishioners ask me for advice. When they do, I give it." Kim put her cup down on the desk. "Are you questioning my talk with the Blalock family last night?"

"The Blalocks?" He asked in surprise. "No. Did you talk with them?" He felt another rise of anger, thinking of Irma Blalock and her unborn child. He made himself speak quietly. "I was talking with Peter Pruitt yesterday. He thinks you have talked to Natalie Pruitt, advising divorce."

"She asked for my advice. I gave it." There was a grim edge to Kim's tone.

"You don't think marriage is a lifetime commitment even if one partner is disabled?" His own voice was beginning to sound a little grim.

Kim spoke with great patience, "Father Leffingwell, I think you have to be realistic about life and people. We live in today's world and if the church can't keep up—"

He lifted his hand. "Just a minute. In my view you have it exactly backward, Kim. The church isn't supposed to keep up with the world. The world is supposed to keep up with the church. And it has never even begun to catch up. And about lifetime commitment—let me ask you this. The other day you told me that your brother and his friend have a lifetime commitment. Is that 'lifetime' only as long as they are both healthy enough to perform sexually?"

Her face flamed, and for a moment she looked stricken. It had been a cruel comment and he regretted having said it.

"Kim," he said quietly. "I don't mean to be at odds with you. We are both here to do God's work. But I must ask you not to do any more counseling on serious problems while I am here. That's my job."

She stood up, her eyes filmed with angry tears. "When people ask me for advice, Father Leffingwell, *I will give it.*"

After she had gone he sat down slowly. The Blalocks. Good grief, what had she said to them? His hands spread out the pink message slips and sure enough, there was one from Mrs. Blalock. He read Gloria's neat handwriting.

*Mrs. Blalock wants you to come to their home tonight. 8:00. Call to confirm. Take packet of tissues if you go.*

He held the slip in his hand. Tonight? He had a heavy schedule today, all he wanted to do tonight was go back to the rectory and collapse. Well, nobody ever said the work was easy. He started to pick up the phone but just as he did it rang. It was Gloria.

"Father, Mrs. Griswold wants to talk to you. Okay?"

When Mrs. Griswold was on the line she said, "Father Leffingwell, I thought about what you said, about little part-time jobs?"

"Yes, yes. Of course. What did you decide?"

"I'd like to do it, if the offer is still open." She sounded uncertain and he wondered if she and Malcolm had had some difficulty.

"Yes. It's open. I'd be delighted to have your help. You'll find the place quite a mess." They talked a while longer and he made arrangements for him to leave an extra key with Gloria for her to pick up. He hung up the phone with a feeling of hope. If the poor woman could just have a little life of her own perhaps her obsession with her son would ease, and they might mend their relationship.

Diane Blalock looked at her mother with baffled anger. "Why, Mom? Why?" Then quickly, "Well, I don't have time. I've got homework to do—I have to keep my grades up," she added sarcastically.

Roger interposed, "Have you already invited him, Irma?"

"Yes." Irma sat down in one of the chairs in front of their

fireplace in the living room. "Just sit down and keep calm. He said he'd be here at eight."

"Irma, you could have warned us. I do have some office work to do," Roger protested.

"Like I was warned last night in advance of Kim Fletcher's visitation?" Her voice was grim and she looked first at Roger and then at her daughter. "It's five minutes to eight. Sit down."

With a heavy sigh, Roger obeyed. It took Diane longer, but she finally sat too, perching on the edge of the couch, as if she only intended to stay a moment.

"Clem," Irma said, "will you go sit by your sister? I want Father Leffingwell to have that chair." The boy obeyed quietly, looking embarrassed and uncomfortable. "Thank you, Love," Irma said and they waited in total silence for the doorbell to ring.

When Father Leffingwell entered he cast a quick glance around the room. With himself and Irma in front of the fireplace, more or less facing the others, he realized the family had reached an us-against-them point, and he was sorry for them all.

Roger, who had risen when he entered to shake hands, looked guarded and apprehensive. The daughter, Diane, remained seated and stared sulkily at her mother. The boy—Clem, wasn't it—stood up too, looking utterly miserable. Father Leffingwell wished he were any place but here. He was tired and very hungry.

He had come straight from the church. Both Claire Gibson and Ralph Prescott had come into the office a little after five wanting to talk "a few minutes" about the search committee and had stayed an hour. Then Newton Crail had come in. Something had gone wrong with the church lighting, and together they had fixed it, but not before seven forty-five.

Roger Blalock seated himself again and started speaking in a rapid nervous manner. "It was good of you to come over, Father Leffingwell. You know our problem, of course. I don't mind telling you, we've had a time with it. Irma's upset, and well she should be. But Deacon Fletcher was here last night—

most helpful. Lovely woman. She straightened out our thinking on a few questions, didn't she, Irma?" He looked at his wife, as if willing her to back him up.

"Actually," Irma said with deliberation, "to my mind, she raised more questions than she answered."

"Mom! How can you say that?" Diane's voice held outrage. "A woman has a right to do what she wants with her own body!"

Father Leffingwell cut in quickly, "Oh, I agree perfectly. Absolutely." He spoke with a calmness he didn't feel. He must keep them from open battle, which would make reconciliation that much harder.

Irma looked at him in astonishment. "You do?"

They were all staring at him. At least he had their attention. He gave a dry little cough. "Could I have a glass of water?"

"Of course," Irma said. "I made coffee. I just forgot it. Clem, would you—"

"Sure." The boy was off the couch like a shot and disappeared through the dining room toward the kitchen.

After Clem came back with a tray, Father Leffingwell took a deliberate sip or two before he began. Setting the cup down on a nearby table he turned to face them. "The difficulty here is that we are not talking about just the mother's body. In a pregnancy there are two bodies, which makes it a different matter completely."

"But not yet," cut in Diane, her cheeks flushed with anger. "Let's have reality check here. Life begins at birth, not at conception—everybody knows that!"

"Diane!" Both parents spoke at once.

"Well, I don't care," she went on defiantly. "There's no way this family should be ruined by a bunch of outmoded ideas that went out with hoop skirts. I know what I know and—"

"Diane!" This time her brother joined his parents, and she stopped, but it was clear not for long.

"I'm sorry, Father . . ." Again both parents spoke at once.

"It's all right. It doesn't matter. Diane is upset, as I'm sure you all are. It's a difficult situation."

There were murmurs of agreement with Clem's mutter of "But some of us can keep our mouths shut," coming through clearly.

"You see, the pro-choice people are usually ardent supporters of women's rights, and it's high time women's rights were considered. But now and again, in their enthusiasm for women's rights, the rights of others are sometimes overlooked—"

"Here it comes," Diane interrupted bitterly. "Are you going to tell us that Deacon Fletcher lied when she was here last night?"

"Of course not. She and I spoke about it this morning. She said she was simply giving you her advice, since you had asked for it."

"Diane asked for it," Irma cut in, with an angry glance at her daughter.

"That was Deacon Fletcher's personal advice. Not necessarily what I would give you," Father Leffingwell said firmly.

"I'll bet," Diane muttered and Clem poked her arm. She jerked away, staring at Father Leffingwell.

"Pregnancy and childbirth are very complicated physical manifestations in a woman—difficult to explain in a little leaflet or a brief conversation. I believe you are several weeks along, aren't you?" He turned slightly to Irma.

"Yes. Almost two months."

"Ah well, then, life has certainly begun."

"That's a crock. Life doesn't—"

"Diane!" Both parents sat forward threateningly and Father Leffingwell lifted his hand for peace.

"You see, nineteen days after conception your mother's fetus had its own heartbeat." He kept his voice tranquil with effort. He held an old anger at the disinformation the pro-choicers handed out year after year. "This is a different heartbeat from your mother's." He had their attention again, even Diane's, but she looked skeptical.

"And after forty days your mother's fetus had its own brain

waves, not your mother's brain waves, distinctive enough to be recorded."

"I . . . didn't know that," Irma said faintly.

He paused a moment and then added the unbeatable piece of evidence of a separate life—two bodies.

"Your mother's fetus has a different DNA pattern than your mother's." He refrained from adding, "And you won't find that in any pro-choice leaflet."

Roger cleared his throat. "Father, with all respect, are you quite certain of that? I've never heard that before." He looked sick.

"Yes. Quite certain. I took the liberty of bringing along some scientific data for you to go through at your leisure. An unplanned pregnancy can be an enormous burden to a family which doesn't want more children, but it's not the end of the world." He handed Roger the material he had brought and resumed his seat.

Diane reached over and plucked the papers from her father's hands, bending over them grimly.

"Tell me how it isn't," Roger said hopelessly.

"Is it absolutely impossible for you to take on raising another child?" Father Leffingwell asked, and they explained to him how drastically their plans would all be changed if they did. He listened attentively.

"Well, in that case," he said gently. "Your lives need only be disrupted for the term of the pregnancy. A healthy, caucasian child from intelligent, personable parents would find an immediate adoptive home and—"

*"Oh, no."*

Both Irma and Roger spoke at once, as he had known they would. In all his counseling on this subject he had never yet understood how two rational parents could consider killing the fetus, but balk at the idea of putting the baby up for adoption after birth. Never had anyone he counseled not objected, at first, to the idea of adoption. Some later changed their minds, but not many. If he could get this baby born into this family, it would be safe, and the family, even perhaps the sulky girl, would close around it.

"I would never adopt out a child of mine," Irma said flatly. "That's that."

"Why not, Mom?" Diane asked weakly, as Clem put his hands to his head and rolled his eyes.

"Diane," Irma said, "nothing on God's green earth could have made me give *you* up for adoption when *you* were born," and Diane had the grace to look embarrassed.

This hurdle seemed to be over. Father Leffingwell got them discussing how it could be managed financially. They all joined in. They seemed to be a close family, which was always a good sign. He was so tired and hungry that his head was beginning to ache. Irma Blalock's coffee had helped, but not enough. He went doggedly on, pointing out different ideas, suggesting alternatives. At least they were all trying.

"The bank will let me work through the seventh month . . ."

"Selling the *Intrepid* would cut our expenses too . . ."

"We could skip using the cottage for a few years and rent it . . ."

"During summer I can work full-time at the restaurant . . ."

"I can check the school bulletin board for a cheaper second-hand car . . ."

It was almost ten o'clock when Father Leffingwell left and Roger Blalock walked with him out the front door. The man looked beaten. It worried Father Leffingwell all the way back to the rectory. His chest felt tight and he fumbled in his pocket for his bottle of nitro tablets.

Once inside the dark front hall of the rectory he smelled the lemony scent of furniture polish and flipped on the light. The old Victorian side table in the hall shone with a high gloss. Mrs. Griswold had come and gone. Bless her. His spirits picked up and he went into the kitchen and read the note she had left on the refrigerator door.

*Dear Father Leffingwell;*
*As discussed, I'll come Mondays and Thursdays*

*after this. Since you use so few rooms, this is a snap. I had some time, so I made baked hash from your leftover roast. I hope you like hash.*

*Faithfully,*
*Hannah Griswold*

The casserole was on the drainboard and he put it into the oven to heat while he said his evening office in front of the fireplace. He had a sermon to write before the noon service tomorrow. Perhaps he could do it early in the morning.

He was sitting down at the kitchen table when someone rapped on the back door. It was Mark. It had started to mist.

"Hi, Father Leffingwell. I came over earlier but there was some old lady here," the boy said. He stood shivering in the damp air. The mist glistened in tiny droplets on his stringy blond hair. No jacket.

"Is it true what Andy said? I can help you with the VW?"

Father Leffingwell felt a rush of keen pleasure at the sight of the boy, at the eager enthusiasm on his still-bruised face. Was a small old blue Volkswagen going to be an instrument for salvaging a wasted child? God did indeed work in strange ways. His fatigue slipped away.

"Yes. Come inside. I'll tell you while we eat."

# CHAPTER 9

Father Leffingwell was putting the finishing touches to his Wednesday sermon while he finished breakfast when the doorbell rang. It was Andrew.

"Oh, come in, Andrew. Have you had breakfast?"

"No. Have you got any?"

"Coffee. Toast. Juice. That do? There is some instant oatmeal if you want to stay on and fix it yourself. I have to get over to the office."

"Coffee and toast is fine. I took a Last Rites call last night, Padre. That is, about four this morning." Andrew rubbed his cold hands together as he followed Father Leffingwell into the kitchen.

"Oh, dear. Who?" Father Leffingwell opened the refrigerator and took out the jug of orange juice.

"Old Mrs. Rhodes in that convalescent home over in Ballard."

"Oh, I am sorry. I remember her. I took communion out there a while ago." He set the jug on the table and went to get some bread and dishes for Andrew. "But how did you get the call?"

"Well," Andrew looked embarrassed. "After . . . your son's funeral, I told Gloria to route any night calls to me with a relay on to your phone if I didn't answer—in case I was over at one of the shelters. I . . . wanted to even up our workloads a little more. I'm a night owl anyhow."

"That was kind, Andrew. I was beat last night. Thank you. And that comes from the heart."

Andrew took the proffered bread and dropped two slices into the toaster. "There's more. She's an old parishioner of

Saint Polycarp's and the family wants the funeral here, but they want to wait until Monday. A son has to get here from another state."

"Monday. I think that's my hospital day." Father Leffingwell put margarine and a jam jar on the table. "I'll have to check with Gloria." He pushed aside his sermon and took a sip of his cooling coffee. He was pensive, remembering Mrs. Rhodes, and his visit to her.

"Thanks for getting the word out to Mark," he said after a while. "It worked. He'll be back Saturday."

"Good. I'm glad." The hot toast popped up and Andrew came to the table, tossing it from hand to hand.

When Father Leffingwell reached the office he found that Gloria was already there again. She was certainly conquering sloth.

"Hi," she said, "Andy left a message about Mrs. Rhodes. Monday is your hospital day, but I called First Baptist and it's okay."

"I'm afraid you've lost me," Father Leffingwell said, reaching for the pink message slips.

"Don't you remember? You took Pastor Abernathy's hospital day? When he had the flu? Well, he doesn't have the flu now, and his secretary said he'd be happy to return the favor."

"Gloria," he said impulsively, "you are a jewel!" and she flushed a bright red with pleasure.

In his office he went through the pink slips. Mrs. Rhodes' daughter wanted to talk with him. Yes, of course, he would call her at home. Ralph Prescott said that both Fathers Bledsoe and Tanner would visit and preach during Lent if that was okay. Yes, it was. There would be an informal gathering at Claire Gibson's home next Tuesday at seven-thirty, and she hoped that Father Leffingwell would join them. Probably the traditionals planning their strategies. He might as well go and help if he could. Kim Fletcher wanted to know if he had any objection to her brother, Jonathan, and his friend, Ross Palmer, serving as acolytes on her ordination Sunday. He thought about it a moment. Pour souls. No, he wouldn't object, certainly, but the traditionals had better get their act together if they didn't want Kim as their pastor.

As he prepared to deliver his sermon at the Wednesday noon Eucharist there seemed to be more people than usual. More men than women, probably from the business community. Mrs. Burris would be pleased. Sunlight streamed through the stained glass windows, splashing color on the floors, the pews, the faces. He felt a moment of deep content.

After the sermon, one of the men lingered to speak to him. He introduced himself as George Kincaid. "I liked your sermon last Sunday, Father. The one on sloth." He had a half-smile on his face.

"Reaction was mixed, I fear," Father Leffingwell answered.

"I don't wonder. My wife and I used to be parishioners here, but . . ."

"Did your wife come with you last Sunday?"

"No. She didn't. I told her about your sermon, and the way Saint Polycarp's is . . . somehow different now." He sounded diffident. "Do you write down your sermons?"

"Oh my, yes. My memory isn't what it was. I have to. Why?"

"Could my wife have a copy? You're not here permanently, are you?"

"Yes, to the first question. I'll have the secretary make a Xerox copy for you. Give me your card so she'll know where to send it. And no to the second question. The Vestry is searching for a new Rector now. I should think he'll be here in a few months."

"I see." Kincaid took out a card and handed it to Father Leffingwell. "Had you thought of publishing all seven of the sermons? It might make a good helpful little book. Remind people that sin is still around. I liked it when you said 'the right things that we don't do are as destructive as the wrong things we do.' Very good, that."

When Kincaid had gone, Father Leffingwell lingered a moment at the church door. Not a bad idea, collecting the seven sermons—expanding a bit, perhaps, to include what he hadn't been able to get into thirty minutes. Not a bad idea at all. He might just try it when he retired.

He had sick calls this afternoon, so he hurried back to the office only to find Andrew waiting for him.

"Gloria says you don't have anything on for lunch, and I'd like to treat you. You've fed me plenty of meals."

"Good. I accept. It will save me driving back to the rectory. I've got two sick calls," he added.

"Three, actually, according to Gloria. She fixed your kit." He picked up the black leather box and handed it to Father Leffingwell.

They went to the nearest place, which happened to be a Denny's, and Andrew asked for a booth. When they had eaten and were lingering over second cups of coffee, Andrew seemed to have trouble beginning.

"I've been doing some thinking," he finally said, "about Mrs. Rhodes."

"The woman to whom you gave Last Rites last night?"

"Yes. If her children don't specifically ask for you, could I take that service?" Andrew sounded diffident.

"Of course. May I ask why?"

"I want to . . . kind of follow through. I was so . . . impressed by that old lady. She died with such . . . dignity. And she wasn't in the least afraid, although she knew the end of her *life* had come. Too late now to change anything, or fix anything—this was it. Neither of her kids got there, and not a word of complaint about that. The daughter, who lives here, hadn't been to see her in a month. She didn't tell me that, the nurse did later. At the last, it was just the two of us and—" He paused for a long while. "I happened to be looking into her eyes and I saw her . . . let go. She was alive and smiling faintly and then . . . she was gone."

Andrew was hunched over, looking into his half-empty cup. "After I was ordained, I was a curate for a while, and then I got this post as assistant priest at Saint Polycarp's. But all that time—because I'm young, I guess—I've only worked with young people. Over at Holy Innocence as curate, I worked with the college kids, now it's even the younger ones on the street." His voice trailed off.

Father Leffingwell had felt a sense of growing satisfaction as the younger man spoke. Maybe, just maybe, Andrew was beginning to realize there was more to his mission than trying to feed and shelter lost children.

"Have you been able to get to know—really know—any of the older people in the parish?" he asked.

"Not really. I kind of know Kim's crowd, of course. She's got quite a following among the liberals. I guess the moderates and conservatives are a blank to me."

"That's too bad. We have a number of good people. I wonder . . ."

"What?"

"There will be a meeting of some sort at Claire Gibson's house Tuesday evening—I'm invited. I think it will be the moderate-conservative group. It's probably about the search for the new rector. I wonder if you could come. Shall I ask Claire?"

Andrew grinned. "Maybe you'd better not push it, Padre. I think if I showed they'd clam up and nothing would get done. Thanks for the thought. How are they coming with the search? I have an interest here—the new guy is going to be my boss."

"Two priests have been invited. A Chester Bledsoe from Boise and someone Greg Talbott knows—Tanner, I think his name is, Harold Tanner."

"You're kidding! Harry Tanner?" Andrew's dark eyes glinted with sudden laughter.

"No. Why? Do you know him?"

"Yes, for a long time. He's ordained, all right, but . . . shall we say that Harry marches to a different drum? And that's not far off." Andrew was laughing now. "He's a musician. He has a rock band. He's never done any church work that I know of besides his composing. He did compose a rock mass. It'll probably blast out the church windows."

"Good heavens. You can't be serious."

"Yes, I'm serious, but I rather doubt that he is. My guess of the moment is that Talbott arranged it to shock the socks off everybody, so Kim will look pretty good to them in comparison, if they put her name forward."

Father Leffingwell sighed. One cross every pastor had to bear was parish politics. Maybe it was God's way of teaching his vicars patience. "What in the world would he preach about?" Father Leffingwell asked.

"Ah. Knowing Harry, unless he's changed in the last month, he won't stick to the script. I'd guess it will be more like a lecture, even a string of accusations, accusing the congregation of intolerance, bigotry, racism, sexism—whatever comes to mind. He automatically thinks that anyone who is clean and neatly dressed is a WASP to be chastised and taught humility."

"I can hardly wait," Father Leffingwell murmured. "Would I be breaking confidence if I told Claire's group?"

"Not at all. They should be prepared. You might also add, and I don't think I'm wrong here, that Harry Tanner wouldn't think of taking on parish work. He's got too much else to do."

"That makes me feel somewhat better," Father Leffingwell said, as they got ready to go. He wanted to leave Saint Polycarp's in good hands. Walking out to his car he realized that the little church and its people were more important to him than he had thought. He dropped Andrew off at the store-front clinic where he had to see someone.

As Father Leffingwell was about to drive off, Andrew called out from the doorway. "Hey, Padre. Harry Tanner wears an earring. And he now and then dyes his hair." He was grinning widely.

"Good grief. What color?"

"We won't know till we see, will we?" Andrew waved and disappeared inside the clinic.

Roger Blalock rinsed his face in cold water. How much longer could he stay in the men's john? He patted his face with two paper towels. He hadn't slept much last night and had finally got up to go into his study and recheck the Martinson data. He couldn't afford to make any mistakes, with Musgrave breathing down his neck. Irma had been awake, pretending to be asleep, but she hadn't followed him. They weren't communicating at all now, circling each other with wary distant politeness. Oh, dear God, let her miscarry—or something.

He stared at his face in the mirror. Stupid hairline. Soon he'd be bald as an egg. Old. Tired. Dear God, how tired. He looked it. Around the eyes. He'd heard a radio commercial the other day. This eye clinic could take tucks or something, make you look younger, more wide awake. They catered to business executives—people who had to face the public. How much did that sort of thing cost? And how long did it take? Could he fit it into a two-week vacation? Maybe? Oh, Lord, he'd better get back into the office. Another of Musgrave's endless meetings.

And they'd all hike up to the third floor. *"Exercise, man. Move it. Good for the old bod."* Of course, Musgrave had just turned forty, and worked out three times a week.

When they got to the conference room, straggling in, some of them panting for breath, he himself would be gasping, his heart pounding so loudly it seemed everyone in the room could hear it. The coffee urn would be there, all ready. He braced himself as he left the men's room to join the others. None of the women would get coffee these days, and he'd make his usual joke of it—as soon as he could speak without wheezing. They would all be seating themselves, jockeying for the seats nearest to Musgrave, leaving him down at the end of the table. And he would be laughing and talking too loudly—why did he do that—making jokes, not really fooling anybody.

*"Okay, you guys, get your bodies in the chairs while I get us our coffee. And don't take my end place—I want to spread out my stuff. Nicky, you're the only one who takes cream, and Josh gets sugar in black. Hey, I got it right this time. Here ya go. Here ya go."* And he would hand around the mugs. Oh, dear God, get me out of this . . . please . . .

Mark arrived at the rectory early Saturday morning, how early Father Leffingwell didn't know. When he went out for the morning paper, Mark was already seated on the doorstep. He was holding the morning paper, still unopened.

"Why didn't you ring?" Father Leffingwell asked, taking the paper Mark handed to him. Again, no jacket. This time he asked about it. "Aren't you cold without your jacket?" The day was dry, but gray and overcast.

Mark got up, shrugging. "Yeah, well. I think I lost it."

"Well, that's too bad. Come inside. We'll have some breakfast before we start to work."

In the kitchen he noticed for the first time that Mark was cleaner than usual. There was no odor of garbage. "Are you still evicted from your dumpster?"

"Yeah. We all are now. The stores got tired of us and put padlocks on. Didn't you notice in the alley? They're all chained shut. If we sleep inside we gotta use the shelters or go stay with somebody we know who lives somewhere. No more 'dumpster divin'."

"Sit down, Mark, and take a look at this book," Father Leffingwell said, as he opened the refrigerator for eggs and bacon.

"Whatzis?" Mark asked, picking up the book. "Oh, wow!" He opened it and started leafing through the pages.

"It's the beetle's repair and maintenance manual."

"Yeah, I see it is." Mark's fair head was bent over the pages. "Look at this. Wow. Will ya look at this?" He was muttering to himself, a skinny finger outlining the schematic of the engine.

Father Leffingwell gripped the handle of the skillet a moment, willing self-control. The sight of the boy's head bent intently over the book had reminded him sharply of Philip in the same pose, over the same book.

"Where'd you get this?" Mark looked up, his face beaming.

"It came with the car—years and years ago." He started to mention Philip, thought the better of it, and added, "All cars have those."

"No kidding."

"No. No kidding. How do you want your eggs?" He put some bacon in the skillet.

"Over easy. You know what? If I could read all those books I could be . . . I could be . . ." Mark was gazing off into the mid-distance. "I mean when I get my gas station and all. I could have this garage attached, see, and I could . . . Oh, wow. Where can I get books like this?"

"Well, the public library would have the complete collection, of course. Maybe not out in the stacks, but available if you request them. Have you got a library card?"

"No. I got no address, see. You gotta have an address to be somebody."

Father Leffingwell felt himself stiffen against a sudden silent wailing in his mind. *Mark, you are somebody. You are made in the image of God.* Deliberately, he tended to the bacon, hearing the toaster pop up the first two pieces of toast.

"Mark," he said steadily. "Would you start buttering the toast and putting in some more bread?"

"Right." He heard the boy get up quickly to obey. He heard the scrape of the knife on the toast as Mark spread on the margarine. How in God's world could this happen? This boy—this delightful, bright, child, how could he be adrift like this? Somehow, with God's help, he had to do something about Mark.

"I can lend you my library card, if you are interested."

"You could? Jeez, that would be great. I'd . . . I'd always take the books back, you know. I mean, I know you'd have to pay for them if I didn't."

"Yes, that's right. How far did you go in school, Mark?" He had wondered this before. Mark spoke rather well, allowing for the adolescent shorthand, of course, but not too many serious grammatical errors. Plus, Mark often obviously censored some of the street kids' saltier all-purpose words for his benefit.

"I woulda been in grade eight, see, but I got in a hassle and got suspended. So when I went back I couldn't catch up and I didn't pass. That ticked me off."

"So did you quit school then?"

Mark paused in his task with the toast, his face suddenly somber. "Not exactly then. Later." There was a note of finality in his tone which made Father Leffingwell drop the subject for the moment.

After breakfast, out in the cold garage, with an extra light rigged up over the motor, Mark proved to be an apt pupil, and they worked well together. Mark seemed to have an almost loving touch when he handled the various parts of the engine.

"Oh, yes, see here," Father Leffingwell said. "I got new sparks. I knew by the way it sounded that I'd need them. Look at that. You see all that buildup there, closing the gap between the electrodes?"

"You mean all that crud in there? Yeah."

"See the wire down there at the bottom of the plug? Twist the boot to free it. No, don't pull the wires. If it's stuck just dig your finger under the bottom to loosen it . . . Fine, that will do it." The boy followed his instructions with a kind of fascinated attention.

"Now notice the numbers, Mark, for future reference. This is a fuel injection engine, so I got Champion L-288s—see here?" He pointed to the rest of the number. "If I had a car with a carburetor engine I'd have gotten . . ."

They worked all morning on the tuning and oil change. Alone he could have done it in half the time but—thank God—it had been time well spent. At some point during the dirty, greasy job a new bond had been forged between himself and the boy. A trust was established.

They washed up together at the tub on the back porch, using the gritty mechanics' soap, guaranteed to get off even the blackest grease around the nails.

"I'm going to have to replace one of the windshield wiper assemblies soon, I think," Father Leffingwell said, drying his hands. "When I do, what I think I'll do is visit some junkyard."

"How come?"

"Often, in the old, wrecked, cannibalized cars, one can find parts in perfect condition, for very little money."

Mark looked at him, his blue eyes wide, "Can I go too?"

"Yes, if you like," Father Leffingwell said, knowing he was holding out the golden apple of temptation to the boy. He recalled how he and Philip had prowled through the dust and junk of partly demolished cars spread out over a large lot. For an instant he saw Philip in his mind, sun and dust on his face, his sweat-dampened hair falling over his forehead. He brought himself back sharply.

During lunch of tuna sandwiches and the rest of the cookies from the freezer, he ventured a few more questions to Mark, and Mark was more open now.

"Are your parents living, Mark?"

"Yeah. I mean no. That is, my mom . . . passed on. But my dad is okay. I guess he's okay."

"How old were you when you left?" Father Leffingwell asked cautiously, praying that the curtain wouldn't suddenly come down and the boy retreat.

"Lemme see," Mark said, chewing a bite of sandwich. "I was twelve, I guess. Maybe almost thirteen. You see, me and Henry—this guy I know, Henry—we ran off together. Sometimes it's easier that way. You know you gotta go. You can't take it around there anymore but it's easier if you got somebody with you. Me and Henry, we were tight, see. Henry is older. I think maybe three years older than me. He's a nice guy. He kinda looked out for me, see."

"Where is Henry now?"

"Oh, God, I wish I knew." The boy put down his half-eaten sandwich and his eyes were momentarily filled with grief so intense Father Leffingwell felt shaken. What had this child gone through?

"What happened, Mark?"

"I dunno. He got some bad stuff. Coulda been angel dust, or acid, or something like that. He went off his nut." Mark's voice broke. "We were in the alley, see, and he started acting crazy. At first the rest of us kids laughed at him. He was running around, yelling, and then we *got it* that something was wrong. Some of the bigger guys tried to hold him so he wouldn't get hurt. He was banging into the dumpsters and that brick wall out there, you know. And finally somebody called nine one one—I think somebody inside the store did. So the rest of the kids ran, of course, cause the cops would be coming. But—I kept holding on—" Mark's voice broke and he took an angry bite of sandwich and chewed fiercely.

Finally he resumed, "The medics put him in the aid car and took him away. I dunno where. I never heard again. I asked and asked around the shelters and all, but nothing." There was a long pause. "I . . . miss Henry." The loss in his eyes was stark.

Henry had been his substitute family. Andrew had talked about how sometimes the kids reached out to each other for someone, anyone. He observed the boy eating doggedly, filling himself up, because he wasn't sure when he would eat again. Maybe there was a way to locate Henry, and Mark could at least have that, or at least know what had happened. He must ask Andrew.

"Why did you leave home? Was it because of not getting to the eighth grade?" Father Leffingwell asked after a time. They had finished the sandwiches and were munching on cookies.

"Nah. Not really. Things got kind of rough at home, you know. Both my mom and my dad had a drinking problem, see. And I dunno how much you know about drunks, Father Leffingwell, but there's four kinds a drunks. There's numb drunks and happy drunks and sad drunks and mean drunks. My mom got sad. Used ta drive me up the wall when she was crying and crying and I couldn't do anything about it. And my dad is really an okay guy when he's sober, but when he's hitting the bottle he turns real mean. He works in construction and I guess he's pretty good at it. He can always get another job when the unemployment benefits run out. They both been in treatment coupla times but . . . it didn't ever take.

"Then, after my mom died, there was this other woman, Evalyn, see, she moved in. At first they had a kind of agreement. They both worked at first. And they had this deal that they wouldn't drink weekdays, but just weekends. They was trying to hold it down, see. They fought a lot, but in a weird kinda way, they got along. I mean they stuck together. It was sorta okay. I was going to school pretty regular then. And I could duck out weekends, when things got rough. You know, me and Henry, could just mess around downtown all weekend. But finally I kinda got the message. You know, if nobody looks at your report card and nobody remembers it's your birthday, you kinda get the message that you don't belong there. So, we cut out. Me and Henry."

Father Leffingwell pushed the plate with the remaining cookie over to Mark. What could he say to this boy? The sins of the fathers were indeed visited upon the sons, even unto the third and fourth generation. Most of these kids were sexually active. It was not unlikely that Mark, at fourteen, even now had fathered an unknown bastard or two, depending now upon the teenage mothers—who were children themselves—the non-families of the future, not living, but existing in the hazy chaos of impossible thin little dreams, supported by drugs and alcohol, day to day, hour to hour, in the concrete wilderness of street living. And more and more families were disintegrating—as Mark's had.

"You okay?" Mark asked.

"What? Oh, yes. Why do you ask?"

"Well, you kinda sighed, you know. And no offense, but you are kinda old and not too healthy. I just don't want ya to get sick or anything."

"Actually, I'm feeling quite well these days, Mark. I'm thinking of going to the junkyard next Saturday. Do you want to come along? Here, eat this last cookie."

"Boy! Do I!" Mark took the cookie and Father Leffingwell wanted to cry. Mark needed *everything*. He needed a whole new *life*, and all he could offer was a trip to the junk yard and the last cookie on the plate.

He picked up the repair manual. "Would you like to have this, Mark? I almost know it by heart and I really don't need it."

"Oh man! Yeah!" Mark dropped the cookie and snatched at the book, his face ablaze with delight. "Father Leffingwell, you are one neat guy!"

# CHAPTER 10

After they had completed the Sunday ten o'clock service, Father Leffingwell got a word with Andrew in the sacristy. The Altar Guild women were in and out, clearing up, so he kept his voice low.

"I was talking with Mark. Did he ever mention his friend, Henry, to you?"

Andrew hung his white alb up in the closet. "Yes, he did. I checked it out." He shut the closet door.

"And?"

"Henry—his name was John Henry McCabe—died a few days after the medics picked him up in the alley. Whatever it was he used, did a lot of brain damage. He was in a coma for a while and then . . . they had to pull the plug. Don't look so stricken, Padre. He'd have died a lot sooner but for the life support systems. They had to keep him alive for a while to see what chance of survival he might have. I'm sorry."

"So am I. Did you think it best not to tell Mark?"

Andrew sighed. "I really didn't know—still don't. I hesitate to load the kid down with more grief then he's got. These kids—when they hurt—reach for relief and they spell it CRACK or ACID. Did he talk to you about it?"

"Yes."

The two priests left the sacristy together. They discussed it a while longer but couldn't decide whether to tell Mark or not. Mark's existence was so precarious. Andrew was very pleased that a real friendship seemed to have been established between the boy and Father Leffingwell.

"Mark tells me he's been sleeping at a shelter, that the dumpsters have been padlocked. How do the shelters operate? Why don't the kids like them?"

"Too much control. Don't forget these kids are life's little misfits—unconnected to *any* form of stability—no rules, no standards. Most of them have been taught nothing, just allowed to survive. They have no guidelines, so when some are imposed, they chafe and want to fight back. In the shelter you are supposed to be on your pallet or whatever by eleven, preferably asleep. No smoking. No drugs. No booze. No sex. You are there to sleep warm and safe, and that's it. There are always two adults to monitor the kids, and one has to be awake at all times, or the building's insurance is down the tube."

"Who runs the shelters? Who pays for them, for the staff?"

"Good question. It's mostly contributions plus whatever grant money they can pick up, and the staff are volunteers—people willing to go the extra mile. To sit up half the night with a bunch of unruly kids, to keep them safe one more night. Saint Polycarp's isn't really big enough to offer overnight shelter. Some of the big churches are, have huge recreation rooms. Even so . . . it's kind of a losing battle." Andrew looked somber.

They were silent for a time. The sound of laughter came up to them from the rec room below and Father Leffingwell knew he should go down, but he lingered.

"That meeting Tuesday night, Andrew. You remember, at Claire's home? If I can get you an invitation, could you change your mind and come?"

"Oh, Padre, I don't know. I've been on her hit list from the first day." Andrew was smiling and shaking his head.

"Wait a minute," Father Leffingwell said, "Don't go yet. Have you considered the idea that maybe Claire needs help in her way, as much as—say—Mark does in his way?"

Andrew laughed. "You got me. That is the one thing I would never in the world have considered."

Father Leffingwell patted his arm. "Well, consider it now. Are you coming down for the coffee hour?"

Andrew looked pained.

"Why not, Andrew? You found out there was more to Mrs. Rhodes than an elderly female WASP when you suddenly got to know her."

Andrew pondered a moment. "Okay. Why not, indeed. I'll see you down there—someone wants you."

Father Leffingwell turned to see Mrs. Griswold, the last person to leave the church. "Good morning. How are you?" Father Leffingwell went to Mrs. Griswold and they sat down in one of the pews.

"How was everything at the rectory, Father? Am I doing all right?" She was smiling, eager.

"Indeed, yes. It's such a pleasure to have everything clean and neat again. And the hash was excellent, but you don't have to cook, you know."

"Well, I had a bit of time left so I just went ahead. I borrowed your copy of the community college bulletin from the hall table. Did you notice?"

"No, I didn't. Keep it if you wish. Are you thinking of taking a course?" This would be an encouraging sign.

"Would it be foolish, an old lady like me?"

"Not at all. Which were you considering?" They had a pleasant talk about the classes offered. He found he enjoyed talking with her. When she abandoned her dedicated-mother role, she was an interesting and charming woman, but when he left her she was faintly troubled. She hadn't told Malcolm yet about her part-time work. He wondered why. Down in the rec room he was again troubled, looking in vain for the Blalocks. They weren't there.

"We should have gone to church," Irma said, pushing aside a stack of Sunday papers surrounding her slippered feet. She and Roger were still sitting on the living room couch in their bathrobes, and it was almost noon.

"I agree," he said. "I never feel quite right if I don't."

They had made love last night and it had eased the tension between them. Somehow or other, during the closeness, she had pressed him about his work and, for the first time, he had told her about the many ugly little truths his pride had kept hidden. With a wife's awareness, she had guessed some of it, but not the snide little comments, the constant small put-downs, the deliberate humiliations. Thinking about it now she felt a surge of protectiveness. *Jerks.* Now that Musgrave creep was beginning to call him "Dad" so nobody would forget that he was the oldest man on staff. *Jerk.*

"Well, Love, I guess I'm going to hit the shower," Roger got up from the couch, dropped a kiss on top of her head, and left. She watched him go. He seemed to shuffle like an old man, but it was just those loose old slippers. It had to be. He was only fifty-five.

He hadn't said anything else about the pregnancy. Father Leffingwell's quiet little list of facts had gotten to them all. It hung like a sword over their heads. And she couldn't seem to think straight. One day she was over-my-dead-body determined to have this baby. The next day she was remembering all the financial problems, *plus* the diapers, the night feedings, the toilet training, the carpooling to and from kindergarten—and she'd be the oldest mother there—the finger paintings on the walls, all the hassle of coping with a small child. *At forty-five years old.*

"Mom?" It was Clem. He looked so good dressed up. At least one member of the family had shown up at church today. Clem was active in the small high school group and was an acolyte. He hadn't served today but had gone anyway. Diane had pretty much dropped out. People often did at nineteen or so. She had, and then come back. Diane would come back.

"Yes, Baby, what is it?"

"You looked so grim. Anything the matter?" He sat down beside her on the couch.

"Nothing that wasn't the matter yesterday, Clem." Even her voice sounded defeated.

"It's a heck of a problem, isn't it?"

"Yes, Clem. It's the biggest problem I've had in a long, long time. And I . . . don't know what I'm going to do. I just don't know."

The rec room was clearing out. Most of the people had left to get on with their weekend. There was the clink of china from the rec room kitchen, and the sound of water rushing through the dishwasher, the murmur of women's voices, occasional laughter.

Father Leffingwell sat down for a moment on one of the benches placed here and there along the walls. Actually, the benches were some of the old pews, painted over. He couldn't recall at the moment who had told him this. He was tired and wished he were already back at the rectory. He had to get together something for the confirmation class he'd promised to teach. For the hundredth time he longed for the books and notes he'd left in Baltimore.

He glanced down at the arm of the old pew-cum-bench. Somebody—probably one of Andrew's kids—had spent time and much effort to carve into the wood, deeply, neatly, and clearly, an obscenity. Father Leffingwell sighed and placed his hand over the words. He'd speak to Newton Crail about it.

"You're looking a little down, Padre." Andrew was standing before him. Andrew was an imposing figure in his clericals. He sat down.

"Maybe I am. Sometimes I get . . . discouraged," Father Leffingwell admitted.

"That's not uncommon for people in our line of work," Andrew said. "You muddle along. One step forward, two steps back, and call that progress. Anything special hit you today? Something about your sermon?"

"Actually, no. I had a couple of good comments on that, but I had another little run-in with Kim, and I haven't heard the last of it, I fear. She's upset—really upset—because I'm going to teach another confirmation class. I didn't realize . . . but I've already announced it and can't cancel now. I've already got an enrollment of five people. Three adults and two teenagers."

"Not bad."

"The two teenagers were taken out of her class."

"Oh."

"And then, I talked a few minutes with little Lucy Pruitt—you know who I mean, don't you, from the Sunday school?"

"I . . . think so. Little dark-haired girl? Ten or eleven? Nervous? Always has her fingers in her mouth? In a couple of years the other kids will be calling her 'Fatso.' That one?"

"Yes."

"I've heard about the Pruitts' marital troubles. I suppose that's it," Andrew said.

"I'm afraid so. She was quite elated today. She was telling me that her parents are planning to take her to Disneyland for her birthday. At first I believed her. I guess I was hoping that things were getting better for them. Then she told me they were planning it as a surprise. She wasn't supposed to know about it. In a couple of minutes, I realized that she was making it up as she went along."

"Fantasizing. Poor little kid. To each his own escape hatch, I guess. What are you going to do?"

"I don't know. I have to think about it. I've left a couple of calls for Mrs. Pruitt, without any response. I may get in touch with Peter again."

"Well, I have something that may raise your spirits a bit. Guess who's invited to Claire Gibson's Tuesday evening salon?"

"You!"

"Me. I've been trying to figure out why. I was circulating around, like a good vicar should, trying to remember names. I have this problem of names here for anyone over eighteen. And somehow I circulated right into the Claire clique. I was about to run for it, but Ralph Prescott started talking to me about the search committee. One thing led to another and—I think it was my clericals. Nobody notices me when I'm in my usual uniform. Anyhow, he suggested I join them Tuesday night. Just like that. And I accepted. I could be losing my mind, of course."

"I'm delighted," Father Leffingwell said. "That does cheer me up. I'd like to make one suggestion, however."

Andrew grinned at him. "I think I'm ahead of you. You don't think I should show up at Claire's in my jeans and dirty sweater, right?"

"Right."

Father Leffingwell welcomed Sunday afternoons as a time of rest. After taking the eight and ten o'clock services, joining the church breakfast between services, and then the coffee hour, he looked forward to the quiet of the rectory. He would rest a while, perhaps take a nap, then think about the coming confirmation class. There was also a Downtown Businessmen's Prayer Breakfast that loomed vaguely in the days ahead. He'd have to come up with a short speech for that. He wondered if he could make a little pitch for funds for Andrew's street ministry. That might not be a bad idea.

It was almost dark when he woke up from an impromptu nap, but it was only four o'clock. It got dark earlier here. He sat forward in his rocking chair gingerly, his back aching. He wished he didn't always fall asleep in the chair. He should have enough sense to go lie down on any one of the four beds when he felt tired.

He had just washed his face in cold water and decided to make a pot of coffee when the doorbell rang. With a sudden hope that it might be Andrew, he hurried to the front hallway.

It was young Clement Blalock. He placed the boy instantly—tall, good looking, with reddish blond hair. Oh dear, he hoped nothing was wrong at the Blalock home.

"Father Leffingwell, I'd like to talk to you . . . uh . . . if possible. Or is this a bad time? I could come back." He looked as if he almost wished to be sent away, but he was carefully using his company manners.

"No. Not at all. I was just going to make some coffee. Do you drink coffee?"

"Yeah. Yes. Coffee's fine. In the restaurant where I work part-time, they have all kinds of coffee. We have an espresso machine. State of the art." He followed Father Leffingwell into the kitchen, and Father Leffingwell had a moment's gratitude toward Mrs. Griswold. Everything was still fairly neat and clean from her Friday visit.

As they seated themselves in front of the fireplace with coffee, Father Leffingwell couldn't help but compare Clem to Mark. Clem was well-dressed, clean, comfortably polite, with the quiet confidence of the cared for. All his life people had loved him enough to *teach* him, to *expect* from him. Nobody had ever neglected to look at this boy's report card, or forgotten his birthday. He was somebody.

"Do you like your job at the restaurant?" Father Leffingwell started off, and Clem took his cue, explaining the job, describing the place, the people he worked with. His boss's name was Tony.

"I've had a dozen jobs—from delivering papers when I was a kid, and then serving my time in the fast food places—Burger King, McDonalds—but I *really* like this job. I don't even mind sometimes when Tony gives me dirty jobs to do. It's all experience, and I want . . . someday I want my own restaurant."

Father Leffingwell had a moment of déjà vu. *I'm gonna have my own gas station. I'm gonna be a boss.*

The boy continued, "I guess you know why I really came over today. It's about my family." He had said the magic words. He belonged.

"Yes," Father Leffingwell said, "they are going through a very difficult time. You all are."

"Man, you can say that again." He sounded almost like Mark. "You see, I know in my gut, that my mom *wants* to have this baby. And I know in my gut that it'll just about kill my dad. Though what the heck—excuse me—we're going to do with an *infant* in a grown up family, I don't know yet." His voice skated upward and he flushed.

"Yes, I understand that. Sometimes people are called upon to make sacrifices—painful ones indeed," Father Leffingwell said gently.

"That's what I need to talk to somebody about. It doesn't have to *be* such a big sacrifice. I've been thinking and thinking about it. But who's gonna listen to a seventeen-year-old kid?"

"*I'm* listening." Father Leffingwell leaned forward. Out of the mouths of babes. He felt a faint flicker of hopefulness.

"You see, they're thinking four-years-plus of college for *both* Diane and me. And we don't need that. *I* don't need that. Diane, yeah. She's got a real thing for math. She wants to be an accountant. She got kind of hooked into it by helping Dad at night. He brings work home most nights. Anyhow, that's great for *her*. And she'll *do* it—I'll give her that. Once she gets something in her mind she's like a bulldog. She *will* make it."

"Wait a minute," Father Leffingwell interrupted. "Why don't you need four-years-plus of college, Clem? Don't discount it. You don't want to be doing those dirty jobs Tony gives you when you are thirty-five and supporting a family."

"But I won't be! I won't be!" The boy's face glowed with enthusiasm. "I've got it all figured out. Look here." He took a sheaf of folded papers out of his jacket pocket. "I just haven't had the guts to show it to anybody yet."

"Why don't we take those in to the dining room table? You can spread them out a bit," Father Leffingwell suggested.

At the dining room table, with Clem's papers spread out under the light, Father Leffingwell was impressed. The boy had put a lot of work into this. He had analyzed two locations, pros and cons, just for practice. There were sample menus he had made out with food costs calculated and overhead costs factored in. There were notes on licenses and permits, on financing, on dealing with labor unions. It was remarkably thorough.

"You see, I've got another little ace, too. Diane's with me on this."

"*Diane* is?" Father Leffingwell had bitten back an astonished "You're kidding!"

"Yeah. Yes. We had one major yelling match. If you can get Diane's mind off Diane for one full minute, she's not too dim. Mom and Dad were both out, or I'd have been grounded for twenty years, but I finally got through to her. I can yell louder, I guess.

"And you see," he rushed on, "I have the best restaurant training of all—in my job. Tony's place is one of the really fine small restaurants in Seattle. And I don't mind telling you that he's making a pile. It takes a while to know Tony, but once he lets you in, he's really a great guy. He got interested in me when I said I wanted my own place some day. He tells me anything I ask—the hard stuff, you know, like getting your start-up costs, that stuff—"

"But Clem, you can't run a business without an education," Father Leffingwell protested.

"I'm coming to that, Father. I'm not jumping off the end of the pier here. I've really worked it out. I've investigated. South Seattle Community College has about the best two-year restaurant management course on the planet. *Complete.* They even have this restaurant over on campus. Man, you should eat there. Some of those guys are real chefs when they graduate. Two years, see? *Two years.* So I finish that before I'm twenty. And Tony says I have a job there as long as I want. He said he's never had such a good worker. When I graduate, he says I can have a shot at assistant manager. I already help him with the think-stuff, like ordering supplies, checking invoices, business things. I'm going into community college next year. Two years there. Then maybe five years working for Tony, full-time, good salary. Then I'm ready. By that time this little new kid—him—her—whatever, is about seven years old. Dad's three years from retirement. *He can quit on schedule. I* can help. I mean financially. Even, say this little new kid is a big brain, see, and wants a Ph.D. later. I could handle it. *I* could pay for it. What do you think?" Clem's face was shining with eagerness.

*I think . . . I think there is hope for the world.*

Father Leffingwell cleared his throat. "I think this is an excellent plan, Clem. Do you want me to go with you when you present it to your parents?"

"Oh, man, would you?" the boy asked fervently. "When?"

"Toward the end of the week, I think, if you don't mind waiting a few more days." It would give him time to check out the course at the community college and perhaps stop for a meal at Tony's. *God bless you, Tony whoever.*

"Terrific. Thank you Father Leffingwell. That's just great." The boy grinned, suddenly looking very young.

"And you know what else?"

"What?"

"*Diane* promised to do my restaurant bookkeeping. For nothing. Nada. Free."

"You're kidding!" This time it slipped out, and suddenly they were both laughing. It was good. It had been a long time since he had really laughed.

On Tuesday evening Andrew picked Father Leffingwell up in his old TransAm, which had been fire-engine red, but was now rusted and faded. The noise and vibration in the old car was astonishing.

"You need new shocks on this, Andrew, for one thing."

Andrew laughed. "I need a new car. This is a relic from my sophomore year in college. One of the old grads, a booster, got it for me at cost, because he was enamored with my probable future with the NFL. I just haven't had the money to replace it with anything else."

On the way to Claire Gibson's, Andrew spoke of Mark again. "If you can get that kid off the street, Padre, he has a chance. Once they hit the street maturation ceases. I judge Mark at about fourteen years old and if, as you say, he's been on the street for a couple of years, he's still probably got the maturity of a twelve-year-old. But he's a bright kid; he could make it."

"Well, I have hopes. He's going to the junkyard with me on Saturday to look for a windshield wiper assembly."

"Good. The thing is to get him interested in doing something. Give him a goal."

"Today we install a windshield wiper. Tomorrow magna cum laude?"

"I know. It's discouraging, but it's a beginning. Hang onto that."

When they reached Claire Gibson's, Father Leffingwell was vaguely disappointed in her home. He didn't know what he had expected. It was a large, old-fashioned frame house up on a hill behind Green Lake. The place was immaculate, of course, but—what? Then he realized that everything was good, expensive, but very old and worn. It occurred to him that Claire probably hadn't changed a thing at all since her parents' deaths. He observed Andrew's quick glance around and knew that he had formed the same conclusion. They were in another shrine.

When Claire came to the door she appeared very upset.

"Come in, you're the last. It was good of you both to come. We're all in here." She led the way from the large entry hall down two steps into an extremely large living room. Several people were there, Father Leffingwell recognized Mr. and Mrs. Burris and a few others. The men stood up.

"Father Cullen, I don't think you know everybody here—since you work mostly with the—er—young people," Claire said. "This is Miss Gillespie, who just retired from the City Library System. And Ralph Prescott you know. This is Mr. and Mrs. McCready, Mr. and Mrs. Brill, and Mr. and Mrs. Bethune. I think everybody knows Mr. and Mrs. Burris. Please help yourselves to coffee and snacks. Oh, dear! I forgot the cream and sugar." She hurried out.

"Is something wrong?" asked Father Leffingwell as he and Andrew found chairs and seated themselves.

"We've been royally had," Mr. Bethune spoke in a grave voice. He put his hand in his pocket and took it out again. A former smoker himself, Father Leffingwell sympathized. He knew the feeling of the dedicated smoker finding himself in a room with no ashtrays and a pretty little china plaque decorated with little pink rosebuds on the coffee table saying "Thank You For Not Smoking." The rosebuds didn't help. Mr. Bethune was looking bleakly at the china plaque.

"Why? What happened?" Father Leffingwell asked.

Bethune spoke grimly, "That jerk Talbott—sorry, Father—conned us into inviting some fool called Harold Tanner for consideration. Now we're hearing all sorts of crazy things about him."

Claire entered with a silver tray holding an exquisite cut glass cream pitcher and sugar bowl. "Claire, I was just telling the good Fathers about that idiot, Tanner."

Claire put down the tray, her hands shaking slightly.

"Suppose that enough people like this man to—suppose Saint Polycarp's ends up with someone like that?"

Father Leffingwell saw his chance to ingratiate Andrew with the group. "Andrew knows Harold Tanner," he said quietly, "perhaps he could advise you." Every head in the room turned to look at Andrew, and without missing a heartbeat, Andrew rose to the occasion. Father Leffingwell was pleased.

"Yes, I know Harold Tanner," Andrew spoke judiciously, as if he had given much thought to the subject—as perhaps he had. He had an appealing deep and mellow voice. "As I was telling Father Leffingwell earlier, Harry marches to a different drum from most of us. Please know that I don't question Harry's vocation. I would never question anyone's vocation. We all know there are a million Christian pathways to God. I know only one pathway—my own." He paused. They were impressed. "You've already invited him to take one service and preach?" he asked.

There were moans of assent.

"Well, then, here is what will happen." They all sat forward intently. "Harry has his own rock band. You will have a rock mass. His vestments you must see to believe. He will look very grungy. He won't have washed his dyed hair for at least a month. He will bring his own communion vessels. The Altar Guild women are in for a shock. They are carved out of monkey pod wood he picked up somewhere in the Pacific Islands. A number of strangers will show up for the service. The guest book will have names like Moonbeam and Meadow Lark, probably all from the same address, as Harry lives in an ever-changing household. But you don't have to worry about Harry ever becoming Rector of Saint Polycarp's."

"Why not?" Miss Gillespie asked in a strangled voice.

"Because my educated guess is—and I'm 110 percent sure of it—is that Harry wouldn't think of tying himself down to a single commitment. He's into a hundred causes: gay rights—although he isn't gay; animal rights; women's rights; minority rights. You name it—he's in it. He also has a large private income so he does it all for love. He wouldn't have any interest at all in giving up his present lifestyle." Andrew was smiling now and there were answering smiles around the room, showing varying degrees of relief.

"I don't mean to ridicule Harry," Andrew said, turning serious. "In with all the slam-bang activity maybe he does some good along the way. Who can tell? Maybe he's one of God's clowns. Remember what Saint Francis said: 'What are the servants of the Lord but his minstrels who raise the hearts of men and move them to spiritual joy.'" He looked around the room. "As I see it, you have two choices."

"What?" They all said it together.

Andrew ticked them off on two fingers. "One, you skip the service that day. Harry comes and goes. You never see him again, and you *don't* get a splitting headache. Two, you *do* attend the service, see the show of shows, *do* get a splitting headache but—you may also have been moved to spiritual joy along the way, as Saint Francis mentioned. Who knows? Life's an adventure, isn't it?"

They were all laughing aloud now, in complete good humor. Claire, flushed and looking quite attractive, picked up a tray of snacks from the coffee table. "I'm so glad you came, Father Cullen. Please have some of these. I made them myself."

As Andrew was driving Father Leffingwell back to the rectory they discussed the meeting. "What do you think of them, Andrew?"

"Well, if you will allow me to quote myself, 'there are a million Christian pathways to God.' I think they are good sincere people, on their pathway, and I hope they get a rector they can live with. They've all put a lot into Saint Polycarp's—that was evident. It means a great deal to them. Maybe this other guy, Chester Bledsoe, is the right one. I was also reminded of another important fact."

"What was that?"

"That Claire Gibson is still the best cook in King County. Did you get any of those little cheese things?"

They sat in the car in front of the rectory a while, talking about the meeting, the people, the parish. It began to get cold in the car.

"Well, I must go in," Father Leffingwell said, but he spoke absently. Did he have another bright idea? He was full of them lately. He turned and looked speculatively at Andrew.

Andrew was looking at him, smiling. They could see each other dimly in the glow from the street lamp. "Forget it, Padre. I know what you're thinking. No way in God's world could I take on the whole parish. Put your money on this Bledsoe guy."

It wasn't until Thursday evening that Father Leffingwell was able to get back to the Blalock living room in support of Clem's master plan. In the presence of his parents the boy seemed less mature, more of a kid, although he had dressed for the occasion in slacks, jacket, and tie. Diane almost spoiled it when she saw him as he joined the group.

"Are you going out?" she asked. "I thought we were having another summit."

"We *are*," he snarled, giving her a poke.

She suddenly understood, looking embarrassed, and snarled back, "Okay. I'm sorry. All right?"

They were all standing in the living room and for a moment no one seemed to know what to do. Clem appeared to have been struck dumb now that his moment had arrived. Roger Blalock broke the awkward silence. "Okay, we're here," he said tiredly. "I'm not sure why, but maybe we'd better get it started. Clem?"

Father Leffingwell rescued the boy. "Perhaps we could use the dining room table. Clem has quite a bit of data to refer to."

"Oh, sure," Roger Blalock led the way into the Blalock dining room, switched on the overhead lights and pulled out a chair for his wife. "Why don't you take the head of the table, Clem, since you called this meeting, so to speak."

Father Leffingwell observed the man keenly for a moment. Was he baiting the boy? Or was he simply exhausted from wrestling with their problem? Clem, his color high, took the chair at the head of the table, and Diane startled everyone by stating: "Maybe Father Leffingwell could start us off with a prayer," and then adding in a faintly defiant tone, "Well, sometimes meetings start with a prayer, don't they?"

"Thank you, Diane," Father Leffingwell said, and bowed his head, knowing that the others would too despite their surprise, and she was right. A prayer was a pretty good way to start anything.

He paused a moment longer to give them enough time to compose themselves, then recited a quickly simplified version of one of the prayers for guidance from the back of the prayer book.

"O God, grant us in all our doubts and uncertainties the wisdom to ask what You would have us do, letting Your wisdom save us from all false choices, and that in your light we may see light, and in your straight path we may not stumble, through Jesus Christ, our Lord, Amen."

"Amen," they all murmured and raised their heads.

It had been a good idea, because Clem seemed able to start now. He cleared his throat and pulled his wad of papers from his jacket pocket. Face flushed, he began what had obviously been carefully rehearsed.

"Not everybody in the world wants, or needs, four-years-plus of college." His hands were unsteady holding his papers and Father Leffingwell felt a lump in his throat. *Please God, keep Roger Blalock quiet until Clem gets going.*

Once started, Clem managed quite well. His confidence returned and he went through all he had told Father Leffingwell on the previous Sunday evening. Interruptions were friendly ones.

"Clem, Honey, that's brilliant, let me see that." Irma reached for one of his charts.

"And Mom, look at his stuff on start-up costs." This was Diane.

"Clem. Show your family those cost calculations for the individual menus," Father Leffingwell contributed.

Roger Blalock remained silent, an expression on his face of mingled pride and dismay. He looked as if he wanted to cry. Gradually conversation ceased and one by one they all turned to look at Roger. He was holding some of Clem's notes, almost lovingly. When he spoke, his voice was husky.

"It's a beautifully thought out presentation, Son. I'm very proud of you. In a way, it makes me a little sad because it tells me that you're not a little kid any more. And I got very fond of you as a little kid." He paused a moment and then went on. "I had already decided—for other reasons—that your mother should not abort this baby, but you go ahead with this plan. It's a good one. And if—when the new little kid is seven or so—I need your help, and you can give it, I'll take it. With gratitude. And thank you."

"Roger," whispered Irma. "Are you sure—about the baby."

"Quite sure." And there passed between them a husband and wife communication which, for a moment, shut everyone else out.

"Well, that's that, then," Diane said, smacking the table with the flat of her hand. "I know what I'll do," she added in sudden inspiration. "I'll give you a baby shower. And I think

I'll give hints to people what to bring. We'd better make a list of what you want."

"Oh, wow." This was Clem, suddenly young again. "What are we gonna name it?" There was a flurry of conversation, laughter, jokes. The strain was over; the decision made, the mood become almost celebratory. Clem went into the kitchen and made delicious capuccino for everyone.

When Father Leffingwell left, Roger Blalock came with him to the front porch. "Thank you, Father. That data about abortions—various types of abortions—was an eye-opener. God Almighty, how can they do it?"

"A form of self-delusion born of fear, I suppose. They don't let themselves know what really happens. They leave that part to the doctors willing to do it. The old good versus evil battle is still with us, Roger."

"But it's so barbaric. I put the data away. I really didn't want Irma to see it. She never wanted an abortion anyhow. I get sick when I think about it. Pulling it to pieces like that. An ear. A hand and forearm. Half a buttock. If I have to plod along a while longer, I can. It's no big deal." He shivered slightly.

Father Leffingwell looked at the other man under the porch light. Middle-aged. Balding. Slightly overweight, but willing to plod along and endure whatever it was about his work he hated. He didn't look much like a hero, but heroes came in various guises, and you couldn't always tell. They bade each other a polite good night.

Father Leffingwell drove away with a feeling of elation. *Thank God. Thank God. Hosanna. Hosanna in the highest!* They would never regret it. They would all work a little harder, give up some things, put up with some things, but in a few months their house would be blessed, and they would be able to say what Martha had always called "those four most beautiful words." *A child is born.*

# CHAPTER 11

On Saturday morning, hoping nobody would need him, Father Leffingwell put on his "work clothes," as Martha and Philip had called them: a pair of old brown corduroy pants, the faded blue plaid shirt he had let Mark wear, and the heavy old coat sweater with elbow patches.

Mark had already arrived when Father Leffingwell opened the front door. He sat on the front step, holding the unopened newspaper. He sprang up.

"Good weather." He pointed heavenward to the gray overcast sky. "We won't get wet or too hot." He handed the paper to Father Leffingwell.

After breakfast they had a glorious morning prowling through a huge auto graveyard just outside the city. They found two windshield wiper assemblies which they could cannibalize to make one in working order. Father Leffingwell also found a much better jack in the trunk of a wrecked car than the one he had, so they bought that too. Pleased, and dirty, they went back to the rectory for lunch.

When they entered the front hallway, the phone on the hall table had all four red lights glowing on the machine. Father Leffingwell's heart sank. He had hoped to go unneeded the rest of the afternoon to have time to install the wiper.

"Mark, you go start washing up, while I get these calls." He began to press the red buttons. The first two were calls from Andrew, the second one stressing urgency. Father Leffingwell stopped there and dialed Andrew's number.

Andrew started without preamble, "Is Mark with you? You said you expected him today."

"Yes. We just got back from the junkyard and—

"Keep him there, Padre. I'm coming over," Andrew cut in. "It's about his friend, Henry. Apparently, when they both ran away—it was from Chicago, incidentally—Henry's parents did file a lost child report. The police between here and Chicago have connected up through computer networks that report with McCabe's death report here."

"Oh dear, what does that mean?"

"They are cooperating with Seattle police because Seattle police are trying to find out what kind of drug it was that was deadly—the narcotics people. They'll be rounding up kids to talk to and I think Mark should hear about Henry from one of us."

"Yes, of course. Come on over." Father Leffingwell hung up the receiver and stood for a long moment looking at the two remaining red lights, not really seeing them. *Dear God, help Mark through this.* The prayer was shattered in his mind, fragments, images in bits and pieces. Mark's ecstatic face. Mark's greasy fingers. *Happiness is pieces of two broken windshield wipers.* To be dashed in a matter of minutes. *It isn't fair.* Father Leffingwell put his hand on the hall table and leaned on it, concentrating on the red glowing lights. He ought to push the buttons.

"Hey! Father Leffingwell. I'm washed up now. You want me to put the kettle on?" Mark's voice rang through the rectory, followed by Mark's footsteps. "Father Leffingwell?" Now Mark stood in the living room doorway.

"Yes, please," Father Leffingwell heard himself saying. "Do that, Mark, while I take these other two calls." He didn't turn around but listened intently to the sound of Mark's footsteps going back to the kitchen. Then he called out, "You can start making the sandwiches. You know where everything is."

The boy's, "Okay!" came back to him.

He could hear Mark clattering around in the kitchen, Mark whistling, and he realized that his chest was cramping badly.

*Oh, no, not now.*

By the time he had gotten his nitro tablets and used one, Andrew was at the door, in his worn jeans and grimy sweater. Andrew's first words were, "Are you okay?"

"Yes," Father Leffingwell answered. He had not told anyone at the church about the chest pains. It wasn't their problem.

"Do you want me to tell him?" Andrew asked, his eyes still intent. Father Leffingwell wondered if he had gone pale, or was sweating.

"Please," he said, turning to go into the living room. "If you don't mind."

"Mark," he called when they were in the living room. "Come in here please. Father Cullen's here. He . . . wants to talk to you a minute."

The boy came in, pausing in the doorway a moment, looking at both priests. He was holding a dish towel. He came in and let it drop onto a chair, his wary blue eyes moving from one to the other.

"Whatja want?" His voice was guarded.

"Some time ago you asked me to see if I could find Henry McCabe, remember?" Andrew said.

"So . . . Didja find him?" Mark stood motionless, waiting for whatever blow was coming, seeming to know that one was.

"I'm sorry, Mark. Henry . . . didn't make it. He died in the hospital a few days after they picked him up."

Mark moved slightly, bent, as if an invisible wind had buffeted him. "Aw-w . . . *Man.*" It was barely a whisper, and he crumpled into a bony heap on the floor, his face pressed against his knees, skinny arms folded behind his head, as if to pull himself into the smallest possible space, as if he could disappear.

Andrew moved quickly to him, getting down on the floor beside him, patting him, gently rubbing his back, trying to comfort. The boy was crying, not the storm of weeping that Father Leffingwell had expected, but softly and tiredly, as one who had cried for a long time and had no strength left.

Andrew lifted him and helped him to the couch, sitting down beside him, continuing to hold him. Father Leffingwell handed Mark something to wipe his eyes with and realized it was the dish towel. Mark took it and blotted at the seeping tears.

Andrew began explaining to him about Henry's hospital stay, making it as tactful as he could, assuring Mark that people—many people, had tried to help, had tried to save Henry. The boy seemed to be withdrawing, answering only in low monosyllables. "Yeah . . . Okay . . . Sure . . ."

When Mark shrugged against Andrew's arm, Andrew moved away from him, still watching him carefully. "Mark, I need to talk to you about something else."

Mark looked at him, his eyes puffy and red, his mouth unsteady. "Yeah, what?"

"The police are trying to find out what it was that was so dangerous, what it was that Henry was using, so that nobody else—"

Mark got up slowly from the couch, as if it cost him great effort. "I'm not talkin' to cops, okay?" he said in a listless voice. "So forget it." He started walking toward the hall. "I gotta go pee."

"Well, it's no big deal, Mark," Andrew said. "I'll go with you. They won't take you in. I promise!" Andrew sighed as they heard the bathroom door shut decisively.

"I should have waited to tell him that," Andrew said, leaning back. "Poor little devil."

"Can you really be sure they won't take him in, send him back to juvy?"

"Yes. He hasn't done anything—that they know of. They have no charge against him. And I'll go with him. They won't push him with me standing there in my clericals." Andrew got up and they both stood for a few moments more, waiting for Mark to come back. They both realized at the same time that the house was too quiet. Andrew rushed into the hall, opening the bathroom door so violently that it slammed back against the wall.

"Gone!"

With remarkable speed, Andrew was at the front door, and down the front steps. "Mark! Wait! Please!"

Father Leffingwell followed to the front door, to see Mark running down the street and Andrew pounding after him, as he must have pounded down the football field, but suddenly the big man stumbled, his solid bulk hitting the pavement with a sickening thud, while Mark disappeared around the corner.

Father Leffingwell hurried to Andrew. "Are you all right?"

"I . . . will be. Gimme a minute." He sat up, clutching his left knee, his face grim with pain.

After a couple of minutes, with Father Leffingwell's help, he got to his feet, gingerly trying to stand on both legs. "That, my friend, was my *own* knee. It just gave way again. It does that sometimes." They began slowly to walk toward the rectory, Andrew limping badly. "My fake knee works great, but both knees got it in my last game. The doctors want to hold off as long as possible fixing this one, but if I can't stay on my feet they'll have to do it sooner than they want to. I'm so sorry I couldn't catch him. If I could have talked to him, maybe . . ."

"Don't blame yourself. You did your best. Perhaps he'll come back later. He has before."

"Maybe. Anyhow, I think he's safe enough in some ways." They climbed the front steps with difficulty. "He'll fade into his group of friends and disappear. They stick together and protect each other, cover for each other."

"What do you mean 'some ways?'" Father Leffingwell opened the door and they went inside.

"Somehow he'll get his hands on crack or acid or whatever and curl up under some bridge or some abandoned house or some place. Oh, Padre, where's it going to end?" Andrew sat down heavily in one of the big chairs. He leaned his head back and shut his eyes. "Do you have any aspirin or anything like that?"

"Yes. I'll get it." Father Leffingwell went to get aspirin and a glass of water.

"Thanks," Andrew said, taking it. "I guess I should count my blessings. I didn't bang up my driving leg, which would have got you an uninvited houseguest or got me back in the hospital."

"Well, don't think of leaving yet, Andrew. Rest a bit. Mark and I were going to have some lunch. Would you like something?"

"No, thanks. I couldn't eat right now."

"Would a bit of Mrs. Burris's tea help?" Father Leffingwell watched Andrew's rugged face. He looked grayish and grim about the mouth.

"No, nothing, thanks. Except maybe a dash of humanity in human beings, for a change. Padre, why don't they raise their kids any more. They don't *care*. How can they not *care*! And as for their everlasting souls, well, forget it. I can't tell you how many times parents have said to me, 'I don't take Johnny to church because I want him to make up his own mind about religion.'"

"Yes, I've heard that one too."

Andrew sounded tired. "Raising kids is a lot of trouble. Nobody thinks of that in advance. It means *teaching* them something. It means taking *time* with them. They seem to think if they can procreate and own a TV, they are equipped to be parents. They can dump Johnny in front of the TV so he can soak up all that garbage. Good grief, half of all you learn in life you get before you're six years old. Then, they dump him into what passes for public schools these days, so he soaks up all that garbage. By the time Johnny is an adolescent, he hasn't any mind left to make up. I'm sorry. I seem to be on my soap box. Maybe falling flat on my face doesn't agree with me. I used to be one good runner . . ."

"Don't be too down, Andrew. The family system is alive and well. It's just that in your work so far you haven't seen much evidence of it. We have families here in the parish who are fighting the good fight, and winning. Trust me. And if you can't trust me, trust God."

Andrew straightened up, half-smiling, rubbing his knee. "I am rebuked. You're right. I'll go back to my little pad, spin my little Rolodex, and start networking. Mark's out there someplace. Maybe I can achieve a minor miracle and find him."

"You may just," Father Leffingwell said, but both men knew that if Mark didn't want to be found, he wouldn't be. "Here, let me give you a hand. I'll tell you something one of my old teachers always told us."

"What was that?" Andrew got up carefully and tested his left leg.

"'God's work is always good, but seldom easy.'" He helped Andrew down the front steps and into the old TransAm.

After he had gone, Father Leffingwell stood in the front hall again. A feeling of lassitude pervaded him. He could recite encouraging words to Andrew, but somehow they rang hollow in his own mind. *Oh, Mark, dear child, come back.*

Two red buttons on the answering machine still glowed. He should push them and listen to the messages. The dirty cardboard box with the windshield wiper parts in it still stood on the Victorian table, and he should do something about that. He looked down at his dirty corduroy pants and shirt. He should clean up and change clothes. And he had left his keys on the table by the box. Stupid old man. He'd be looking for them the next time he left the rectory. He went slowly across the hall and picked them up, his thumb smoothly passing over the plastic fob on the key chain, on which there was printed a motto. Martha had given him the key chain as a stocking stuffer one Christmas. "*Words to live by,*" she had said, laughing. And amid the crumpled Christmas wrappings, the scattered opened boxes around the Christmas tree, he had read the words the first time. Now he read them again. *How I live today makes all the difference in the world.* He reached over and pressed a red button.

By mid-February Mark had not come back, nor had Andrew been able to locate him. The boy remained a haunting shadow, always in the back of Father Leffingwell's mind, and he knew Andrew felt the same way, but the work had to go on.

Good things happened. Father Leffingwell discovered yellow and white crocus pushing up around the back steps of the rectory through a late, light snow. Newton Crail found a copy of John Donne's exquisite sermons in an odd-lot of books he purchased and gave it to Father Leffingwell. Andrew was walking again without a limp. Ralph Prescott, retired high school teacher on the search committee, volunteered to help Andrew with the street kids, was remarkably good at it, and Gloria had started to change, looking somehow different, better.

"Andrew, does Gloria look different to you?" Father Leffingwell asked in the sacristy after they had finished a service of Evening Prayer.

"Yeah. She's losing weight."

"That's *it*! Wonderful. I'm so glad."

"You should be. Your gluttony sermon did it. I thought you went a little far, myself, but apparently she didn't. She quoted you to me, verbatim."

"Dear me. What did I say?"

"You said—lemme get it right now. You said, 'We hold our minds and bodies in trust from God, and it is our bounden duty not to corrupt, damage, defile, or degrade them."

"You think that was going too far?"

"No. Just kidding. Another woman who has changed is—what's her name—Mrs. Blalock. Could she be pregnant? She's got grown children, hasn't she?"

"Yes. She has. And, yes, I think she is pregnant."

"I knew it. She has that look some pregnant women get, a kind of inner glow, as if they knew some splendid secret, and you don't."

They left the church together and walked out into the evening. It was six o'clock and full dark, but there seemed to be a hint of spring in the air, a warmth that hadn't been there a day before. It wouldn't last, of course. Pacific Northwest weather went its own way, Father Leffingwell had learned that much.

"Oh, I forgot to give you this." He took an envelope from

his pocket and handed it to Andrew. "One hundred and sixty-four dollars for your street ministry. I spoke to a businesswomen's group. I've already dictated a note of thanks from you to Gloria. Stop by the office and sign it."

"Thank you, Padre. This is getting to be a good thing." Andrew put the envelope in his pocket. "So far you've hit Rotary, Kiwanis, Downtown Businessmen's Prayer Breakfast, and now the women. Keep up the good work." They had reached the church parking lot.

"It seems so little . . . for so big a need." Father Leffingwell got out his keys for his car door.

"Day by day," Andrew said. The phrase from the old twelfth-century hymn had become a kind of password between them when either was tired or discouraged.

Driving home to the rectory, Father Leffingwell thought of Andrew. During the months he had been at Saint Polycarp's he had learned a good deal more about Andrew, a many-layered personality. He knew that when he returned to Baltimore, he would keep in touch with Andrew and count him a friend for life. He thought he knew the man now, as well as anyone may know another, stopping short, of course, of that private center self in every person, known only to God. He wished . . . he wished he might live long enough to see Andrew come into his own, although he wasn't sure what that might be. Andrew always surprised him. Andrew's continuing friendship with Harry Tanner had surprised him; the two men were so different. He had been surprised, though why he didn't know, that Andrew was seeing his estranged wife again. And he had been surprised when Andrew had suggested that they—just he and Andrew—hold a brief memorial service in the empty church one night for the soul of John Henry McCabe. Andrew was a worldly man, a strong man, a sensitive man, and a deeply spiritual man . . .

Father Leffingwell stopped the car sharply. He'd driven a block past the rectory, his mind miles away. Was it safe to back up? Or should he drive around the block? Silly old man.

During Lent, with the altar stripped of flowers and the beautiful gold crosses covered with purple draperies until Easter, Harry Tanner's guest sermon at Saint Polycarp's was a nine-day-wonder.

The church was packed. The conservative-to-moderate block arrived in force, partly because they were curious and partly because word had gotten around now that Harry Tanner would come and go and was no threat. The liberal-to-radical set came to show solidarity with the political correctness of a rock mass and because they wanted to watch the conservatives be totally shocked. Both sides were more than satisfied, and the coffee hour was a sell-out. The women had to send out for store-bought cookies—unheard of at Saint Polycarp's—and more coffee and tea had to be brewed.

The decibel level was deafening. People who had coolly looked through each other before gathered in groups, talking and laughing.

Then Harry Tanner, who had chastised them all from the pulpit as unfeeling WASPS, gave them a solo musical performance in the rec room. It left them breathless with wonder, and the feeling—one couldn't quite put one's finger on it, but—that there was so much *more* to God than one had thought—the vastness, the unknowableness—one couldn't really explain. And he did it by playing his guitar, which he did superbly, and singing songs. His repertoire of Christian music, ancient and modern, was astonishing. It profited them greatly to have heard him, dirty hair and all.

# CHAPTER 12

Father Leffingwell's confirmation class would be meeting two evenings a week around the dining room table at the rectory. He had thought he would be too tired, but he was looking forward to it. It would be pleasant to again review the history and doctrine of the church in an organized manner. Another surprise from Andrew was that he had asked to sit in on the sessions.

"Of course, Andrew. Maybe you can help."

"Nope. This is your show. I just feel like taking a refresher course. I'll keep the coffee cups filled or whatever. Why are you meeting twice a week? And why here?" They were having coffee in the rectory living room after dinner. Andrew had splurged and bought two steaks, a bag of ready-made salad, and some frozen potatoes.

"One, because my group must be ready for the bishop's visitation, and Kim's class has been going on longer."

"And two," Andrew said, "Kim's class meets at church and you are being tactful."

"Or cowardly. Are you and Kim past your icy-polite stage yet?" Father Leffingwell asked.

"No." Andrew sighed. "And I don't think now that we are going to be. Kim's a better grudge-holder than I thought. I'm sorry about it."

"So am I," Father Leffingwell said. He regretted that he had alienated Kim, but they were worlds apart.

"Can you take another student? You've still got only five, haven't you?"

"Six, actually. Yes, I can take another. But *please* don't tell me it's another one from Kim's class."

Andrew laughed. "No. This is a young guy who's been working as a volunteer at the shelter, name's Francis Foster. About twenty. Bright. He'll graduate from college next year. He thinks he wants to be a priest."

"But he's not in the church now?"

"He's been coming to the services. He's a new convert, Padre, and he's still in that state of elation and euphoria people enter when they finally focus in and understand."

"Oh yes, bring him, by all means. He may well have a vocation. He'll know in due course." Father Leffingwell knew a moment of deep satisfaction. Regardless of the world's madness, the Christians would keep coming. He wondered if Christ had been a physically able man like Andrew, striding strongly along the dusty roads in Palestine. *Follow me.*

"Hey, Padre, come back. You're a thousand miles away. I want to tell you something, and I want you to hear it."

"Sorry. What is it?"

"About Kim. I've heard—not from Kim—but I've heard that the bishop is very pleased with the idea that she wants the rectorship here at Saint Polycarp's. He wouldn't openly come out for one candidate over another, of course, but he's letting it be known quietly that he thinks she can do the job."

"Too bad. That's going to influence a lot of people in the parish."

"Greg Talbott is delighted, of course. Kim's kind of a protégé of his. When's her ordination?"

"The second Sunday after Easter."

"When is this Bledsoe coming?"

"Soon, I think. You'd have to ask Gloria. Oh, there's the doorbell."

"Mark, you think?" Andrew asked in quick hope, as Father Leffingwell got up to answer it.

It was Malcolm Griswold. As Father Leffingwell ushered him into the living room, Andrew got up and picked up the coffee cups.

Malcolm was saying, "I must apologize for coming here to the rectory unannounced, but I have to talk to you." His face was flushed and his mouth tight with anger. He gave a jerky nod of his head toward Andrew.

"I was just leaving," Andrew said agreeably. "I'll stash these in the dishwasher as I go," he added to Father Leffingwell.

"Please sit down, Malcolm," Father Leffingwell said when Andrew was out of sight. "You needn't apologize. How can I help you?" He had had a tiring day, but from long practice his voice didn't reveal it.

Malcolm took one of the big chairs but didn't relax into its comfort, sitting tensely forward. He was nice looking in a bland way, but was clearly disturbed. Father Leffingwell recalled a meeting with him early in his tenure at Saint Polycarp's. Had the man finally found the courage to seek whatever help he needed?

Malcolm spoke suddenly, harshly, "Father Leffingwell, my mother is not a charwoman."

"I beg your pardon?" This certainly wasn't what he expected.

"I just learned that my mother has become your scrub lady. She won't be back, I can assure you. I absolutely forbid it."

"Just a moment," Father Leffingwell said quietly. "Didn't you know that she was working here at the rectory four hours a week? It's just a part-time housekeeping job. She seems quite happy with it. There is no heavy work involved, Malcolm."

"I am quite capable of supporting my mother in her old age." His voice was tight with suppressed anger.

"I'm sure you are, but, if I may say so, your mother is not in her 'old age.' She is in her early sixties, intelligent and active. She is a woman who has worked all her adult life. Perhaps just keeping house for one son isn't really enough to keep her occupied. Hadn't you thought of that?" He kept his voice gentle.

"My mother was a widow, and she supported me all alone, brought me up, saw that I was educated. I certainly don't begrudge taking care of her now." His voice shook slightly.

Father Leffingwell let a small silence stretch out between them. Poor devil. He did begrudge it, every day of it, and felt the more guilt because of it, and how quickly guilt turns to hate. He'd have to go carefully here.

"We were trying it as an experiment, Malcolm. I called on your mother one day and she mentioned she liked to keep busy, that she sometimes becomes bored. I suggested that, since I'll be here such a short time, she might try a little part-time housekeeping. Just to see if she liked it."

"She's got the ridiculous notion that she wants to take a course over at the community college," Malcolm said tightly.

"What course was she thinking of taking?"

"I don't know. Some sort of word processing course, I think." His voice was sullen, but he was calming down.

"Well, that's the coming thing. Almost no one uses a simple typewriter any more."

"But what *for*!" Malcolm exploded. "What possible reason could she have . . ."

"Perhaps she intends to do some volunteer work over at the church office. We fill in with volunteers for all sorts of things, you know."

Malcolm was silent a moment.

"You think she might be interested in that?" This was obviously a more acceptable idea than that of his mother doing menial labor.

"I shouldn't be surprised. And I rather think she took on my little job because she felt sorry for me. She is a kindly woman. I did mention to her that this big old place wasn't what I had expected when I took the post at Saint Polycarp's."

Malcolm looked around the big, shabby room. There was a small white bowl of purple crocus on the coffee table.

"Those are pretty, aren't they?" Father Leffingwell asked. "Spring can't be far off, I guess. Your mother found those out behind the garage. There are only white and yellow ones by the steps. You know, Malcolm, I think she rather enjoys getting out twice a week, and doing for me here. I'll soon be gone. Perhaps by the time I am, she'll have enough skill at word processing to do something else. People shouldn't limit themselves if they don't need to. And," he went on softly, "if she decides to take on another part-time housekeeping job—or more than one—who are we to disdain that? Any labor done well is honorable, and worthy of respect. If your mother wants to work a while longer—why shouldn't she?"

The other man seemed to sag in his chair. "It isn't that . . . exactly. It's that . . . it's that . . . it's so awful . . . what is happening. I loved my mother. I mean I love my mother now. I'll always love my mother but . . . but . . . I was going to be an attorney but . . . I want to marry but she sacrificed. She gave up her whole life for me. She worked . . . so hard. Sometimes I woke at night . . . eleven or twelve o'clock and she would be ironing in the kitchen . . . ironing after working all day . . . I owe . . . I owe . . . and she denied herself. I saw her cutting cardboard to put into her shoes because the soles . . . Oh my God . . ." He covered his face with shaking hands and Father Leffingwell's heart went out to him. He had seen this before. The too-close relationship that started to bind, with neither captive knowing how to break or ease the bonds. He waited patiently for the other man to regain a measure of composure.

When he was sure that Malcolm would hear him, Father Leffingwell began in an easy conversational tone. "If we have wrestled with a problem for a long time, we begin to see nothing but the problem—and we stop seeing any possibilities, any options."

Malcolm leaned forward, resting his arms on his knees. "What if there aren't any options, Father? What if—"

"Usually there are, if one can find them. Forgive me if I invade your privacy, but I believe that you and your mother must have talked in the past of how, when she finished working, it would be your turn, and you would take care of her. Did you think that as a child? Did you say it?"

Malcolm looked up. "Many times, I guess. I thought it would be . . . would be . . ."

"And it isn't, is it?" Father Leffingwell said gently. "Well, project that idea forward a bit. Have you considered that perhaps it isn't what your mother wanted either, after she got it? Maybe you both needed something different. Do you think your mother and you and I could get together and talk about it?"

"Oh, I don't know. I wouldn't want . . ."

"You wouldn't want your mother to know how you feel?"

"Of course not. I would never want to hurt her."

"Malcolm," Father Leffingwell said, "Don't you think she already knows that things aren't right? Is she happy? Is she oblivious to your tension? Your—rebellion?"

The other man was silent a long time. "What do you suggest?"

"I suggest that it isn't necessary for you and your mother to live together, if it isn't comfortable for you both. I suggest that there is no reason your mother can't use part-time work to supplement her pension benefits if she wants to. I suggest there is no reason why you can't still go into law. Have you inquired? Perhaps with your paralegal work experience it wouldn't take you the full three years."

Malcolm spoke hesitantly. "I never considered . . ."

"Well, think about it. There are many options, Malcolm, for both of you. Your mother enjoys this little part-time job at the rectory. She likes doing things for others. She was as pleased as a kid with a new balloon when she found that patch of purple crocus. Every once in a while, if she has extra time, she cooks something and leaves it for me. Yesterday she found half a loaf of stale bread and made a pan of the best bread pudding I've had in years. Father Cullen and I finished it off tonight at dinner. Draw back from your situation and try to get a perspective. Can you do that?"

"Yes," Malcolm said slowly, "I want to. I just don't think I can tell my mother that—"

"Why don't I talk to her—not mentioning this talk we've had. It is absolutely privileged. But perhaps she might *like* to discuss it. If she does, we could take it from there."

"Yes. Could you do that? Maybe—"

"Have you actually forbade your mother to continue working here?"

"No. I haven't yet. I was going to when I got home. I just learned about it from Kim. She was kind of worried, Kim was. About how it might look. She was worried about you, mostly. She stressed that, well, you know you are about to retire. Maybe you wouldn't have as much energy as someone younger, and you would certainly need some help with this big old place. But she thought, you know, that it might look as if you were exploiting Mom. Kim said you probably couldn't afford to pay very much, with all the expense you've had. She knows you would never, of course, exploit anyone, but it just might look that way. That sort of set me off, I guess. I'm sorry I barged in like this. But I'm not sorry I came, Father Leffingwell. Just maybe—"

"Hope, Malcolm. Always hope. Never give up hope." Father Leffingwell said, smiling. "I'll talk to your mother. We can all think on it, explore the possibilities."

"Yes. Yes, we can. And thank you. Thank you." Malcolm's bland face was alive, excited, and he went down the front steps buoyantly.

Father Leffingwell shut the door after him and paused a moment in the hallway, a little saddened. Andrew had been right. Kim was a good grudge-holder.

Sweating, crying, twisting, Diane Blalock fought with her tangled bedsheets as she struggled up out of her nightmare. "Oh . . . Oh . . . Oh."

Still half-caught in sleep, she groped her way to the edge of the bed and found the switch on her bedside lamp. Her pretty bedroom sprang into view and she managed to sit up on the edge of her bed. She could hear her mother padding hurriedly down the hall. She shuddered. "Oh . . . Oh."

"Diane, what is it? What's wrong, Sweetheart?" Mom was

there beside her and Diane wrapped her arms around her mother's thickening waist and clung for a moment.

"It was a nightmare. It was hideous—horrible. Horrible."

"Oh, I'm sorry, Darling. How strange. You stopped having bad dreams when you were about six."

"It wasn't a bad dream," Diane said fiercely. "It was a nightmare! Horrible!" She shivered and swayed a little, her eyelids drooping.

"Don't go back to sleep, Baby. You might go back into the dream again. Look, it's almost five. Come in the kitchen. I'll make us some hot Ovaltine. No, put your slippers on. The kitchen floor will be cold. And here, blow your nose." Irma took some tissues from her robe pocket.

Diane sopped her tears away and blew her nose and followed her mother to the kitchen. Mom didn't show too much yet, but she was walking like a pregnant woman. They had that kind of backward tilt.

In the bright kitchen, Diane sat down at the table and watched her mother pour milk into two mugs and spoon in the Ovaltine, then put them into the microwave. "Do you remember any of your nightmare?" she asked.

"Some," Diane said somberly. "It's fading a bit, but I was . . . running around . . . there were a lot of people. Strangers. Lots of people milling around. I had this baby and I had wrapped it up so they couldn't see it but I was trying to give it away . . . and nobody would take it because it was dead already."

"Diane. That is horrible."

Diane huddled at the table. "You see, you had the abortion, and it was that saline kind, you know, where they take a big needle and put salt solution into the fluid. You know, around the fetus. And the fetus swallows it and moves around in it and . . . it takes hours, of course, but finally the baby dies . . . and then, of course, there is a miscarriage . . . and it's all burnt, the baby is all burnt . . ."

"Diane! Where did you hear all that?" Irma took the

steaming mugs from the microwave and came to the table. "Don't drink that yet, Baby, it's too hot."

"I read all that abortion information that Father Leffingwell gave to Dad. Dad didn't want you to see it, so he hid it. Mom, why don't the pro-choice people give all that information? If the pro-choicers don't tell you all the facts, it isn't really a choice, is it?"

"No, I guess not. Try to put it out of your mind. Don't think about it. I didn't realize your dad had all that."

"He didn't want you to see it. Too gross. You'd both already decided anyhow, but I had to dig it out. You know me. If Daddy puts anything in his hidey-hole I've got to see it."

"What hidey-hole?" Irma asked, laughing.

"You know that bookcase in his study with all those accounting books and business books? Well, one of them isn't a book. It just looks like a book. It's really a little box, with a combination lock on it."

"Diane! You are the limit!"

"Well, I first got into it about a year and a half ago. You remember that Christmas I desperately did need new skis, and I had to see if I was getting them, because of that ski trip up to Crystal Mountain in January."

"Skis in a hidey—"

"No, of course not. But that's where he stashes his charge slips around Christmas. How do you think I can always guess right what everybody is getting under the tree?"

Irma began to laugh. "But how did you figure out the combination to the lock?"

"Mom, don't you know anything about Dad? There's that little string of numbers he can't remember, written in the back of his checkbook. You know, his PIN number for the cash machine—numbers like that. I figured it would be there and it was." Diane paused and looked at her mother. Mom seemed to be getting better looking. Was that possible in someone of her age? Should she tell Mom what else she knew? Or not? She began to sip her Ovaltine. Mom was always so good to everybody. Okay, she would tell.

"When I took the stuff on abortions out of the book I saw he had stashed another charge slip in there."

"Why? It's almost spring. Christmas is long past."

Diane took her time. "Well," she said, putting down her mug. "You said you wanted that old-fashioned carved wooden cradle for this baby, and you passed it up because it was too expensive?"

"It is too expensive."

"You're getting it anyhow."

The Reverend Chester Bledsoe came in mid-March, was interviewed by the Vestry and several other parishioners, and preached a very good sermon. He was a personable man of middle age, with a wife and two grown children. His views, which he spoke very freely of, were moderate. He was, Father Leffingwell thought, that solid middle-of-the-roader who might keep both conservatives and liberals fairly satisfied with their pathways to God and their parish activities in general.

Saint Polycarp's liberal-radical spokesperson and Kim's mentor, Greg Talbott, was the only one who gave him a hard time. Talbott was so critical that some of the other liberal members became annoyed at his carping and seemed inclined to support Bledsoe in retaliation.

After Father Bledsoe went back to Boise, there were several meetings about whether or not to appoint him. But before the parish could decide, Father Bledsoe took the decision out of their hands by withdrawing his application. He wrote to Father Leffingwell about it privately, as they had gotten along splendidly. The letter said in part:

*. . . reason I must make a change is that my parish here is split down the middle—a real schism, enough to render my work here largely ineffective. I see the same thing developing at Saint Polycarp's so I don't think . . .*

Father Leffingwell sighed, and laid the letter down on his desk. He wished Bledsoe well. He was sorry for Claire Gibson and Ralph Prescott, who were deeply discouraged about the search, but they were soldiering on, preparing to visit another parish, this one in California. Maybe their luck would change.

To most of the people involved, it was clear now that Greg Talbott was going to hold out for Kim to have the post as soon as she was ordained.

Father Leffingwell tried not to let it worry him. There was too much work to do, and the work must go on. He was feeling good, which was a help. He hadn't had to use any of the "little whites" as Mark had called them, for quite a while. The weather might have had something to do with it. Seattle had moved into a spell of early spring that fairly lifted the soul. It would be brief, of course, but for now the buds on the countless flowering trees in the city were showing bits of color, the clean, clear air glistened and Seattle-ites were saying, "The mountains are out," meaning one could see the massive snow-covered peaks in almost any direction.

Father Leffingwell tidied up his desk. It was about time to go home to the rectory, and he came again upon his application for the retirement home in Baltimore. He should fill out the blasted thing and send it off. There was bound to be a waiting list. After hesitating a moment, he put it back into the drawer. Soon. He would do it soon.

Lucy Pruitt woke up just before six. *Oh no! Now-I-lay-me-down-to-sleep-I-ask-the-Lord-my-soul-to-keep-If-I-should-die-before-I-wake-I-ask-the-Lord-my-soul-to-take.* She moved and felt the wetness. *I'm sorry, Mommie. It just happens. I can't help it. I don't even know. Don't yell. Please don't yell.* But Mommy was coming. Her high heels were clicking and clicking down the hall. She was going to say, *Get up Lucy, you don't want to be late for school.*

Eyes squeezed shut, Lucy tensed as her bedroom door opened. "Get up, Lucy. You don't want to be late for school."

Answer. Answer. Say okay, or she'll be coming to the bed, but the word wouldn't come. And she felt the covers jerked up.

"Lucy! You've wet the bed again! What on earth is the matter with you. Get up! Get *up*! I've got to strip this bed."

*Don't surrender to anger, Mommie. Don't surrender to anger. Father Leffingwell said.* Lucy scurried out of the bed and into her bathroom. She would take her shower and not get her hair wet this time. She would brush her teeth—do everything right. She was so hungry. Maybe Daddy would cook sausages. Sometimes he did, with his chair turned sideways in front of the stove.

There were no sausages for breakfast, and Lucy ate her cold cereal as fast as she could because they were going to fight again. She could feel it coming. They were just holding it in until she left for school. She must hurry, hurry, hurry. There was still eighty cents in her purse. What could she get to eat for eighty cents?

With Lucy gone, Peter Pruitt put his coffee cup down, looking at his wife on the other side of the breakfast table. Still a knockout. No wonder that Driscoll wanted her. Had her. There was something remote about her this morning and he went sick for a moment. *This is it,* he thought. *This is it.*

"Lucy wet the bed again?" he asked, just to get her to speak, to come back from wherever she was.

"Yes. I've put the sheets in the washer. Can you see to it after I go to work?"

"Of course, good house husband that I am. Father Leffingwell says Lucy is withdrawn, possibly disturbed. He says our fighting is getting to her."

"Don't talk to me about Father Leffingwell!" Anger flashed in her eyes and a flush rose up her elegant neck. "That old relic is still back in the last century." Her voice shook with fury, and she rose from the table and started stacking breakfast dishes with an angry clatter.

"I take it you are quoting your good friend, Kim."

"Never mind who I am quoting." She was facing the sink, and there was a jerking movement to her shoulders. He knew she was crying. Natalie almost never cried. *This is it.*

"You wouldn't think he was out-of-date if you'd go talk to him as I asked. And asked. And asked."

"There's no point," she said, still facing the sink.

"Turn around, Natalie!" He had to see her say it. He had to be looking at her exquisite Madonna face when she told him.

She turned around. She was crying. How did she do it?

"Natalie, you're the only woman in existence who can cry and still look beautiful. Why don't your eyes swell up and get red? Why doesn't your nose run?" He was filled with a crazy anger because Natalie could cry and still look beautiful.

She raised one hand and wiped at the tears. "I've had it, Pete. I'm leaving you, divorce or not. I know I'm a rotten wife. And I'm a lousy mother. But I'm thirty-five years old. Time is passing. Life is passing by. I've got to have a life and . . . this isn't it. I'm . . . sorry."

He felt as it he had been hit in the belly with a pile driver. For a moment he couldn't speak, only shake his head.

"Don't do it, Natalie. I warn you. You'll regret it. You'll regret it as long as you live."

Andrew stopped by the rectory after dinner, as he often did now. Small wonder, Father Leffingwell thought, having been in Andrew's apartment. It was a cramped, grubby three rooms in a run-down neighborhood. His first thought had been that surely Andrew could have afforded better. Then he realized that probably much of Andrew's stipend went into his ministry. The rectory was a much more comfortable place and Andrew referred to it as his second home.

One thing that helped to deepen the growing friendship

between the two men was that they both had eclectic tastes in recreational reading, and often traded books.

They were finishing off the last of a pot of cocoa-flavored coffee with a whipped topping—Father Leffingwell's experiment in making latté. And Andrew picked up the book which Father Leffingwell had been reading. "What's this?"

"That's the one I told you about. John Donne's sermons in London in the sixteen hundreds, the one Newton Crail found in that odd-lot of books he bought."

Andrew was leafing through it, reading bits here and there. "Could I borrow this?"

"Yes." Father Leffingwell was pleased. "You may have it when I go back to Baltimore. I have a copy there with my other things in storage. But you were saying something about Ralph Prescott."

"Oh, yeah." Andrew put the book aside. "I was surprised when he volunteered to help me with the kids. Now I am absolutely amazed at how terrific he is at the job. It's a marvel."

"That's wonderful, Andrew. You'd think that having taught teens all his professional life he'd feel well out of it now that he's retired."

"That's what he was saying. He told me he couldn't wait for retirement those last two years. He was looking forward to all those wonderful empty days, when he could just stand and stare, and after a couple of months he was going out of his mind. That's why he was willing to serve on the Vestry and the search committee and any place else he was wanted."

"Well, thanks be to God you got him. Oh, there's the phone. Excuse me a minute."

Father Leffingwell stepped into the front hall to answer it there, and when he answered, he recognized Peter Pruitt's voice, before his caller identified himself.

"I'm sorry to lay this on you, Father, but I had to call you." His voice was shaky.

"Of course, Peter. That's what I'm here for. What can I do

for you?" Father Leffingwell felt himself tensing at the obvious stress in Pruitt's voice.

"You see . . ." There was a long pause. "Natalie has left me."

"Oh, I am sorry, Peter. I left several messages for her but she didn't—"

"She's left me . . . my wife. She's gone. My . . . wife." This last was a disbelieving whisper.

"Listen," Father Leffingwell said. "I'll come over and we'll talk. Maybe something can—"

"No, Father. No point. But . . ." There was another long pause and Father Leffingwell felt Andrew's presence behind him in the hallway.

"What's wrong, Padre?" And Father Leffingwell put his hand over the mouthpiece. "It's Peter Pruitt. His wife has left him. He—" Then Pruitt started talking again.

"I really apologize for this, Father Leffingwell," he said with a strange formality. "But you see I—caved in. I'm going to kill myself as soon as I hang up . . . and I thought . . . somebody should know, you see."

"Peter! Listen to me. Peter—" He turned to Andrew saying softly, "He's talking suicide." Then into the phone. "Peter? Are you there?" He should have forseen this. The man had given him enough clues.

There was no sound for a long moment, then a whispered, "I apologize," and the final click of the receiver being replaced.

Father Leffingwell disconnected quickly and started to dial. "Have you got the address? I'm dialing nine, one, one."

Andrew had squatted down and snatched the phone book from the shelf under the table. He was flipping pages and muttering, "Pruitt, Pruitt, Pruitt. Here it is, Padre."

The emergency operator had answered.

"This is Father Leffingwell of Saint Polycarp's Episcopal Church. I have reason to believe a suicide is being attempted. Just a second, I'll give you the address."

Andrew read it to him and he repeated it to the operator. "Yes, thanks. I'm going over there, too."

Father Leffingwell willed himself not to panic and hurried

to the hall closet where he kept an extra stole. "Get my prayer book from my bedside table, will you?" he said to Andrew, folding the stole and putting it into his pocket.

They went in Andrew's TransAm because it was parked in front on the street. It started with a roar and Father Leffingwell inanely thought, *I should do some work on this thing. Andrew's never going to.*

As they arrived at the Pruitt house they heard the dying whine of a siren. The white aid car and red fire engine were already on the scene, their engines droning, their radios squawking, the rotating lights bathing the night street with gaudy splashes of color. House lights began to go on up the block.

The medics, five or six of them, in their baggy canvas-like jackets were loping up the walk, carrying their various tools of life. One was already on the porch, ringing the doorbell.

"Door's locked," he said, turning to Father Leffingwell and Andrew.

"Step back a second," Andrew said and, raising one strong leg, he kicked the door with a powerful thrust. It crashed inward. All the men poured into the house, ranging through the rooms.

"What's his name?" one asked.

"Peter Pruitt," Father Leffingwell answered.

Several began calling his name and then one said, "Here he is." They all crowded into a hallway and peered into a bathroom. Splashes of blood gleamed on a wall.

"Could you two stay back, please?" one said to Father Leffingwell and Andrew.

"Let me know if I'm needed. I'm his priest," Father Leffingwell said, as he and Andrew went back a pace into the living room. They could hear the men working as a superbly trained team.

"Can you reach it? Can you feel it?"

"Here, tie this. Got it?"

"Yeah, he kinda flopped over."

"Right. Maybe we can get him out of here."

And another voice was talking into the radio line to the hospital, "We have a middle-aged male attempted suicide. Both wrists cut. Arteries severed. Vitals . . ."

"Get the gurney."

"Okay. Right. Let's get him out of the chair."

"Gimme that blanket."

"Okay get the strap."

"Here's the drip."

And all the time through and over the other men's voices another voice, "Peter? Peter Pruitt. Can you hear me, Peter? Listen to me, Peter."

It seemed an interminable time, but Father Leffingwell knew it was only minutes until the medics had Pruitt strapped onto the gurney, connected to monitoring devices and the hanging bag. Peter Pruitt's face was gray and still.

The man on the hospital line was saying, "Okay, we're bringing him in now."

Then another medic said, "Good God," and they all looked to where he was looking.

Lucy Pruitt stood in the doorway to the hall in her pink cotton pajamas, staring at the scene with round tranquil eyes. She walked into the room and sat down on a chair, clasping her plump nail-bitten hands in her lap.

One of the medics swore under breath, "He did this with a *kid* in the house."

Father Leffingwell turned to Andrew. "Will you go with Peter? I'll see to Lucy." He took the stole from his pocket and handed it, along with the book, to Andrew. "I'll join you at the hospital later."

When they had gone, he went over and smoothed Lucy's sleep-tousled hair. "Your father is hurt, Lucy. They've taken him to the hospital."

"Yes, I know. I heard the sirens coming."

There was a rapping on the door, and a man in a bathrobe came hesitantly in. "I'm from next door. Can I help? What happened?"

"I'm Father Leffingwell, the family's pastor. Yes, you can. Peter Pruitt has been taken to the hospital. I'll be taking Lucy to someone who can care for her. Could you somehow secure that door? When no one answered we had to break in."

"Yes, I can do that. Where are you taking the girl?"

"I believe to one of our other parishioners. Do you see a phone book anywhere?"

"I'll get it," Lucy said. "You can use the kitchen phone." Again the composed, quiet little voice.

Mrs. Burris would undoubtedly take Lucy in. She had taught Sunday school for years and often spoke of grandchildren spending the summer.

"Lucy, Mrs. Burris is your Sunday school teacher, isn't she?"

"Yes."

"Would you like to go and stay with her until we find out how your father is?"

"Yes."

He was disturbed at her monotonal responses. She should be showing a far different reaction.

"Do you think you could dress and pack an overnight bag?"

"Yes."

He called Mrs. Burris, who agreed instantly to take Lucy in for as long a time as needed.

Father Leffingwell's clericals and Lucy's mention of her Sunday school teacher allayed any doubts the neighbor had, and he and Father Leffingwell exchanged names and phone numbers.

"I've got some wood in my garage. I'll just board up the door for now. The neighbors are all probably awake anyhow."

Father Leffingwell thanked him and drove Lucy over to Mrs. Burris's house in Andrew's TransAm, thinking idiotically that even the headlights needed adjusting. One beam was sweeping along the tops of trees.

At Mrs. Burris's home, Mrs. Burris was waiting for them at the door. "Come in, Father Leffingwell. Come in, Lucy dear."

It was a lovely home, and they went into the softly lit, well-appointed living room. Lucy obediently came in and put her bag down. She stood a moment, looking around the room, then turned to Mrs. Burris and smiled. "My mother and dad are going to take me to Disneyland for my birthday. It's supposed to be a surprise."

# CHAPTER 13

On the drive to the hospital Father Leffingwell had to fumble in his pocket for his nitro tablets. Too bad. He'd been doing so well up to now.

At the hospital, he found Andrew in the emergency section's waiting room. Andrew saw him enter and came to meet him, handing back the folded stole and book.

"Didn't need them. At least not yet. He's in surgery. Been in for about an hour. They think it will take another hour to complete things. Did you get Lucy settled in someplace? Poor little kid."

"Yes. I did. Let's sit down. I want to talk to you about that. The child has got to have psychiatric help. Immediately." As they found chairs and sat down, he told Andrew what had happened. "Mrs. Burris called her daughter-in-law, who is a medical doctor. She was on her way over when I left."

"Where's the child's mother? She must be someplace. You were counseling him, weren't you?" Andrew asked.

"Trying to. Let me think a minute. Driscoll. Evan Driscoll. It's possible that she's with a man named Evan Driscoll. He's a member of our parish."

Andrew shook his head. "You know, Padre, even in my heyday, before I got religion, I had enough decency not to sleep with other men's wives. Even as a pagan, it just didn't seem to me to be the thing to do. Lemme get you a phone book."

They looked up Evan Driscoll's number but got his answering machine. All they could do was leave a message for Natalie Pruitt that Peter was in the hospital, and asking her to call.

They waited another hour and a half before they were told that Peter Pruitt was in the recovery room. He had a good chance of survival if he'd work at it. Father Leffingwell went in and stood by the bed. The big frame of Peter Pruitt lay motionless and gray-faced, connected to plastic tubes and purring flickering monitoring devices which were electronically cosseting him back toward living. Faceless persons in other rooms were aware of his functions minute by minute. Two or three nurses went silently here and there about their business.

Holding the bed rail, Father Leffingwell closed his eyes and prayed silently and intensely for Peter. When he finished and looked again at the man in the bed. Peter's eyes were open and he had been watching.

"Thank you," he whispered, "for whatever it was you just did on my behalf . . . I don't deserve it." His eyes closed slowly and he seemed to drift off.

In a few minutes he woke again. "There *is* a long passage," he whispered. "And a great light. Endless light . . . I didn't want to come back. . . . You know one thing I can't forgive myself for?"

"Don't, Peter. You must forgive yourself," Father Leffingwell said gently. But the relentless whisper went on.

"I forgot Lucy was there. Can you believe that? I forgot my child? How can you forget a child? . . . Where is Lucy now?"

"She's with Mrs. Burris, her Sunday school teacher. Mrs. Burris will care for her as long as needed. You mustn't worry. We'll talk about it later."

Watching the ravaged man on the bed, Father Leffingwell thought of Newton Crail, making a good life for himself with what he had. If only he could give this man some of Newton Crail's hard-won wisdom. Once, Newton had said to him with his crooked, ugly smile, *You play the hand you're dealt, Father.* Somehow Peter Pruitt would have to make his peace with what he had left. And somehow he must be helped to do it.

A nurse came up briskly to the other side of the bed, smiled at Father Leffingwell and said too-brightly, "How are we doing, Peter? I think you're about ready to go up to your own room now, don't you?"

"Whatever," Pruitt murmured. His voice sounded a bit stronger. He turned his eyes to Father Leffingwell again. "Can you come back tomorrow? I . . . need to talk to you."

"Yes. Of course. Have a good night, and don't worry about Lucy."

It was almost three o'clock when he went back to the waiting room. Someone, sometime had smoked a last cigarette in a pack and had twisted the package and tossed it to the floor. Andrew had picked it up and was turning it in his fingers.

"I used to smoke, Padre," he said glumly. "Coach gave me grief and I quit. How's our patient?" He tossed the twisted packet accurately into a nearby trash basket.

"Awake and asleep by turns. They are taking him up to his room now. I'll come back tomorrow."

Andrew stood up. "Did he ask about his child, by any chance?"

"Don't be judgmental, Andrew. Come on, let's go. Tomorrow is another work day."

"You look exhausted, Padre."

"I've been exhausted before and survived. I'm a tough old bird."

The next day about noon, Father Leffingwell went back to the hospital and found Peter with more color in his face.

"I'm not feeling too bad," he said in response to Father Leffingwell's inquiry. "Better than I deserve."

"Stop whipping yourself, Peter. Concentrate on coming out of this. What do your doctors say? Have you talked to them yet?"

"Yes. The right arm's going to be okay, which is good, because I'm right handed. But I messed up the left by cutting some tendon or other. It's iffy whether I'll have full use of it or not. How's Lucy?"

"Well, I talked to Mrs. Burris this morning. We tried to call her mother last night but didn't get through."

"No, you won't for a couple of weeks. They went on a little

trip. Possibly a honeymoon of sorts. I'm sorry—I was going to put that behind me. I woke up at about six this morning and I've had some time to think. My . . . experience with this has . . . made me see things in a different way. I am . . . able to accept this now. God knows it took me long enough. I'm going to try to put my house in order, meet my responsibilities."

"I'm glad, Peter. With God's help you can do it. Is there anything I can get for you, or do for you?"

"Yes. I'm very clear on things now. And I'm tougher than I look at the moment, connected to all this equipment, so you can tell me—really—how Lucy is. Things have been going bad for her for some time. But I was so wrapped up in my own rage and frustration that I . . . forgot about her."

Father Leffingwell looked searchingly into the other man's face for a moment. "Lucy's in trouble, Peter." And he told him, as kindly as he could, about Lucy's reaction to his suicide attempt. "Mrs. Burris said this morning that her daughter-in-law has recommended a child psychiatrist and pediatrician. Together they can help, but it may take a while."

"I've got the rest of my life. I've got a pretty fair income from disability insurance and Lord knows, I've got time. I may have to get some household help. There are things I can't do too well in the chair."

Father Leffingwell felt a tightening in his throat. He wanted to cry. Another unlikely hero. "I may know someone, if you're thinking of part-time housekeeping. Her name is Mrs. Griswold," Father Leffingwell said. "Would you like me to inquire?"

Spring exploded in the city in a burst of color from the flowering trees, it seemed, on every street.

"You haven't seen anything yet," Newton Crail told Father Leffingwell as he brought in the morning carafe of coffee. "In May, the rhododendrons start—you have to see it to believe it. And in June, the city rose garden in Woodland Park, well, you have to walk through it at least once a week to get all the varieties."

"I'll do that," Father Leffingwell said, but he spoke absently. He had just seen another message from Claire Gibson among the pink phone messages. His heart sank.

> *Father Thornberry decided he didn't want us. Can you come to a meeting at my house tonight at 7:30 P.M.? If you can't make it, we'll set a different date.*
>
> *Claire*

Father Thornberry was the last of three applicants who had come and gone in the last three weeks. The Reverend Hugh Ledbetter from Southern California had tried and been found wanting by the liberals. The Reverend Brian (everybody-calls-me-Bri) Gilmore had tried and been found wanting by the conservatives. And now the Reverend Judd Thornberry had tried Saint Polycarp's and found it wanting.

Holding Claire's note and thinking about it, Father Leffingwell considered putting it off so he could take Andrew but decided against it. Andrew was busy tonight. He didn't want to inconvenience Claire if she had already set things up. He'd tell Andrew about it tomorrow.

Driving to a sick call later he thought he saw Mark and turned the little car around. He sped up in the opposite direction until he passed the slim blond boy, only to find that it was not Mark, after all. *Dear child, where are you?*

There were more people at Claire's house this time than there had been before, at least thirty, he thought. Claire was holding this meeting in a basement family-room, and had rows of chairs facing a speakers' table. She had set it up as a proper meeting. There was a table at the side with coffee and tea urns, and trays of snacks.

Ralph Prescott was Chair. Father Leffingwell was invited to sit at the speakers' table with Ralph, Claire, and another man he recognized but couldn't put a name to. He'd probably remember it when he got back to the rectory and was thinking about something else.

Ralph Prescott took the floor. "Father Leffingwell, we had a meeting—we, meaning all here tonight—last week when Father Thornberry was here. We decided that if we struck out with him, we'd try another course." He paused and took a sip of water.

"Since last November, when you came to us as priest-in-charge, Saint Polycarp's has been doing very well. In checking through attendance records, we find that attendance at all services has increased—not dramatically, but slowly and steadily. We've had some criticisms on your traditionalism, but these have been outnumbered by the approving comments we've had. We've all been impressed by your dedication and faithful performance, even in the face of your own personal loss when your son passed away." He took another sip of water. For a rather shy man, he was doing quite well as Chair.

"There has been a total increase in communicants at Saint Polycarp's of eight single people and six families. Most of these are dropouts returning. Two are single men who happened to come to Wednesday noon service with business associates. In addition, there has been one family, and one single come to us on letters of transfer from other parishes. Father, you have done good work for our parish, and we thank you for it."

Father Leffingwell was deeply touched. "How very kind of you to tell me this. I am sorry that the search has been discouraging so far, but please don't give up hope. Saint Polycarp's is a fine parish and you will find the right person.

"I can stay on until you do find a new priest. I told Claire that some time ago. A couple of weeks ago I sent in my application to a retirement home in Baltimore, and I was advised that there is a six-month waiting list. If you don't find someone in that time I'll stick around until you do—they can move me down on the list."

A murmur of good-natured laughter moved through the group.

"Actually, Father, we had a different idea. We were thinking things are working so well that . . . er . . . can't you stay on permanently? We feel sure that we have enough backing for this to outweigh any group Greg Talbott can get together. We know the Vestry has the final word, but they are listening to us."

Father Leffingwell was stunned, and at the same time deeply pleased. There was life in the old man yet. He stood up.

"I thank you all. From the bottom of my heart, but I'm almost seventy. At best I'd only be able to work a few more years, and then you would have it all over again. Much as I appreciate this heart-warming offer I . . . must decline." He was about to sit down again amid a stir of protest from the group when he straightened. "I do have one suggestion," he said. *Forgive me, Andrew but I have to do this.* "Have you considered Father Cullen?"

There was another stir of discussion throughout the group. He caught some of the comments.

"He'd be good. I like his sermons . . ."

"Who's Father Cullen? Oh, him, I know who you mean . . ."

"Has he applied . . ."

"Doesn't he spend most of his time in the street ministry?"

Ralph Prescott rapped for order. "Actually, I've thought of Father Cullen, myself," he said, "but I don't think he'd give up the street ministry. Has he said anything to you about it, Father Leffingwell?"

"Yes," Father Leffingwell admitted. "He has. I mentioned it to him some time ago, and he didn't seem interested then and I haven't brought it up since. Do you want me to?"

There was more discussion, and it was decided that Father Leffingwell would mention it to Father Cullen, just to see if he had changed his mind and might indeed be interested.

Ralph Prescott cleared his throat. "It is my understanding that Deacon Fletcher will also be making application as soon as she is ordained."

This met with dead silence and then an explosion of discussion, people talking over each others' voices. The consensus was, at least with this group, Deacon Fletcher would not be a popular choice. Father Leffingwell didn't pay too much attention. He was thinking up persuasive arguments for Andrew.

"Padre! You didn't!" Andrew said when Father Leffingwell told him the next morning about the meeting. They were in the church itself, where Father Leffingwell had again found Andrew kneeling at the rail. Andrew laughed and shook his head.

"Andrew. I'm just asking you to think about it."

"But there's no point. What about the kids?"

"You've got Ralph Prescott now, and you didn't have him before. Maybe he could do more. Maybe you could find his clone somewhere."

The empty church was very quiet. The morning sun came through the round rose window above the altar. They both watched it for a few moments, appreciating its beauty.

"Seriously," Andrew said, "I don't think I have the experience yet to run a whole parish. The administrative work would get me, I think. My work, so far, has been almost exclusively with youth—kids. I don't know how much help I'd be beyond that. I objected to the idea of Kim taking over because of her lack of experience, so I couldn't very well—"

"On the other hand," Father Leffingwell interrupted. "Actually, you've had more experience than you realize. Ever since Philip died you've been assisting with most services. Well, many services. And you're getting pretty good on the coffee hour circuit. How do you plan to *get* full parish experience if you don't plunge in and do it?"

Andrew laughed. "You don't give up. Do you?"

"You don't get anywhere by giving up. I learned that a long time ago. When I suggested your name last night nobody objected."

"Nobody?" Andrew turned and looked at him intently. "Nobody?"

"If you are thinking of Claire, no."

"Don't tell me she jumped for joy."

"Well, no. Actually, come to think of it, I wasn't looking at her when I made the suggestion, so maybe I'm not positive of her reaction, but she didn't say anything. Or I'd have heard it. One person didn't know who Father Cullen was, but that was all."

"Sometimes I don't know who Father Cullen is," Andrew muttered.

"Well, just think on it, Andrew. I'd hate to see this small part of the Body of Christ in schism. It needs to be pulled together, to heal. The fact of your street ministry work would make you acceptable to the liberals in the parish, but I think your views are really moderate enough to keep the conservatives satisfied."

"You mean I could pass as your solid middle-of-the-roader?" Andrew's dark eyes glinted with laughter.

"Think, Andrew. Think."

"All right, but not today, okay? I've got a million things I have to do."

Easter Day was a brilliant *Alleluia*.

The gardens along Father Leffingwell's street were a blaze of color, and at church the women had outdone themselves with the flowers. In addition to altar flowers, they had banked yellow daffodils on the window ledges below the stained glass windows. Never had the little church looked so beautiful.

"It's not extravagant, Father Leffingwell. They all go to hospitals later," Claire told him in the sacristy. It was her turn on Altar Guild. She looked out the partly opened sacristy door into the church proper and added testily, "All the Easter Bunnies are here."

Andrew, in his white alb, was tying the cincture around his waist, the heavy white cordlike thread in his hands. "Standing room only," he said.

"I suppose coming to church one day in the year is better than not going at all. At least they remember annually that there is a God. And don't be judgmental, Andrew," Father Leffingwell added, grinning.

He picked up his stole—white for Easter—his face sober, kissed it reverently, and placed it around his neck.

Everything went well. It seemed the organ music swelled more magnificently, the singing was more beautiful, the sun through the stained glass glowed more richly and, of course, the Easter liturgy would always lift the heart.

*He is risen. He is risen.*

After the service, changing in the sacristy, Andrew seemed remote, his dark eyes dreaming. "You know, Padre," he said softly, "it's at the Easter festival that I sometimes feel I may be getting . . . close."

Father Leffingwell looked at him in quick understanding. *A man of God, this. Oh, verily a man of God.*

The downstairs coffee hour was also crowded. It was a happy time, with reaching out and laughter, and the Sunday school children in their Easter finery. The long, white-covered refreshment table had been decorated with a scatter of brightly-colored Easter eggs, which the children made short work of.

As the rec room cleared, Andrew came to Father Leffingwell. "Well, I'm off. My in-laws in Bellevue invited me over to lunch. I'm going home to change first. It'll be casual, out on their terrace if it stays warm enough."

Father Leffingwell told him good-bye, wondering if his estranged wife would be there. Andrew's situation worried him. He turned to Newton Crail who was approaching him.

"Yes, Newton?"

"Father, two young . . . er . . . persons are upstairs and want to see you. They seem to think it is urgent."

"You mean in the church?"

"That's right. They didn't want to come down here—I think the crowd intimidated them." There was a quizzical look on his homely face.

Upstairs, two girls stood just inside the church door.

"Good morning. I'm Father Leffingwell. What can I do for you?"

The girls turned. One was rather thin, and seemed to be a

natural blond, but her hair was slicked up to form an imitation spiky Mohawk, streaked with light green. Her face—she couldn't have been more than fifteen—was heavily made up, dark maroon lipstick, green eyeshadow and false eyelashes.

The other girl, somewhat shorter, had a mop of crinkly hair down to her waist, an improbable red, and was similarly made up.

Both wore tight black body suits. The blond girl had on a long see-through skirt of printed yellow fabric and the other a red imitation leather mini-skirt. Both wore excruciatingly high-heeled-shoes.

"Hi," the blond girl said. "Uh—I'm Crystal, and this here is Tiffany." Her manner was rather grand, and she looked around the church imperiously. "This is the first time I bin inside, actually inside, of a church. It is inneresting, I'll say that, but I don't go for all that God stuff."

*Oh, my dear, dear child.* "What can I do for you, Crystal?" Father Leffingwell asked kindly.

"Well, actually, it's what you can do for Mark. Mark says you are a friend of his."

"Yes," he said steadily. "Mark and I are friends."

"Okay. Now so you'll know I'm on the level, here's the liberry card I took off him." She held out the orange plastic card from the Seattle City Library that he had loaned Mark.

"Where is Mark? How is he?" *Dear God, don't let Mark be dead.*

"Now see, he's kinda in trouble. I met 'em on Aurora. Me and Tiffany was out workin' on Aurora and we met Mark, see."

Father Leffingwell felt sick. "Out working on Aurora" meant these children were prostitutes. One strip along North Aurora Avenue was a favorite place for young prostitutes, male and female, to work their ancient trade. Andrew had complained about it bitterly.

The thin blond girl was still talking, ". . . he's a nice kid, actually. And he was couch-surfin' around, see, staying here a while and staying there a while, with people who lived places.

I got my own place, see. And I let 'em stay with me a while. Mark ain't cheap. Once he gimme seven dollars and once he gimme ten. But then I got tired of 'em bein' around, so I tole 'em to get lost. Now I wisht I didden do it. Because, see, he's doin' too much. He hadden oughta do so much. He could O.D. like Henry done. You know about Henry?"

"Yes. I know about Henry. When you say he is 'doing' too much, you mean he's doing drugs too much?"

"Yeah. And it ain't good for 'em. You gotta control it. You always gotta stay in control, see."

Father Leffingwell looked at the thin girl, twisting her red-nailed hands together, believing pathetically that she was in control of anything.

"And Mark's outta control. He's bin outta control since he found out Henry died. So when I'm not too busy, I start lookin' for Mark, see. And I found 'em."

"Where is Mark now? Can you give me the address? I will certainly help him." He kept his voice steady and firm.

"Address?" She turned to look at the girl called Tiffany, and they stared blankly at each other. She sighed deeply.

"Okay, see. I dunno what address, actually, but I know this here squat where he's at. Out past Northgate. I can take you there, if you want."

"Yes. I want you to take me there, if you please." He thought frantically for a moment. Andrew wouldn't have reached his apartment yet, so he couldn't phone him. And there was no address to leave on the answering machine.

"Do you girls know Father Cullen? Andrew. Andy?"

Both girls' faces brightened. "Andy, yeah. We seen him around a lot," Tiffany said.

"I need to get hold of Andy. I can't get him on the phone right now because he's on his way home. Tiffany, do you know where this squat is?"

"Yeah, I know. Everybody knows."

"Fine. I'm going to ask you to go along with someone to Andy's place and tell him where Mark is, and show him the way there. Will you do that?" As he spoke, the two girls moved close together, and looked quickly at one another. After a moment, Tiffany shrugged elaborately.

"Sure. Why not?"

"Come with me a moment," he said, and herded them before him up the aisle toward the sacristy, fearing they might run like frightened rabbits.

Claire was the only Altar Guild woman left in the sacristy. She had just put away the Easter vestments and was shutting the drawer marked 'White.'

"Claire, I need your help," he said.

She turned and at the sight of the two girls a look of faint astonishment crossed her face.

"This is Crystal, and this is Tiffany. Girls, this is Miss Gibson," Father Leffingwell said.

Claire managed a wooden, "How do you do."

"Hiya," Tiffany said in a strangled voice.

And Crystal said grandly, "Likewise, Okay?"

"Claire," Father Leffingwell said, "I have an emergency, and I need Father Cullen's help with it. He's en route home—you can get his address from the Rolodex in the office. I would like you to take Tiffany there so she can show him where I'm going. Will you do that, please?"

For a moment she looked stunned, but managed to collect herself. "Yes, of course," she said. "I'll be glad to. Perhaps Tiffany could help me carry down these flowers for my hospital trips later. It's the gray Buick Regal parked in the corner of the lot, Tiffany."

And Tiffany, with an anguished glance at Crystal, reached out for the mass of daffodils.

Father Leffingwell thought fleetingly: *There is a soft side to Claire that nobody has seen. I must . . . I must . . . but later. Now I must go to Mark.*

With Crystal directing him, Father Leffingwell drove the VW out several miles past the Northgate Shopping Mall into a hilly wooded area on curving streets where the paving was a strip of worn asphalt down the center, with rough ditches on each side. Here and there were frame houses in sad disrepair, usually hidden back among trees, an occasional battered pickup truck or car was parked along side the road. He wondered if they were outside the city limits. It looked like it.

"Slow down now," Crystal directed. "Lemme see. No, not yet. See. Up there where the sign is." She pointed to a FOR SALE sign, which looked as if it had been there a long time. He drove on.

"Here. Stop. Here. Now, I'm gonna go just as far as the door, see. I can't take the stink, okay?"

He looked up the unpaved driveway to a one-story frame house which may once have been white. There were piles of trash on the sagging front porch, and the screen door hung crookedly.

"Perhaps you'd better stay in the car," Father Leffingwell said, opening his door to get out.

"No. It's okay." She got out and walked up the sloping driveway, teetering on her high heels because of the rough surface. He took her arm to steady her. Together they mounted the steps and went to the door.

"Here's where I get off, okay? Last I seen Mark he was in the kitchen, sleepin' on the floor. It's way to the back. You can't tell it's a kitchen actually because all the stuff like sinks and stuff was ripped off already. But that's where Mark was. I'll wait."

Entering the filthy house Father Leffingwell gagged at the vile stench, and placed his hand over his nose and mouth. It was dim inside the house. What remained of the window shades were all pulled down and, torn as they were, still kept out most of the daylight.

*This is Easter Day*, he thought a little madly.

He felt the presence of others. "Mark?" He called out loudly. "Where are you?"

He crossed the room to raise a windowshade, walking through the trash of fast-food containers, countless wine bottles in twisted paper sacks, bits of rotting garbage, and here and there a broken hypodermic needle. Roaches scuttled and scurried about among the rubbish. The ammonialike odor of old urine and feces was everywhere.

"Mark!" He raised another windowshade. Where was the kitchen? Dappled sunlight from the window fell on a roll of rags or bedding in the corner where a man lay sleeping, or dead.

Father Leffingwell went to him, leaned over and touched his shoulder. The patches of sunlight lay on the man's face. He was a young man, not more than thirty, and Father Leffingwell was deeply shocked at this. There was a growth of reddish sandy beard. His hair was matted and gummed with filth. He opened his eyes and looked vacantly at Father Leffingwell from under puffy lids. His fingernails were long and black with dirt. He made a sound, half-moan, half-sigh, and closed his eyes again.

"Is a boy named Mark here?" Even as he said it he knew it was useless. He doubted that the man even heard him. He felt a deep pervasive sorrow. *Let us make man in Our image . . . according to Our likeness . . .*

He straightened up. He was getting used to the stench now. He went through two more rooms. There were other people there. He approached each, hoping it would be Mark. One seemed to be a woman, who muttered curses at him. The other was a man who was breathing but couldn't be roused. He raised another shade and heard a skittering sound which made him shudder. *Rats.*

He felt a kind of inward weeping. He found the kitchen but Mark was not in it. He went out onto the front porch again. "Mark isn't in there, Crystal." He was surprised that he could speak so calmly.

"Then he went unner. The stink got too much."

"What do you mean?"

"Unner the house. It's kinda open unner there."

"Oh, I see." Father Leffingwell went down the steps. The house sat rather high, and the crawl space beneath it was enclosed only with a lattice of slats, once arranged in a crisscross pattern, but now many were broken or missing. He walked around the side, with Crystal following him on her teetering heels, until he found a broken place big enough for an entrance. He bent down to peer underneath but couldn't see much, odd lumps and shadows.

"Crystal, there's a flashlight in the glove compartment of my car. Could you get it for me?"

"Sure."

When she came back with it, he directed the beam under the house and swept it this way and that. *Mark, dear boy.*

"Crystal, will you hold this light? Keep it on Mark. I'm going to get him."

"Okay." She gripped the light in her pale thin fingers with their talon-like nails. "You watch out, now. There's rats unner there. You get bit and you can ketch rabbies. Rabbies'll kill ya."

Father Leffingwell crawled under the house. He felt spider webs hit his face and cling. Stones cut into his knees and hands, and a cramping began in his chest. *Oh, no, please.*

He reached Mark. The boy was curled into a fetal position, facing away from him. Bracing himself on one arm, he pulled at Mark's shoulder, the boy moved slightly, straightening, until Father Leffingwell could see his face. He had been in another fight, and recently. There were dark ugly bruises, and scabs of blackening blood around his mouth. He was breathing shallowly, and muttered something Father Leffingwell couldn't understand. Mark's eyes were open now and he looked dreamily at Father Leffingwell. His swollen mouth attempted a smile and he spoke in a raspy whisper.

"Did you . . . call me?"

# CHAPTER 14

The chest pains were growing sharper. He let go of Mark's shoulder and fumbled in his pocket for his nitro tablets.

"Hey, Padre. I'm coming in."

*Thank God. Thank God.* He crouched back, bracing himself against an upright so he could unscrew the cap of the tiny brown bottle. He could hear Andrew approaching. Then Andrew was there, hunkering down beside the boy. He hadn't even delayed long enough to change but was still in his clericals, minus the jacket.

Father Leffingwell put the tablet under his tongue and capped the bottle. Wordlessly, Andrew reached over and plucked the bottle out of his hand, looked at the label, and handed it back. "I thought there was something," he said somberly. Then he turned his attention to Mark.

Mark's eyes were open again and he was looking at them dreamily.

"Mark, are you all right?" Father Leffingwell asked, but Mark's eyes closed and he seemed to drift away. His swollen cracked mouth moved again in a half-smile.

"I'm . . . flying," he murmured.

Andrew reached over and silently slid his fingers into Mark's front pocket, withdrawing what looked like small squares of crinkled paper, hanging together with perforations, somewhat like postage stamps. He put them in his own pocket.

"Acid. LSD. He's flying out in Never-Never Land, but he'll come down soon, or he wouldn't be talking to us. The LSD is impregnated into the paper. Soak it in a bit of water, or anything you intend to swallow, and you're off to the moon. I'll get rid of this. He'll think he used it. Are you feeling okay now?" Andrew asked Father Leffingwell.

"Yes. Or I shall be in a couple of minutes. What are we going to do?"

Mark opened his eyes, he whispered, "Hi, Andy."

"Hi, Mark. How'd you get beat up?" Andrew asked gently.

There was a long pause before Mark answered. It seemed a struggle to focus long enough to get the words out. "Some rough trade . . . happens . . . " And then he was gone again.

"I guess," Andrew said, his voice husky. "The first thing is to get him out of here. Okay to take him to the rectory?"

"Yes, of course."

"We'll have to get him some medical attention, in case he's been badly hurt. His reference to rough trade scares me. He's very likely been raped."

"Oh, dear God."

"We have to make a choice here, Padre."

"What do you mean?"

"We can take him down to the Sexual Assault Center, and he'll get first rate care. But then he's back into the system and they have no choice but to shuttle him into another foster home—where he won't stay. Or, I can get hold of Doug Ahern. He's a medical doctor friend of mine. He and two other doctors run a storefront clinic for street people. He's sort of laid back and he won't mind forgetting the paperwork. Then maybe you wouldn't have any hassle about keeping him at the rectory—at least for a while."

"Yes. Let's do it that way."

"Fine. Now you go ahead and get out of here and I'll bring Mark."

"Can't I help? I'm all right now, really. Can you manage?"

Andrew looked pained. "Padre, two-hundred-pound men have trembled when they saw me coming—"

"All right. Point taken." The chest pains were gone and there was the rapid beating of the heart which always followed use of the little whites. This would diminish soon and he would be back to normal.

He crawled toward the broken slats around the entry hole. Crystal still held the flash and he tried to avoid getting in Andrew's light.

"You okay?" Crystal asked as Father Leffingwell emerged into the bright sunlight. "Oh, you got your suit all dirty. Tiffany, you got something to help him brush his suit off?" Tiffany, who now stood by watching, delved into her large plastic handbag and withdrew a brush. She pulled off several long red hairs and handed it to Father Leffingwell. He began brushing at his clothing.

"Here, lemme help you," Tiffany said, taking some tissues out of her bag. "Wipe your face. You got spider webs and stuff." She had a bright yellow daffodil pinned to the front of her skin-tight black body suit up under her chin. "Miz Gibson gimme a flower. I got one for Crystal too."

"That was nice of her," Father Leffingwell said, wiping at his face.

"How's he doin'?" Crystal asked, as Andrew emerged from beneath the house with Mark. He was crouched over, on his knees, and holding Mark clear of the ground. Dear God, Mark was so *thin*. He looked so *fragile*.

"I gotta hand it to ya, Andy. You sure got the muscle power." Crystal turned to Father Leffingwell, "We're always tellin' Andy he can have a freebie, but he didden never take any yet."

"He's coming down," Andrew said, laying Mark on the ground.

"Oh, look at him. Look at his face," Crystal said, "he can't work lookin' like that."

"No. He needs medical help, Crystal. We're taking him to Father Leffingwell's house. We'll take care of it."

"Yeah. I guess that's best." The girl stood, gnawing her vivid lower lip. "When he gets okay tell 'im he can come stay with me a while, if he wants, okay?"

"Thanks, Crystal. We'll tell him," Andrew said. "Padre, my

car's bigger than yours, so why don't I take Mark to the rectory while you drop the girls where they want to go?"

"Yes. Let me give you the key." He turned to the girls. "Thank you both, very much, for coming to me about Mark. I appreciate it. It was good of you."

They both looked embarrassed. Crystal managed to reply, "Yeah, well, he said you was his best friend, next to Henry."

Andrew picked Mark up and carried him down the sloping drive. Father Leffingwell and the two girls followed. "Where would you two girls like to go?"

"Just to Northgate. They gotta shoe sale." At the Trans Am, Tiffany retrieved the other daffodil from the dash and gave it to Crystal. Crystal had no pin, nor did Father Leffingwell, so they decided to slip it under the waistband of her flowing filmy skirt.

"Don't that look nice?" Crystal said, very pleased. "It kinda matches the yella in my skirt."

"Yes, it looks very nice, indeed," Father Leffingwell said, helping the two girls into the VW.

Now what would happen to them? He would drop them off at the mall, where they would spend some of their accumulated cash on more spiky-heeled shoes. Tonight they would walk up and down the dark stretch of highway that was North Aurora. Strange cars would stop. They would go up to the strange cars, speak to the strange men behind the wheel. Bargain for what he wanted and how much it would cost him. Then get in. The risk. The terrible *risk. I can't let this happen. How can I help them? What can I say? Will they listen?* Suddenly he understood very clearly Andrew's deep frustration with his work.

At the mall he couldn't let them go without saying something, "Thank you both again. It was good of you to help Mark. If either of you ever need any help—my help, do please let me know. Please remember my name, Father Leffingwell." He stopped, because they were acutely embarrassed. They hurried out of the car.

"Yeah, thanks, bye-bye, now."

"Bye-bye, Pop. You take care."

Back at the rectory, he found Andrew and Mark in the big bathroom. "He's filthy, Padre. We can't put him to bed like this, but I don't think he's awake enough to bathe without drowning. Will you fill up the tub? I wish you had a shower so I could just stick him under."

Mark was standing up, weaving slightly, his blue eyes looked almost black, the pupils were so dilated. "I always liked this bathroom," he said vaguely. "I always did."

"Well," Andrew said to the boy,. "you sure got dirty under that house. You want to clean up now?"

"Yeah, I guess."

"Can you undress?"

"Yeah, I guess," Mark said, making no move to do so.

"Here, lemme give you a hand." Andrew helped Mark pull off the sweatshirt, spilling onto the floor the things Mark had underneath it. Father Leffingwell stooped to pick them up. The beetle repair and maintenance manual, a grimy and dog-eared Christmas card—the one he had slid under Mark's door Christmas Eve, and two color snapshots: a woman with blond hair, squinting into the camera and smiling; a lean and sinewy man in work clothes and a hard hat that cast a shadow on the top half of his face. Mark's treasures.

Mark staggered while Andrew helped him with his pants, and Father Leffingwell had to steady him. The boy tried to help, but his hands fumbled uselessly.

"Is that the doorbell?" Andrew asked. It had sounded dimly over the rushing of water into the tub.

"Oh dear, yes. I'll get it." Father Leffingwell straightened up, and hurried to the front hallway. The oval door glass showed him Claire Gibson and a bunch of daffodils. His heart sank.

"Come in, Claire. What can I do for you?"

"I wondered if everything was all right. Did the girl, Tiffany, find the place—where you were?" She seemed startled more than upset.

"Yes, she did. And thank you very much for your help. Would you like to come in?" He felt a moment of sheer panic.

Was she going to tell him Mark couldn't stay? What had the girl Tiffany told her? Well, he would just have to take a stand.

"Tiffany said you—one of your young friends was in trouble."

"Yes," he said stiffly. He would just have to defy her, house or no house. This was his house as long as he was rector.

"I gathered he might be—sick?"

"Yes. He's been badly beaten, for one thing. We have a doctor coming. He can be salvaged. I will do what I can to help him. I am determined about that."

"Yes, I understand. I was just thinking that during my mother's last illness, my father bought a hospital bed. He thought it would be more economical. I still have it stored in my basement. If it would be easier to tend to the boy in a hospital bed, you are welcome to it. Newton has a pickup truck and he could bring it over. You've been so good to us here, so helpful, I wanted—" She faltered to a stop.

He was astonished, and suddenly ashamed. "Thank you, Claire, from the bottom of my heart. I don't know yet what we'll need, but if we do need it I'll let you know. Thank you for your kindness."

"All right, you let me know." She extended the daffodils. "Take these. They're so bright, they're good in a sickroom."

"Thank you, Claire. Thank you." He reached out and took the flowers.

When he got back to the bathroom, Andrew had Mark into the tub. The boy was shivering and gagging. "What's wrong?"

"LSD does that. He'll have some tremors. Some nausea. Dizziness. He tried to throw up in the toilet, but nothing would come. Probably hasn't eaten in a while. He's still hallucinating a little. He said I was in a pink cloud. Who was at the door?"

"Claire Gibson."

"Oh, Lord. Does she know Mark's here?" Andrew was soaping a wash cloth.

The boy murmured softly, "Mark's here."

"Yes, but it doesn't matter. She's offered her mother's

hospital bed if Mark needs one. Tiffany talked to her about Mark, apparently."

"You're kidding!" Andrew's soapy hands went still in surprise. "She knows he's a street kid?"

"Yes. I had the same reaction, for which I am heartily ashamed. She even gave us these daffodils. Said they would brighten up the sickroom."

Andrew sat back on his haunches by the tub. "The ways of the Lord. Claire, I apologize in absentia. Now, there's the phone. Will you get it? I called Doug Ahern as soon as I got in the door. He was with a patient. That may be him calling back."

It was Doctor Ahern. Father Leffingwell explained the situation and Ahern said he was just about to break for lunch, and would come right over.

By the time Ahern got to the rectory, Andrew had Mark clean and in bed in a pair of Father Leffingwell's pajamas. And Father Leffingwell had made sandwiches and a pot of coffee for lunch.

Doug Ahern's greeting to them was, "You guys are both dirty, do you know that? I didn't think Anglicans got dirty."

"We crawled under a house to get your patient," Andrew said. "He's in the back bedroom. Come on back." Andrew turned to Father Leffingwell, "I wonder what Claire thought."

"Whatever it was, she was too polite to mention it."

Douglas Ahern was about Andrew's age and size, but with sandy hair and a beard. He was wearing a similar uniform—worn jeans and a grimy T-shirt. When they reached the bedroom, Mark was curled in the middle of the bed with the covers obscuring his face.

"Do you want us in here?" Andrew asked.

"I think not. No point in embarrassing the kid in front of his spiritual advisors. Examining a rape victim gets pretty personal. Show me your bathroom so I can wash my hands."

While Ahern was with Mark, they both took the opportunity to clean themselves up as well as they could. "Hadn't you better call your in-laws, Andrew?" Father Leffingwell asked, suddenly recalling Andrew's luncheon date.

"Good grief, yes! I completely forgot."

"Will they be upset?"

"They won't. Melanie might. They're pretty laid back."

So, Father Leffingwell thought, Andrew's wife was there too. What in the world was Andrew going to do about that situation? It worried him. His and Martha's marriage had been so good, so right for both of them. He wished—

No sound came from the back of the house for quite a while, and then Doug Ahern could be heard washing his hands in the bathroom. He came into the living room.

"He's sleeping. He will for a while."

"How is he?" Andrew asked.

"Not too bad, fortunately, though he's had some rough treatment. My guess is he was too doped up to resist much, which kept down the tearing. The bruising is deep all over him. Some animal gave him a real going over. Malnourished, of course. I'd say at least fifteen pounds underweight. Says he's been using acid pretty heavily, and crack, of course. I'm going to leave you some medication." He began to put several plastic medicine bottles along the mantel. "Antibiotics to preclude infection, if we can. Anti-depressants—he may need these for quite a while, if you are getting him off the acid."

"Father Leffingwell's going to try," Andrew said, looking at the bottles.

"Good luck, Father," Doug Ahern said. "I took a blood sample, and after it has been run through the tests I'll give you a call. So many kids pick up HIV. I can't tell how heavily he's addicted, but I'm leaving you these." He put another bottle on the mantel. "He'll have withdrawal symptoms—this will help him get through it. If these are not sufficient I can put him on methadone, but try these. And watch the depression—the LSD itself brings that on. Be sure to keep him on the antibiotic for the full series."

Father Leffingwell picked up one of the bottles. "He's entitled to severe depression without the LSD," he said.

Doug Ahern shook his head and snapped his bag shut. His

eyes held infinite sadness. "I'll leave you my phone numbers. Call me if you need me, anytime."

"You can stay for lunch, can't you, Doug?" Andrew asked. "Father Leffingwell has it all fixed."

"Andy, no. I've got a room full of people waiting. But if it's ready, I'll take along a sandwich. Is there coffee?"

"Yes."

"Okay, I'll go get my cup." He loped out the front door, moving as Andrew did, big and graceful. He came back with a stained coffee mug, the big-bottomed kind that won't tip over.

Father Leffingwell and Andrew ate lunch after Ahern had gone. "We were in college together," Andrew explained. "We were both athletes, although Doug never made varsity. He was good though. We're kindred spirits in another way too. He also married too young. His wife also thought she was getting a famous NFL star. Then he went to med school and she thought she was getting a rich and famous surgeon. When he opted for his storefront clinic, he lost her."

Father Leffingwell sat staring at his half-eaten sandwich. There were good people out there, helping, healing, picking up the pieces. And making hard sacrifices to do it. There was hope.

"Hey, Padre. Come back."

"Sorry. What were you saying?"

"Can you deal with Mark, or should I stick around? My in-laws said come over anyway if I could."

"Yes, Mark and I will be fine." He suddenly remembered what day it was. "Andrew, this is Easter Day. Does Doug keep his clinic open all the time?"

"Padre, sometimes street people don't know what day it is. You have to be there when you're needed."

When Andrew had gone, Father Leffingwell sat down in his favorite rocking chair. No fire in the fireplace these days. It was too warm and springlike. Mrs. Griswold had swept it clean of ashes and had put in a large vase filled with some sort of artificial fernlike leaves. It made a pretty picture. He was suddenly very tired. Looking at the leaves, he slowly fell asleep.

When he woke it was almost dusk, and Mark was standing

in the doorway, shivering in his old blue-striped pajamas, which hung like a tent around him.

"Mark!" Father Leffingwell started up from the chair too quickly, a pain shooting through his shoulders. *Why did he always fall asleep in the stupid rocking chair!* He stood, bending slightly, easing his back up straight.

"Are you okay?" the boy asked, hunching his shoulders over.

"Yes. It's just that old people sometimes have achy bones. How are you feeling? Are you cold? You're shivering again."

"No. Just shivery. After a trip, you know, you can get shivery. But achy bones, that I got." He began to walk carefully into the room and sat in the other rocker. "How come I got here?"

"Father Cullen—Andy, and I found you under that house, that squat, out in the North End. Your friend, Crystal, came to the church and told me you had been hurt." The boy's battered face broke his heart. *Animal.*

Mark's swollen mouth attempted a grin. "Crystal came to your church, huh? Did the roof fall in?"

"No, the roof's fine. And you should be glad she came. She cared enough to get some help for you."

"Yeah, Crystal's okay."

"Would you like something to eat? Doctor Ahern said you were about fifteen pounds underweight."

"Eat. Maybe later, okay. I keep havin' the dry heaves." A shudder went through him.

"I think you are cold. I'll get you my bathrobe."

"Could be, I guess." Mark stayed huddled in the rocking chair while Father Leffingwell got his old maroon bathrobe. In it, the boy at least looked more comfortable.

"That's pretty," Mark said, indicating the leaf arrangement. "But I kinda miss the fire."

"I do too. We'll have one this evening, if you like. Doctor Ahern left you quite a bit of medication. I'd like to explain to you which is which. Are you up to taking that in?"

"Yeah, I guess." Mark sat up straighter. The pupils of his

eyes appeared to be of normal size. He explained carefully and Mark obligingly repeated directions after him, so he knew the boy's understanding seemed unimpaired.

Bracing himself, and saying a silent prayer, he put the bottles back on the mantel and sat down again. Now or never.

"Mark, you've had a pretty bad time lately. As your friend, I want you to take it easy for a while. Get better. Gain the weight you need to. I'm going to be here a couple more months, maybe a bit longer. I want you to be my houseguest for that period. It would give you time to—get on your feet again. Will you do that?"

"Houseguest?" The term seemed to appeal to the boy. "Houseguest. Yeah. I guess. How 'bout that lady who don't like street kids? The one I hid from before? I don't wanna getcha in trouble at Saint Whatszits."

"I think the lady has changed her mind a little. In fact, she left a bunch of flowers for you. Said they would brighten up your room since you're sick."

"No kidding. That was real nice."

"No kidding. And I could use some company. A big house like this can be a pretty lonely place. I miss my grandson, too. Timothy. I told you about Timothy."

"Yeah." There was a long pause while Mark stared at the leaves in the fireplace. "How come he don't come see you sometimes?"

"He's in Baltimore, with his mother. She . . . She's married again. She has another child. And she thinks it best if . . . Timothy identifies with that family. I don't—I'm not in touch with Timothy now."

"You mean she won't let ya be?" Mark asked, straightening up a little.

"You could put it that way, I suppose. She thinks it's best for the boy."

"I think it stinks," Mark pronounced. "*Stinks.*" He sat back in the rocker. After a long time he said, "Maybe we could have some soup later. Maybe that would stay down." He closed his eyes and seemed to doze. "Houseguest," he muttered.

They had a simple supper of soup and crackers in front of the fire that Father Leffingwell had built. "I think that's gonna stay down," Mark commented, putting his bowl down on the floor beside his rocker. It had been painful watching him eat, his mouth was so swollen.

"Did you get the windshield wiper fixed?" Mark asked.

"No. That's still to be done."

"Maybe we oughta do it while I'm your houseguest."

"Good idea."

"Gimme a coupla days to heal up. How long does a houseguest stick around?"

"It varies. Maybe while you're here you can put on that fifteen pounds the doctor said you're lacking. Build yourself up. I'm a bit underweight myself. We really ought to go on a definite fitness regimen."

"What's regimen?"

"A definite program or plan. A steady routine. I used to drink a cup of hot Ovaltine every night before going to bed. It helped keep my weight up to normal. That, and regular well-balanced meals. Living alone, I just make do. I work evenings sometimes, going to meetings and such. Often, I just eat a quick sandwich—not exactly the way to keep fit."

"Maybe while I'm here, we oughta both do a whatchamacallit—regimen," Mark said, shivering again.

Father Leffingwell had a sense of near-elation. The boy was interested. It was a start. *Please God, keep Mark interested. Don't let him run away again.*

Monday, Father Leffingwell bought a bathroom scale, in addition to the Ovaltine, whole milk, and other things on his list. He and Mark had sat at the dining room table and worked out their separate regimens. And Father Leffingwell had measured Mark's height against his bedroom wall, as he and Martha had marked Philip's. *Forgive me, Claire, for marking on the rectory bedroom wall.*

Monday went very well. Mark had immediately accepted the idea of the medication, various pills for various purposes. He lined them up on the kitchen windowsill, so he wouldn't forget any. He was quick. Told something once, he had it. And he *wanted* to recover—that was a big plus. When Father Leffingwell came home, Mark told him in some detail how his day had gone. He had had to take pain pills every four hours. Father Leffingwell asked him about the withdrawal from drugs—did the yellow capsules work?

"Pretty good," Mark said. He had run his clothing through the washer and dryer and was dressed. "Not exactly perfect. But I gotta stick it out, see. I bin thinkin' a lot. Crackheads don't get gas stations."

"Mark! That's profound. You just hang in there. Nothing is easy!"

"I already figured that out, Father Leffingwell. No offense."

Tuesday things didn't work so well. Mrs. Griswold came on Tuesdays and Fridays, and she and Mark took an instant dislike for each other, which promised to develop into lasting enmity.

In the kitchen, Father Leffingwell explained Mark's presence. Her sympathy was ready, but qualified. "I do pity those poor street children," she said. "But you know, if Malcolm had been orphaned, he would never have run away and gone on the street."

The night before he had explained to Mark about Mrs. Griswold. "Is that the same old lady I saw here before?" Mark had asked apprehensively. Father Leffingwell hoped for the best as he left for work, but hoped in vain.

"That old lady is a pain," Mark said furiously that night. He was seething. "*She moved my pills* off the kitchen windowsill. She has no *right* to move my pills. I hadda put 'em in here on my bedroom windowsill. She's gotta keep her hands off my pills!" They were in Mark's bedroom and Father Leffingwell glanced around. The beetle manual was on the bedside table. Mark's two snapshots were stuck in the dresser mirror. *Please God*, he was settling in.

"Mark, Mrs. Griswold is a friend of mine, and certainly one of my parishioners. And you must admit that living in a neat house is better than living in a messy one."

"Yeah, I guess."

"You probably wouldn't be so impatient with her if you weren't hurting so much."

"Yeah, maybe."

"And what's wrong with leaving your pills in your own room?"

"And that's another thing! She messes around in my room! I am your houseguest, and as long as I am your houseguest, this is my room, my place." He was almost crying.

"I agree," Father Leffingwell said gently. "This is your room, your place. I'll tell Mrs. Griswold that you can take care of it yourself. You do. Each time you've stayed here you've left the place neater than you found it. And I've appreciated that. She won't come in here again. Okay?"

"Yeah, I guess." He seemed sullen for a moment, then he fairly hissed, "I hate fussbudgets. Evalyn was a fussbudget. 'Mark do this. Mark do that.' Fuss. Fuss. Fuss. Drove me nuts."

Evalyn? Evalyn? Father Leffingwell had to think a minute. Oh, Evalyn who had been Mark's father's live-in girlfriend, who tried not to drink on weekdays, only on weekends. That Evalyn. What a terrible life this boy had had.

He placated Mrs. Griswold by telling her he wanted Mark to have the responsibility of keeping his own room. She sniffed but accepted it. It was clear, however, that she didn't have much use for street kids, Mark included.

This was a petty nuisance only. What worried Father Leffingwell, in the days following, was Mark's visible slide into deep depression. He talked to Andrew about it. They were just leaving the sacristy after the Wednesday noon service.

"He has trouble sleeping. He gets up at night—stays up for hours."

"He doesn't go out, does he?" Andrew asked, sounding apprehensive.

"No. I don't think he's even been out the door as far as the porch. His body's healing up, but his mind isn't. I find him in the living room, on the floor in front of the TV. He keeps it low so I won't be disturbed."

"What does he watch? The night talk shows?"

"He's not watching it, that's the point. He has on anything at all. Just motion and sound. Sometimes not even that. Last night—morning, really. It was almost three o'clock. He was sitting there on the floor, staring at the TV screen. The channel had signed off and all there was was that flickering gray light with no sound. Apathy *is* depression, Andrew."

"I know. Is he taking the anti-depressants?"

"Faithfully."

"I'll call Doug. Maybe he can give us something stronger."

"And I think . . ." Father Leffingwell hated to say it. "I think he may have more LSD. I got the feeling last night at dinner that he was hallucinating. When I asked him, he admitted he was. I helped him to get to the couch and lie down."

"Did you ask him if he had used any?"

"Yes. He denied it. Would he lie? I've thought . . . that Mark wouldn't lie to me."

"He probably didn't, Padre. He was probably telling you the truth. LSD revisits."

"What do you mean?"

"A user may quit. Be clean for days. Everything is fine. Then suddenly his friend's head is melting away. Or a thousand beetles are crawling up the wall. He may know it's not really happening, but still he sees it. LSD is powerful stuff. It acts directly on the brain. It takes the human body a while to get rid of it. I think I'd trust Mark on this, if I were you."

Doug Ahern changed the medication for depression and Mark obediently took the new capsules, but he had lost his passionate interest in the VW and said nothing more about the windshield wiper. He stopped making his bed, doing it only on Tuesdays and Fridays, when Mrs. Griswold was coming. The only thing he seemed to hang on to was their health regimen. "I'm gonna get healthy," he would say doggedly, taking his vitamin tablets.

Father Leffingwell and Andrew talked about it again. "He

has nightmares, Andrew. He wakes up crying, terrified. That's why he goes in to the TV. What has that boy been through?"

"Plenty, Padre. I don't know how long he has been hustling but that's a pretty hard life. Have you tried to talk to him?"

"Yes, but I got nowhere. He closed up. The curtain came down."

"Why don't I try? I haven't stood you to a meal in a long time. I'll pick up three T-bones today and go over to the rectory to put them in the fridge. While I'm there I'll get into a conversation with Mark, see what I can find out."

They had a very good dinner that evening, the three of them. Mark showed a bit more liveliness and joined in the table conversation.

The next day the two men discussed it. "He opened up fine, Padre. I think it did him some good. The kid's had a rough time of it, that's for sure."

"I knew you could do it. You're much better with the young than I am."

"Not really. You have reached Mark. The reason his curtain went down shutting you out was, I believe, an act of kindness on Mark's part. At least he perceives it as that. Sometimes we shortchange kids and their motives."

"What do you mean?"

"He said he wanted to talk to you but—and I quote—Father Leffingwell is too good, see. He wouldn't know about all this lousy stuff. Unquote. He was protecting you."

Father Leffingwell wanted to laugh and cry. "That poor child."

"Well, one thing you can be thankful for, Padre. I think he's through hustling. He's had it. I think even with me he may have deleted some of the grimmer things. But he's been . . . badly used. Badly used." As Andrew said it his voice shook slightly, and his big hands curled into fists as if he must smash something. Smash it. "If he can be kept off the drugs long enough, maybe, just maybe, he'll make it. Hang in there. I think Mark is a survivor. So be patient. We've just got to be patient."

# Chapter 15

Kim's ordination was postponed yet another week, until the third Sunday after Easter, because Bishop Jackson's father died suddenly of stroke, and the bishop had to join his family for the funeral. Father Leffingwell deeply regretted Richard Jackson's death. They had been friends for so many years. It had been a good friendship. Each time they met, regardless of how long it had been, they seemed able to take up where they had left off the time before. A comfortable friendship. And—it didn't really matter now, of course, but he hadn't answered Richard's last letter.

"Was he your best friend?" Mark asked at the breakfast table. Mark was finally showing some improvement.

"No, not exactly a best friend. But an old friend. I'll—send some flowers. I'll stop at the florist on my way to work."

"I'll go with you and help pick 'em out," Mark offered, and Father Leffingwell felt a lifting of the heart. To his knowledge this would be the first time Mark had gone outside the rectory.

"I can even pay some, if you want,." Mark added, spreading jam on his toast.

"I didn't know you had any money."

"I got five dollars. Miz Gibson gimme five dollars."

"What! When did you meet Miss Gibson?" Father Leffingwell was astounded.

"Yesterday. Newton was over again. He started cuttin' the grass last week. He says it's warm enough now for the grass to start growin' again, so he has to cut it. I went outside this time and helped him. Around the edge, see. You have to get down, and it's kinda hard for him. Last week I saw him out the window. I wasn't gonna take money from Newton. I figure he's got his problems, so I was just cutting the edge and Miz Gibson came."

"Why did she come, do you know?"

"Yeah. Newton told her the garage needed paint, and they went around back to look at it. They shoulda made it outa rocks like the house. Then it wouldn't need paint." So, he had met Claire. At least he was looking better. Most of the swelling was gone, and the bruises were fading.

"I told her I was your houseguest 'til you quit Saint Whatz-its. So she said I could cut the edge for Newton when he cut the grass, and she gimme five dollars. I hadda make a contract with her, though. Her and Newton. So I signed it. I can't spend the money on any controlled substance—that's what she calls crack and pot and acid, you know. So I made the deal. A deal's a deal. I never went back on a deal in my life. It's not my policy." He began to eat his toast.

*Thank you, Claire. Thank you, Newton.*

"So how much do flowers cost?" he asked, swallowing. "I could pay five dollars. Would that help out?"

"Yes, Mark. It would be a great help. We'll go pick them out after breakfast. Thank you."

"Don't mention it."

Andrew assisted the Bishop at Kim's ordination, with her brother, Jonathan, and his friend, Ross Palmer, serving as acolytes at the Eucharist which followed. Greg Talbott, Kim's mentor and friend, and another of Kim's friends, carried the wine and the wafers up to the altar. Father Leffingwell observed the ceremony from the front pew.

The ceremony itself, of course, touched him as always, but he was saddened as he listened to Kim's quiet, confident voice reciting her vows. She sounded as if she truly believed what she was saying. " . . . I do solemnly engage to conform to the doctrine, discipline, and worship of . . ."

He tried not to be angry and silently prayed for forgiveness. Kim would only conform to her personal interpretation of the doctrine and the discipline. The Gospel of Saint Convenience again. He gave up praying. It was no use. The disappointment and anger wouldn't go away.

Bishop Jackson preached the sermon, which sounded somewhat like a lecture on how the church could keep up with the world, the gist of which, if one listened closely, was that Saint Polycarp parish would indeed be lucky if they could get Kimberly as their next rector.

As the congregation—which had been large—left the church, most to go downstairs for Kim's reception, Andrew sat down beside Father Leffingwell. The church was empty now and the beginning of the sounds of celebration came to them from below.

"We'll have to go down, wish her well," Andrew said easily, settling back. "But no hurry. She's got all her fan club around her." Then he added in a different tone, "That Ross Palmer, now, he really turns my stomach. Why do I feel the place needs to be reconsecrated?"

"That's too harsh, Andrew," Father Leffingwell said sadly.

"I'm sorry, I was out of line," Andrew said, obviously remembering Philip. "I know gays have a tough time. Today, during The Peace, I should have embraced Ross Palmer. I didn't. I couldn't. Twelve inches from Christ's altar and I turned away from another human being. And he knew it. And he knew why. Maybe I'd better have another session at the rail."

"Now you're judging yourself a little harshly," Father Leffingwell said, "but a session at the rail never harmed anybody."

Andrew wasn't finished castigating himself. "Right now. This minute. If Jesus Christ walked into this church *He* would embrace Ross Palmer."

"He would also tell Ross Palmer to go and sin no more,"

Father Leffingwell said drily. "That's what he told Mary Magdalene."

A slow grin appeared on Andrew's face. "Padre, you just made my day. Let's go down and eat some of the cookies and stuff."

Downstairs it was a real party. Kim's friends had done a very attractive job of the decorations. Flowers were everywhere. The long refreshment table, covered with white linen, was filled with platters of snacks and sweets. Mrs. Burris was seated in her accustomed place at the coffee end, and Claire Gibson was in her accustomed place at the tea end. And they were using the best china because the Bishop was there. Father Leffingwell felt a moment of love for them. They both worked so hard. So many did. Year after year they had done all the work behind the scenes. Baked for the bake sales. Gathered rummage for the rummage sales. Made casseroles for the church suppers. Carried flowers to the sick. Filled and emptied the dishwasher—thousands of times. And they came, faithfully, to the church service every Sunday, walking along their pathways to God. Trying to live the Christian life. They faltered. They stumbled. They made mistakes. But they kept *trying. Come before Me, and be thou perfect.*

The Bishop was surrounded by people, of course, and so was Kim. Father Leffingwell and Andrew parted and began to circulate. Father Leffingwell went to Kim and wished her well. She was radiant. He must pray for Kim. She had such a long way to go.

He managed to get to the Bishop and offered his condolences on Richard's death. For a moment, Dick Jackson seemed shaken. And Father Leffingwell liked him better. It had been a revealing instant. For all his pretenses, Dick Jackson had loved his father. It had come through clearly.

As the crowd cleared out and the party wound down, Father Leffingwell and Andrew came together again. They sat down on one of the old pews against the wall.

"Nice bash," Andrew commented. "I won't be able to eat

any lunch though. What are you doing with the rest of your weekend?"

"This afternoon Mark and I thought we'd have a picnic in the backyard at the rectory. It's warm enough. Mark is supposed to be fixing the lunch now. So I held back on the goodies today. Are you going over to Bellevue?"

"No. I promised to help Doug out at the clinic. They're short-handed today. I'm no medic but I can keep order in the reception area and mind the phones. Ah, here comes Greg Talbott."

They both stood up. Every time Father Leffingwell saw Greg Talbott, the old-fashioned word *dandy* came to mind. Of medium build and height, he wore his dark hair slicked smoothly back, and a hairline mustache. His clothing was impeccable.

Andrew muttered, "I always think he just this minute pressed everything he's got on. It must be against the law to be so *neat*."

"Father Leffingwell," Talbott said heartily as he came up to them. "Father Cullen. Glorious service, wasn't it?"

"Yes, indeed," Father Leffingwell and Andrew nodded agreeably.

"Well, our girl's on her way," Talbott said. He was more beaming than smiling. He rubbed his hands together happily. "And she doesn't let any grass grow, not that girl. Do you know what I've got in here?" He patted his breast pocket.

"No, what have you got in there?" Andrew asked, not quite smiling.

"Kim's application to the Vestry for the rectorship here at Saint Polly's. They couldn't do any better, and that's a fact. So, Father Leffingwell, you'll soon be laying down the burden. I'll bet you'll welcome that, won't you?"

"I've enjoyed being here at Saint Polycarp's," Father Leffingwell said noncommittally, and Greg Talbott hurried off to speak to someone else. He was spreading the word.

"Well, well," Andrew said. "That was quick. I suppose it

was to be expected. Dick Jackson practically endorsed her this morning from the pulpit."

"Yes, he did. It will probably influence a lot of people. I thought Dick looked good today though, considering he's just come back from attending his father's funeral."

"Padre, he had his toup today," Andrew said. "And don't look so blank. His rug. His toupee."

"You're right. That's it. Well, he certainly looked good."

For a time they observed the diminishing crowd. The women began to clear the refreshment table and gather up the flowers. The party had blended into a casual work session with the usual cleanup crew. The Bishop had long gone and Kim's group had left also.

"Wonder what Claire wants," Andrew said. "She's been good about Mark, I'll give her that." Both men stood up again.

Claire looked almost pretty today. She was dressed in an elegant light summer suit of sage green. Her face was flushed attractively and her eyes fairly sparkled. She stopped before the two men and said precisely, in very ladylike tones, spacing her words for emphasis, "Over—my—dead—body."

Both men laughed. They couldn't help it. They knew exactly what she meant.

"Won't you join us?" Father Leffingwell said in sudden sympathy.

"Actually, I'm just leaving," Claire answered, and Father Leffingwell realized that the sparkle in her eyes was the sheen of tears she refused to let fall in front of anyone.

"So are Father Leffingwell and I," Andrew said quickly. "We'll escort you out to the parking lot." So he had seen the tears too and responded. Andrew always surprised him.

Out in the church parking lot, Claire fumbled with her keys, and Andrew took them from her and unlocked the door of her elegant car. She paused before getting in, as if reluctant to leave them. She turned to Andrew.

"Father Cullen, would you . . . consider applying to the Vestry for the Rectorship?"

Andrew was silent for a moment, studying her. "I have

considered it. Father Leffingwell saw to that. Yes, I will apply. And thank you for suggesting it."

"You're welcome," she answered formally, and got into her car. They watched her drive out of the lot onto the street, her head held high.

"Sad lady," Andrew commented softly.

"Not as sad as she used to be, though," Father Leffingwell said slowly. Then he turned to Andrew. "Congratulations! I am elated. Delighted. Euphoric. When did you decide?"

"Actually, just now," Andrew said with a look of faint surprise on his face. "And suddenly I'm scared spitless, but there—sometimes she's a pain in the neck, but—sometimes she's sort of . . . gallant. And then Kim." He sighed. "Kim would really screw things up. I can't let that happen. You're going to have to help me write out my application, you know."

"Gladly. Gladly. We'll work on it together."

"Well, I'd better cut out to the clinic. They're expecting me. I'll talk to you later."

At the rectory Mark had prepared a very good picnic lunch which they carried out to the back yard, spreading an old blanket on the grass. It was a brilliant day but with a slight chill in the air, so they both wore sweaters. A couple of trips to Value Village, the thrift store, had enhanced Mark's wardrobe, and so far nothing had disappeared. Mark was looking better and, even in the short time he'd been at the rectory, he looked healthier. For one thing, he kept himself very clean. In the spring sunlight, his long fair hair almost glowed.

Father Leffingwell was so pleased with Andrew's decision that he told Mark about it without thinking.

"So you're gonna quit Saint Whatszit's?" There was quick fright in Mark's eyes, just as quickly veiled. "I guess you're pretty tired of workin', huh?"

"Well, it's going to be a good while yet," Father Leffingwell said. "The Vestry has to decide, and they usually take a long time about it. We've got a couple of months yet here anyway."

When they had eaten, Father Leffingwell braced himself and plunged in. He had to talk to Mark sometime. It may as well be now. "I've been thinking about the future a lot lately. My future and also yours. We get along rather well together, don't you think?"

"Yeah, I guess."

"I'm an old man, but I've thought of your future a lot. Where you're going. How you're going to get there."

"I'm gonna have my gas station," Mark said in a small voice.

"If that's what you really want, then you'll probably get it. Father Cullen said you were a survivor."

"He did? That was real nice." They had eaten everything but the cookies and Mark held one in his hands. He was crumbling the edges of it and dropping the crumbs into the grass beside the blanket. "I gained another pound."

"Good! You're getting there!"

"It's just so slow. And I'm not any taller. If I could just look about eighteen I could get a real job. In a gas station. Get my start, see?"

"It will be a while before you look eighteen, Mark. But speaking of age, I'm sixty-nine, but I have several good years left. When I leave Saint Polycarp's I was thinking that I may not go back to Baltimore. I may just stay on out here. Next month I will have paid off the last of my son, Philip's, debt to the hospice. And I have my pension. I could live out here as well as I could back in Baltimore."

Mark was looking up at him, his eyes questioning, guarded.

"I was thinking that perhaps I could get a smaller place, and we could just go on along as we are now. If you could keep off the drugs—and you're doing so well, I think it would be good for both of us. I would hope that you would consent to go back to school—"

"No!" Mark threw down the rest of the cookie. "I *can't* go back. I told you and told you! I couldn't even get out of the lousy seventh grade." He had started to cry, trying not to.

"It's all right, Mark. I wouldn't insist on school," Father Leffingwell said quickly. He shouldn't have brought it up. The boy had been through too much trauma; he was still so vulnerable. "It's okay, we'll forget about school. Okay?" It took a minute for him to get through to the boy.

Mark raised his fair head. "It's okay? Honest? I could live with you and not go back to school? Oh yuck, my nose is runnin'. Gimme a napkin."

Father Leffingwell handed him a paper napkin and Mark blew his nose and wiped at his tears. He was trembling. *Oh, dear God, help me. The future of this boy is in my hands and I cannot make a mistake.*

"See, Father Leffingwell, I'm startin' to read again," Mark said. "I took your library card and got two more books. I'm movin' on from just the beetle now, movin' on to other kinds a cars, see?"

"Good. Excellent. That's a start. That's just fine. But there is one thing. I know you're working on cleaning up your language a bit but once in a while you slip. You're going to have to deal with the public, you know."

"Yeah, I guess. I guess I better work on that some more, huh?"

"It would be a good idea."

"I'll do it!" Mark rolled up the paper napkin and threw it out over the grass. He was suddenly exuberant with relief. "Man, Father Leffingwell, you are one neat guy! And I'm doin' better! I'm makin' my bed every day now. And I promise you, I promise you, I will keep out of Mrs. Griswold's way And I'm givin' you my word on that. And Newton says I can help him paint the garage, and I'll get paid for it too. And I'm not usin' my paint money for controlled substances. Come look at that garage. It's a mess. It shoulda been painted before."

The boy leaped up and Father Leffingwell struggled to his feet, feeling every one of his sixty-nine years, but his heart was singing. Surely, Mark would be all right now. And surely, surely, Andrew would come into his own. Was there such a thing as too much joy?

"Did you know there's mint back here?" Mark asked when they reached the garage at the rear of the lot. "Newton found it. Big bunch of it. There's this drippy faucet, see, and the mint grows up around it." The boy went to his knees and pulled up a sprig of mint and put it between his teeth. "Tastes great. Here, take some." He pulled another sprig and handed it to Father Leffingwell. Father Leffingwell bit down on it and tasted the freshness of it. They stood by the side of the garage, looking at the peeling gray paint and chewing the fragrant mint.

*God's in His heaven. All's right with the world.*

Gloria came into the rector's office with pink messages—she certainly *was* losing weight. Father Leffingwell couldn't help commenting. "May I say you are looking wonderful these days, Gloria?"

"Thanks. You may. Eighteen pounds wonderful, but a way to go yet. And I've got a message for you you may not like. I have requests for two letters of transfer *out* of our parish."

"Who's going?"

"Natalie Pruitt and Evan Driscoll." She paused a moment before the desk, her eyes questioning, which he pretended not to notice.

"All right, type up the letters and I'll sign them." Neither had been back to church since the Pruitt marriage breakup. He was glad that at least they were trying to keep up a church connection. Better than just dropping out.

This brought Mrs. Griswold to mind. She and Peter Pruitt had hit it off very well, but part-time work wasn't enough. She had apologetically given her notice. She would work full-time for Peter. Lucy needed her. Mark had been elated, of course, and was doing most of the housework—and making a good job of it. "And I'm free, see. I don't charge my friends, okay?"

When he left Saint Polycarp he'd have to go over his finances, make some sort of budget so he could put a bit aside for Mark's college—just in case.

Father Leffingwell and Andrew had worked hard and carefully on Andrew's application, and Andrew made a good impression when he was officially interviewed. They already knew he was good behind the pulpit.

Mrs. Burris dropped in at the office on her polish-the-brass day for a chat. "I'm so glad Father Cullen applied, but I don't think it's going to be a shoo-in. A lot of people were surprised that Kim was such a good preacher. Some had the impression she was a far-out liberal, but she didn't sound like one."

No, Father Leffingwell thought, she hadn't. Kim's first sermon as a priest, the Sunday after her ordination, had been a masterpiece of moderation.

Mrs. Burris went on, "Between you and me and the gate-post, Father, I thought she was trying to split off the moderates—she's already got her own crowd nailed down."

"On the other hand, perhaps there is a chance she's given some thought to ministering to all sides of the parish." It sounded a bit hollow to his own ears, but from long practice he tried not to openly take sides.

There was laughter in Mrs. Burris's brown eyes. "And I'm the Queen of Rumania," she said, starting to laugh, and Father Leffingwell had to laugh with her.

Beyond congratulating Kim on her ordination, Father Leffingwell hadn't tried to talk to her when he realized that she was obviously trying to avoid him; now he rose to seek Andrew out. It was early. Andrew might still be in the empty church, where he stopped off most mornings. Now he was there again. Father Leffingwell sat down and waited for him to leave the rail. When he did, he looked sad and somewhat grim. Sometimes prayer didn't help if you couldn't focus.

"Oh, dear, what's the matter?" Father Leffingwell asked as Andrew sat down in the pew in front of him, leaning over the back of it to face him.

"Kim's the matter," Andrew said. "She's furious that I've applied to the Vestry. We had quite a confrontation. That is, she confronted. I listened. I'm not only anti-gay now, I'm also anti-feminist. Maybe I *am* sort of anti-gay, but anti-feminist I'm not. I have no problem with Kim becoming a priest on that basis. I'm also a false friend, incidentally. Well, no point in wasting time hashing it over. I've got work to do. I didn't like the . . . undercurrent of it, though. I'm uncomfortable with it."

"What do you mean?"

"I'm not sure. It was as close to threatening as Kim could get without coming right out with it—whatever it was. She doesn't think I'm 'fit' to be the Rector. Unless being semi-anti-gay has become a felony, I don't think I've committed any."

"Put it out of your mind, Andrew. She was probably just upset enough to exaggerate. I wouldn't worry about it." But Father Leffingwell worried about it when they had both resumed their duties.

After Mrs. Burris had polished the brass, she popped into the rector's office again. "I meant to clue you in about something for the next Vestry meeting, Father," she said. "Have you been comfortable in the rectory?"

"Yes. It's old fashioned but certainly very comfortable. I've enjoyed it. And Newton keeps it up."

"Claire pays for that herself, as an extra contribution."

"That's generous of her."

"Would you be willing to kind of back her up at the next Vestry meeting, then? What's happening is that those who want to sell it and offer the next rector a housing allowance are making another pitch. You see, that neighborhood has been rezoned—there's a fourplex on the corner. Perhaps you didn't notice. The land is worth a lot more than the house now."

"Ah, I see." He felt a pang of regret. He'd come to like the old house. Somebody would buy it now, pull it down and build a neat fourplex. Progress. People had to live somewhere, still . . .

"I don't think the church needs the money that badly," Mrs. Burris went on. "It wouldn't hurt the church to wait another decade or two—Claire's in her fifties."

"I see what you mean. I'll do what I can, certainly."

*Poor Claire. Yet another battle.*

Father Leffingwell wandered through the rectory that evening. How silly to become fond of an old house. He went into the study, as he usually did after the evening news. He and Mark had different tastes in TV, so he had decided that Mark's birthday gift—coming up on August 15th—would be his own personal TV. He himself had a pretty good set with his things in Baltimore which would be shipped out when he sent for them. Maybe he would get a VCR for Mark's. How much did they cost?

In his study he saw again the letter from Richard Jackson that he hadn't answered before Richard's death. He picked it up to re-read. Richard had been in a mood to remember old times. He had written of one of the general conventions and what a disaster it had been. With a full agenda, as soon as the first meeting convened, someone had jumped up and demanded an adjournment. There was a protest in progress two blocks from the hotel and they, in conscience, should go and join in. There was an immediate outcry in support, so the meeting was adjourned and more than half the people rushed out in wild glee to show solidarity with the protestors—without even knowing what the protest was about. A whole morning was wasted.

> *. . . remember, our crowd was so disheartened. We wandered into the coffee shop and took a big table. Martha asked for your pen and scribbled one of her nonsense verses on a paper napkin. It caught the very essence of our Church's ridiculous hierarchy and got us all laughing, at least. I'll never forget it . . .*

Smiling, Father Leffingwell dropped the letter to his desk. He wouldn't forget it either. That was one verse that came to mind more often than he wished.

*The bishop went into a trance*  
*He filled his mitre*  
*With apple cider*  
*And everyone started to dance.*

His mind was miles away, and Mark put his head in the door and said, "Miz Gibson wants to see you." She had probably heard about the Vestry plot. He hurried into the hall.

"Come in, Claire. Let's go into the study. We can talk there." And when they were seated in the study, he added, hoping for the best, "Now, what can I do for you?"

"Two things," she said, settling herself. She wasn't as upset as he had expected she would be, but was tense about something. "I want to ask you first if you will speak at our upcoming anniversary dinner—May 3rd? Any subject you choose will be fine with us."

"Yes, certainly, May 3rd?" He thought a moment. It sounded familiar.

"It's the anniversary of the finding of the true cross. I remember my father telling me there was a disagreement at the very beginning, since—coincidentally—our church was consecrated the same day, there were some people thought the name should be Holy Cross instead of Saint Polycarp's, but my father prevailed. You will speak, then?"

"Gladly. I've enjoyed being at Saint Polycarp's."

"Well, there's something else." A slow color mounted to her face. "It's rather hard to explain."

He took the plunge. "Is it about the rectory?"

"No. It's about . . . Father Cullen. It's difficult, but you should know—I mean, you must know about it. You have in a way, sponsored him and . . . could we have Mark in here?"

"Mark?" This was the last thing he had expected.

"Yes. It's about . . . the street children."

"Why don't you tell me about it first, Claire?" He could feel apprehension building. "I've been a priest for more than forty years. I've heard it all, my dear. You won't surprise me or shock me."

She sighed and relaxed. "Well, it starts with Kim Fletcher. And it's so hard to pin down. She's—forgive me—but she's sly about it in some ways. People talk a lot about the search for the Rector—they've been talking about it for five months. But I keep hearing odd disturbing . . . bits." She paused.

"Tell me the bits," he said, his voice sounding hard.

"I'll try to get it right, but it's so subtle, so well, sneaky. I heard one person say, 'He was married, at last he's supposed to be—' And someone said, 'I'm not sure it's a dedication to kids, more like an obsession—' And the other day someone remarked, 'Well, you find it a lot in athletes. They look so macho but—' Father Leffingwell, I think . . . it sounded as if they were talking about Father Cullen—being . . . gay?" She sounded disbelieving as she said it.

"Claire, I can give you my unconditional guarantee that Father Cullen is heterosexual. But what makes you think that Kim is responsible?" He felt a rising sense of dread.

"It's hard to pin down. The conversation is always connected in some way to what Kim said, or thinks, or something. Like 'Kim's worried, but—' Or, 'Kim's protective of him but—' Or, 'He's Kim's friend, so she's defensive—' I'm doing a terrible job of explaining this."

"You're doing a good job," he said a bit grimly. "Am I to infer that the gist is that Andrew is molesting street kids?"

"But that's it! It's never actually *stated*—at least I've never heard it stated. But then . . . I guess sometimes things don't have to be stated—" Her voice dwindled off.

He felt sick. *If this ends Andrew's career, may God forgive you, Kim.* He got up and went into the living room. "Mark, can you leave that for a minute?"

"Yeah, I guess." The boy got up amid a burst of canned laughter and the commercial break. He followed Father Leffingwell into the study.

"Mark, Miss Gibson heard something unpleasant and I want to ask you a question about it."

"Okay." The wary look had suddenly returned and Father Leffingwell was sorry. Mark hadn't looked wary for some time. He was glancing guardedly from one to the other.

Father Leffingwell began carefully, "Mark, when adults work with children, there are sometimes abuses. Father Cullen has been working with children for several years. Miss Gibson heard someone hint that there might be some—molestation—"

For a long moment Mark looked blank, simply not understanding. Then suddenly he did. "Andy?" His voice cracked and skated upward in outrage. "Come on! Andy gropin'—messing around—no way! You gotta be kidding. Miz Gibson, you are lookin' at an ex-street kid. I knew Andy for two years now, give or take. Andy never put the move on any kid—male or female. *Never.* And man, does he ever get the chances. He gets chances every hour on the hour but it's like you know, he's deaf, dumb, and blind. Okay, granted, Andy can be a pain when he's workin' in a shelter. He's a certified *nut* on shelter rules, okay. You screw up and you're out. But that's plain looney—only a nut case would say—"

Father Leffingwell cleared his throat.

"Sorry," Mark said quickly. "Things just slip out, but oh, man." He looked at Claire Gibson pityingly. "Miz Gibson, just don't sweat it, okay. You don't have to worry about old Mister Clean. Really, you don't." The boy was almost pleading.

"Thanks, Mark," Father Leffingwell said, intending that the boy should go back to his TV, but he lingered, looking troubled. Father Leffingwell turned to Claire. "I'll follow through on this, and thank you for coming to me." He saw her out, and turning from the door saw that Mark had followed them into the hallway.

"You're really ticked, right?" Mark asked.

"Mark, I have never been so angry in my life." He went to the hall phone and picked it up to dial Andrew, hoping he wasn't off in some shelter. The phone was slippery in his hand. He paused a moment, puzzled.

"Father Leffingwell?" Mark's voice sounded dim.

He tried to grip the phone. Sweat?

*Sweat.*

He was shaking. *Oh, dear God.* He stood there waiting, waiting for something. His arm was becoming numb. The numbness was moving up into his jawline. *I haven't time for this.* He tried to put the phone back into the cradle and dropped it. He must try to keep his voice steady, not alarm the boy. "Mark . . . could you dial nine, one, one for me?"

Pain engulfed him like a great wave and he blacked out for an interval. Then he knew he was on the hallway floor amid some great activity. A man's voice was speaking.

"We have a male, sixty-nine years old . . ."

He had been in recovery rooms before so he knew where he was. There is a sameness to recovery rooms. There were the various attachments to his person. A greenish monitoring screen was there with little lines and blips. There was the faintest hiss of oxygen into his nostrils. They were making a thorough job of it. Someone was adjusting the line from the drip connected to his hand. He should thank them, but he was too tired.

"Father Leffingwell? Father Leffingwell?"

He should tell this voice that he was here and awake but it was such an effort. He managed to say something. He hoped it was the right thing.

Now, this was an ordinary hospital room, so obviously he had drifted off again. He wasn't so tired now. And Andrew was sitting beside the bed. *Bless you, Andrew.* It took him a moment to get his voice working, then he asked, "How is Mark taking this latest hassle?"

A smile lit up Andrew's face. "So, you're back among the living. I'm glad. Don't worry about Mark. He's a survivor. I told you that. And he's pretty good in the crunch too. He was determined you'd stick around, so he got you help. He called nine one one, dug your insurance card out of your wallet for the hospital. He gave everybody any information they needed.

He tracked me down at the shelter. It's well into tomorrow, you know, and he's still up. You've been out of surgery for about an hour and a half. He and I have been taking turns sitting in here with you. I get in because I'm your priest. He gets in because he's family—your grandson. Kid can think on his feet."

"Bless the boy. You mentioned surgery. Do you want to expand on that a bit?"

"I'm supposed to tell the nurse when you wake up so she can call the doctor, but I can give you a preview."

"Please do."

"You had a heart attack, which you've no doubt already guessed. They used a procedure called angioplasty to clear the appropriate arteries—quicker and easier than a bypass. Do you know what I'm talking about?"

"Yes. I've heard of the procedure. That's good news. It means I won't be laid up for weeks and weeks."

"No. You'll be out of here probably before you want to be."

Father Leffingwell closed his eyes, resting a moment. It was so peaceful, but there was something . . .

"Andrew, there is something I must—"

"Forget it, Padre. Mark filled me in. Don't worry about it. I shall, in the fullness of time, take care of it. But now I'm supposed to get the doctor and nurse in here. First things first. Okay?"

"Hold up a minute. Send Mark in first. He's been so good."

"Right. I'll do that. He's been worried sick, and there is something on his mind he's dying to tell you."

Out in the waiting room—Mark had been in with Father Leffingwell about five minutes now—Andrew stretched again. He'd give Mark a few minutes before he got the nurse. What he needed was a good workout. The thing was to try not to think about Kim, his disappointment. Did she want the post so badly that she'd do anything to get it? It was hard to believe—they had been such good friends. He tried to put it away but couldn't. It clung in his mind, hovering among all his other thoughts. There was no feeling quite like knowing you had been let down by someone you liked and trusted.

Okay, get another cup of hospital coffee. He went to the cart beside the wall. He had just filled his plastic cup with more of the thick black liquid when Mark came back into the waiting room.

The boy looked solemn. His fists were jammed into his jacket pockets. When he put on some more weight he'd be a nice-looking kid. Mark was going to make it. One down, a million more to go.

"You feel better now? You've seen him and he's going to be okay."

"Yeah, looks like. What a relief. Man, I was scared. People get sick, they die and . . . he's such a neat old guy. I . . . guess . . . I guess I'm gonna . . . I guess I'm gonna go back to school," he finished in a small voice.

For a moment Andrew couldn't believe what he was hearing.

"*School!* Mark! That's wonderful. When did you decide that?" He had slopped hot coffee all over his hand and grabbed a paper napkin from the cart to start mopping at it.

"When I was out here waitin' forever, you know. He keeps bringin' it up alla time. So I figured, you know . . . so I thought, okay. I'll do it. So I told him it's a deal. I said . . . I made the deal . . ."

A look of mingled alarm and disbelief began to dawn in Mark's eyes.

"O-o-o-oh-h-h, yuck!"

# CHAPTER 16

The Saturday morning after Father Leffingwell was released from the hospital, he and Mark put together the replacement windshield wiper assembly. They stood in the garage watching it swing briskly back and forth, as they scrubbed the worst of the grease from their hands with Father Leffingwell's collection of wipe rags. Mark got into the VW and turned off the wipers and then the engine. Father Leffingwell had never felt better in his life.

"You know, Mark, it isn't going to be that much trouble going back to school," he said, resuming a conversation they had started while working.

"You never had a problem getting out of seventh grade," Mark said, suddenly glum again. "When do I hafta go back?"

"Not until the fall term, in September."

Mark brightened. "How come?"

"I want you to be ready. I'm going to get some textbooks and tutor you all summer. And, if I do say so myself, I'm a very good teacher. When you go back to school you will be ready and you can handle it."

"Man. Can you really do that?"

"Yes. Trust me." Mark didn't know it yet, but, among the daily lessons would be an extensive vocabulary drill which, Father Leffingwell hoped, would replace Mark's saltier, all-purpose words not normally suited to the classroom. Mark was an intelligent boy, and opening up his lively mind to the joys of language and learning was going to be a labor of love.

Maybe by the time Mark's birthday came around, he would be ready for a Scrabble set as well as his new TV.

The boy wasn't out of the woods yet, but he was having fewer nightmares and fewer sleepless nights. Doug Ahern had been able also to diminish the strength of the anti-depressants.

"You're getting company again," Mark said, as a car drove into the driveway. "Lotsa company," he added as a van with several people in it stopped at the curb.

"Good Heavens, what's this?" Father Leffingwell said.

"More handouts, maybe," Mark answered hopefully. Since Father Leffingwell's release from the hospital, there had been another deluge of home-cooked food from the parish women and the fridge and freezer were well stocked. He and Mark had been eating very well or, as Mark put it, "high on the hog."

Mark ducked back into the garage, and Father Leffingwell walked around the side of the house to greet the people getting out of the car and van. He began to recognize parishioners who seemed to be led by Greg Talbott. His heart sank. It was a good representational group from the church's liberal to radical contingent. Were they going to attack Andrew?

"Good morning," he said cordially. "Forgive my appearance. I've been doing some work on my car." He was in his old corduroy pants and plaid shirt. "Come inside and give me a minute to wash up a little better."

"Forgive us, Father," Greg Talbott said, "for barging in on you like this unannounced, but we've been having an impromptu meeting and we needed to talk to someone about it." Greg Talbott was stressed. He didn't look as impeccably neat as he usually did.

Father Leffingwell took the crowd in by the front door, with a quick glance around. Mark had dusted yesterday and vacuumed the day before. The place looked pretty good. "While I clean up, perhaps some of you could put a few of the dining room chairs into the living room." He was recognizing more faces now. "Would you like me to make a big pot of coffee?"

"I can do it," volunteered several people, as others began to rearrange the living room.

He washed as quickly as he could and then hurried into his bedroom to change his clothes. They could wait another five minutes. If he was going to have to do battle for Andrew, he might be more effective doing it in his clericals. Thank Heavens he had shaved.

When he came into the living room, two men and a woman were bringing in a tray of the white crockery mugs plus milk and sugar, and he could smell the coffee. It was almost noon and he had a ton of food so he could probably invite them all to lunch. But prudence dictated that he wait until he heard them out. There might be fireworks. Unobtrusively, he took a count. *Eleven* people. Eleven people were a committee, no doubt about it. And it could only be about Andrew.

When everyone was seated he took the initiative. Long experience had taught him this was the way to go when in doubt. "I'm delighted to see you all on this non-Sunday morning," he began, and there was a murmur of appreciative laughter. "So let me do my priestly thing and open our meeting with a prayer. Shall I?" Without waiting for an answer he bowed his head, and began an abbreviated version of the prayer to be used in times of conflict. Trust the beloved prayer book for whatever you needed.

"O God, You have bound us together in a common life. Help us, in the midst of our struggles to confront one another without hatred or bitterness, and to work together with mutual forbearance and respect, through Jesus Christ, our Lord. Amen."

The soft "amens" of eleven people echoed his and there was a rustling of movement among them. They wanted to get down to business. Greg Talbott stood up, holding his coffee mug with his hands clasped around it like a child. "I guess I'll come right to the point. First, of course, we're glad you're doing so well. If you weren't we wouldn't bother you with this. But, you see . . . are you aware of some . . . of the talk, the gossip, going around about Father Cullen?"

"It has come to my attention, yes."

"Well, we . . . those of us who were hoping that Kim . . . we've been feeling pretty upset about all this . . . all this . . ."

"Say it, Greg!" This came from a young woman in jeans with crinkly blond hair. What's her name? Culpepper? Margo Culpepper.

"Okay," Greg Talbott resumed. "I'm doing a bad job of this, but, you see, Father Leffingwell, we don't like this. We don't like any of it. And we think . . . some have said . . ."

"It's not true. None of it." This came from a man named William Kimbrough who was a regular volunteer with the FOOD PLACE people. "I've known Andy Cullen ever since he came to this parish. Everything they're saying is a bunch of lies. He's a decent, hard-working man. He's a good priest. I wanted Kim because I wanted a woman priest—I'm all for the feminists making their mark, doing anything they want, but—not if they have to smear somebody else to do it."

"Don't be so hard on her, Bill," Talbott said, looking miserable. An almost angry murmur ran through the group.

A woman in the back spoke up. Alice? Agnes? Agatha Sloan? She stood so everyone would hear her.

"Father Leffingwell, most of us know Andy Cullen and respect him mightily for the work he's doing so well. The more the dirty little rumor circulated, the more we realized how unfair it was, because it's not true. We all know this. So we got together to talk about it. There are probably more of us who feel the same way. We're a kind of ad hoc committee to tell you that we—this group anyhow—have decided to switch our support from Kim to Andy for the rectorship. Greg's going to handle it because he's on the Vestry."

"Thank you, Wilma," Greg said fervently. "You said that a lot better than I could have." He turned to Father Leffingwell. "It's just that we're so . . . sorry about Kim."

There was another angry murmur from the group. It was clear they felt let down, betrayed, and their mood was unforgiving. Poor Kim. She had gambled and lost. Father Leffingwell lifted his hand for silence.

"If Kim was indeed responsible, it was bad judgment,

surely. But I think when she's had time to think it over and pray about it, she'll probably regret it. Let's not stand in judgment. Any harm done, if any has, is to Kim herself, and she's a good learner." There was grudging agreement to this.

"Will the Vestry then formally accept Father Cullen's application?" Father Leffingwell asked.

"Yes," Greg Talbott nodded, still clasping his coffee mug. "We'll work out the details. There's the business about the street kids. He's got Ralph Prescott now and Kimbrough says he knows another person who'll help if she's approached. Then there's the business about the rectory. We can resolve that all right. Then we heard that you're not going back to—uh—Baltimore. And we were wondering if you'd consider part-time. With Cullen as rector, and you assisting, things could be arranged. What do you think of that?"

"That comes as a bit of a surprise," Father Leffingwell said thoughtfully. "Let me think about it a while. Have you mentioned it to Father Cullen? He may have other ideas, you know."

"No. Not yet. We wanted to run it past you first."

"Well, I suggest you speak to him about it first." A great wave of relief was engulfing him. *Andrew was coming into his own.*

They discussed it a while longer and he felt an inward reaching out to them. They had backed Kim so fervently, yet when she fell short, they had the courage to swallow their disappointment, admit their mistake and try to correct it. As Andrew had said—a million pathways. His pathway wasn't theirs. He didn't understand or have any use for their feel-good, anything goes religion. Christianity was not an improvisational faith. You didn't make it up as you went along to accommodate your current wishes. The Ten Commandments were not the ten suggestions or the ten debatable points. They just didn't get it. But he had to like and respect them for hanging on and trying. Maybe some day they would get it.

On impulse, he invited them all to stay for an *al fresco* lunch, courtesy of the church ladies' contributions. All but two could accept the invitation and it became something of a party. The dining room table was large enough, with all the leaves in it, to seat everyone. Mark, immaculately clean now, with his long gleaming blond hair down to his shoulders, pitched in to help. Being liberals, they didn't seem at all surprised that their rector had acquired a street kid as a ward, and Father Leffingwell was pleased that Mark watched his language. At first a bit timid, Mark was soon at ease in the group. Some of the people he already knew from their work in the FOOD PLACE. He did so well that Father Leffingwell began to wonder if *panache* was something you got through your genes and didn't have to learn.

After the ad hoc committee had gone, Father Leffingwell called Andrew and invited him over. They discussed it. "You don't know what a relief this is," Andrew said. "I was really sweating it." They could use the living room, as Mark had dropped out of sight and the TV was silent. They were seated in the rocking chairs in front of the now fireless fireplace. It was the beginning of May and warm enough for the windows to be open. A slight breeze brushed vivid purple rhododendron blossoms against a screen. The rectory garden had masses of rhododendron and azalea as well as other flowers. Newton Crail had pointed out to Father Leffingwell a little patch of wild violets which grew near the garage by the mint patch and the drippy faucet.

"You really do want this rectorship, don't you, Andrew?"

"Very much. Although when you first suggested it, I was positive that parish work was the last thing I wanted." He shook his head.

"I know I've pushed you about it," Father Leffingwell said. "I hope I haven't been too much of a nuisance."

"Well, you're a gifted nag, I'll give you that. But yes, I do know it's what I want now. I pray to God I can handle it. I like their idea about you coming in part-time as assisting priest."

"I'll be seventy soon, and I've already had that one heart attack."

"But they fixed that, Padre. You're good for a lot of years yet. Tutoring Mark isn't going to take that much of your time. He's a smart kid. He's not going to need that much help once he gets going. And remember what Billy Graham said."

Father Leffingwell had to laugh. "Billy Graham's ministry has been a lot broader than mine. You'll have to clue me in on what statement you have in mind."

"I heard him once in a TV interview. The interviewer asked him when he planned to retire. Billy Graham thought about it a moment then he answered. He said, 'I haven't found anything in the Bible yet about retiring.'"

"That's right! That never occurred to me," Father Leffingwell said.

"Of course he's right. This retirement gimmick is fairly recent. People have their God-given talents and abilities, plus their acquired wisdom from just living out the years. Why in the name of Heaven should they suddenly stop using these gifts at an arbitrary age. It doesn't make sense."

"I think you're right. Good. When they offer me the part-time place, I'll take it! We've been a pretty good team so far."

The front door slammed. Mark hadn't yet got the habit of shutting doors quietly, and they both looked at him as he entered the room. There was something different about him.

"Mark!" Father Leffingwell said, "You've had your hair cut!"

"Yeah, what d'ya think?" Mark came into the room with almost a swagger, a look of pleased embarrassment on his face.

"What made you do it, Mark?" Andrew asked in admiration.

"Aw, I dunno." Mark shrugged elaborately. "I thought, well, y'know, goin' back to school and all. Why not? Why not go all the way and look, you know, like a real straight. Like you and Father Leffingwell. How d'ya like it?" He turned this way and that, posing.

"You're a very nice-looking boy," Father Leffingwell said. "And I must say I like you in short hair better than long."

"Yeah." Mark paced up and down the room with satisfaction. "Maybe I won't get a gas station, after all. Maybe I'll be a male model. Who knows? If I can get outa seventh grade, I can do anything."

Both men had to laugh. Mark was, indeed, going to make it, and God bless him.

For Father Leffingwell there ensued an interval of joyful peace. The Vestry made the offer to Andrew of the rectorship and Andrew accepted. They ironed out the details of stipend and housing allowance. He began working with Father Leffingwell rearranging their schedules. Father Leffingwell was feeling so well he was again taking some services and counseling. He moved into the smaller office, leaving the Rector's office to Andrew. Kim took some earned vacation time so they didn't have that worry for the moment. Newton Crail and Mark were scraping old paint off the garage in preparation for the new paint job. Newton also collected second-hand textbooks for several seventh-grade subjects for them and the tutoring sessions were going surprisingly well. And for the first time in Saint Polycarp's history, the Anniversary Dinner of May 3rd was put forward until May 15th so Father Leffingwell could still be the speaker of the evening. He was busy writing his speech in odd moments.

The week after the Vestry called Andrew to the rectorship, Claire Gibson came to the rectory. Father Leffingwell had a good idea what her problem was. He and Mark had finished dinner. He took her into the study. Mark had worked hard in the tutoring session and deserved to relax with his TV programs.

"Sit down, Claire, my dear. Can I get you anything?"

"Nothing, thank you, Father. I just need to talk to you. I need your help." She had been crying and her carefully applied makeup did not completely hide the fact. It had to be about the rectory.

"Sarah Burris told me that you have been very comfortable here," she began tentatively.

"Yes, indeed. I'm sorry things didn't go as you wished. I realize they wouldn't have offered Father Cullen a housing allowance if they hadn't decided to sell this place," he looked around as he said it. "I've really enjoyed living here."

"They've already sold it," Claire said, her lips tight.

"So soon! How could they sell it so quickly?"

"Because I bought it," she said grimly. "I sold some stock and offered them the appraisal price. They accepted, with the approval of the Bishop and the Standing Committee, so I wrote them a check."

"Claire! You didn't. Oh, my dear, what in the world are you going to do with two houses? I suppose you could find a tenant, a large family possibly . . ."

"No! I won't have a lot of strange people running about in here, damaging things . . ." She stopped, on the verge of tears. She strove for control and Father Leffingwell watched her helplessly. Like most, she probably remembered selectively, blotting out the bad things, remembering only the good things, building for herself an idealized version of the past so that she yearned always for that which was long gone, or never had been.

She reached over and passed her well-manicured hand over the surface of a lamp table. "I was with my mother when she shopped for some of these furnishings. I was just a little child, but it was so important that everything in the rectory be just right. I . . . remember this."

"This," the lamp table, was scarred by two deep cigarette burns and multiple scratches and nicks. He doubted if Claire really saw the scars. Her elegant hand left the battered table and she leaned back tiredly in her chair.

"What I wanted to ask you," she said, "is—will you stay on here? They say you're not moving back to Baltimore. I can't leave the place empty. What were your plans exactly?"

"I was going to look for a four-room apartment," he said. "I have the boy now. I've taken on Mark Bascomb as my ward.

I feel quite well after my surgery. I'm confident I can see him through college, at least—get him started. As you know, I'm staying on at Saint Polycarp's part-time."

"Yes, yes. But will you stay *here*, in this house? I must hire some sort of caretaker—and you are already here. I will pay you, of course."

"Claire, no! Certainly not. I couldn't possibly take such advantage of you."

"But I can't leave it empty,." she wailed desperately. "Thieves would carry off everything in a week. Vandals would come and mark up the walls. Squatters would creep in . . ." She began to cry.

Yes, the squatters. For a moment Father Leffingwell could almost smell the stench of the squat where they had found Mark. He got up and went to her, patting her shoulder, giving her his handkerchief.

When she had become calmer, he sat back down. "I might rent it from you," he offered, tentatively. "I'm not sure how much rent would be appropriate for this much room."

"It doesn't matter how much rent," she said tiredly. "If you insist on paying . . . just pay whatever amount you would pay for the four-room apartment. That would probably cover taxes and upkeep. I don't need the money anyway. My father left me . . . well provided for. I have a lot of . . . money." The bleakness in her voice saddened him and told him she had little else.

"Claire," he said gently. "At some point you will have to give this place up. You must begin to think of this."

Her green eyes narrowed. "Vestries come and vestries go. Another Vestry group, down the road a few years . . . I'll just wait them out."

He sat back hopelessly. Claire would stay in her dream world. "All right," he agreed. "I'll rent it from you. It would certainly be a convenience, not having to uproot again and move."

He remained uncomfortable about it after she had gone. They had looked in the rental ads and made a few phone calls to arrive at a figure. But he was resolved that somehow, in the months ahead, he would have to help Claire come to terms with just letting go.

He talked to Andrew over a long lunch the next day. Andrew had brought two deli sandwiches for them to eat in the rec room. There was the faint odor of solvent from Andrew's latest cleaning of graffiti from the NO SKATE-BOARDING sign. Tentatively, he brought up the subject of Melanie, Andrew's estranged wife, hoping not to offend.

"I'm getting a lot of advice on that from my elders lately," Andrew said, trying not to smile. "Theron—my father-in-law, Theron Forbes—brought it up just yesterday."

"Oh, did he? I don't mean to intrude, of course."

"It's no intrusion, Padre. It's okay. Melanie and I have talked about it." He took a bite of sandwich and chewed a while, taking his time. "She wants to try again," he said finally.

Father Leffingwell hardly dared to ask. "And what do you want?" And when Andrew didn't answer immediately, he added, "The honeymoon always ends, Andrew. And you go on from there."

"For better or for worse?" Andrew was quiet again for a longer interval. "I agree, Padre. And I've leveled with Melanie—we've always been honest with each other. If she comes back, it has to be as the Vicar's wife, so she knows that. And she still wants to come back—so wish me luck." From his tone, Father Leffingwell knew that the matter was closed for now. *Trust Andrew. He would deal with it.* Quickly, to change the subject, he plunged into Claire's and his arrangement about the rectory, which still troubled him.

"Take it, Padre. You're doing her a favor. But I agree, Claire could use some counseling on this living-in-the-past thing."

"I'm going to try, but counseling someone who doesn't want to be counseled is a bit iffy."

Andrew laughed. "Well, give it a shot. You'll have more time anyhow. And I went over for my interview with the bishop today. He seemed pleased that I've been called to the parish, and he gave me a lot of advice, some of which I'll take.

I got the feeling while I was there that he's not as much of a wild card as he used to be."

"Perhaps not. People change, grow."

"Which brings me to Kim." Andrew put down his half-eaten sandwich for a moment. "While I was there I brought up the subject of Kim to him."

"Does he know about the business here?"

"He seemed to. I guess his information network is alive and well. He was disappointed in Kim, and he didn't trouble to hide it. But Padre, I don't think Kim should be written off because of one bad judgment call. Mean-spirited though it was."

"I don't either. I've worried about it."

"So I asked Dickie-boy if he could find a place for her, and he thought about it a while, and said he could."

"That's encouraging."

"I told him she intends to resign from Saint Polycarp's as soon as she comes back from vacation. I got that yesterday from Greg Talbott. I told Dick she has no job to go to. Dick said he could make a place for her on his staff. He was going to hire someone anyhow. He's been involved in that ridiculous sexuality study so he's come to know a lot of people in the gay community. He needs someone for outreach to the unchurched gays with AIDS, and also help out in the AIDS hospice."

Father Leffingwell looked off into the distance, remembering Philip in the hospice. He remembered Philip's thin fingers moving the letters on the Scrabble board. Playing little games to hold thinking at bay. He had spoken to a number of the other men there. He remembered the hopelessness behind the wisecracks, the this-is-all-there-is-left undercurrent, the once-strong bodies decaying, and over and under and through everything the relentless smell of dying. *Dear God, they needed hope. Some kind of hope. Maybe Kim could give them that.*

"She would be good at that, I believe," he said, and a silence stretched between them.

"Hey, Padre, come back."

"Sorry. I was thinking about Philip."

"I thought you were. Well, cheer up now. I have a really good bit of news for you."

"Fine. Let's have it."

"I mentioned your work with Mark while I was there. Dick was impressed. I told him I was worried about Mark going into public school in September."

"Why? He'll be well prepared. He's doing just fine."

"It isn't that, Padre. It's that so many public schools are awash with drugs. I've seen too much drug use. I'm not convinced that there is any such thing as full recovery from it. I don't think they can ever kick it completely. Mark's doing well now. He's on medication. He's motivated, and he's leading a sheltered stress-free life. But he has depended on drugs in the past. When he gets out into the world again, has to compete, it's going to be an ongoing struggle for him. I thought if you could get him into a Christian school it would be easier for him, safer. Drugs wouldn't be available from every third kid he passes in the hallways."

"Of course it would be better, but could I afford it?"

"No. But that's not a problem. Dick can get him a scholarship at Saint Aiden's Academy. And he said he would. It's a private church school. Class size—ten pupils, max. Ideal."

"Good heavens, yes! But isn't that a bit posh for Mark? I'm working on his vocabulary, but would he fit in, do you think?"

"Mark's a survivor. He'll fit in. And I think he'll get a charge out of wearing a school blazer with a crest on the pocket."

Father Leffingwell laughed, seeing Mark in September in a crested blazer. Somehow, it seemed absolutely right.

On the evening of the 15th of May—a Thursday—the women had worked all afternoon, setting up the tables in the rec room beneath the church. These were long folding tables, stored folded, between use, in a series of closets along one wall.

Would eleven be enough? They thought surely that it would. Not everybody came to the Anniversary Dinner. At ten place-settings per table, this allowed for a hundred and ten people.

They had covered the tables with white cloths and set out the best china again. Each table had a centerpiece of brilliant spring flowers—one wondered how many gardens had been stripped, and how many hospital rooms would be decked with flowers tomorrow, surprising how many patients.

There was a Eucharist service scheduled for five-thirty and by six-thirty people would be coming down to dinner. Meanwhile, Newton Crail knelt in front of one of the old pews with a hair dryer. He had filled up another lewd carving with plastic wood, painted it quickly and set the dryer to HOT, hoping for the best. Snatches of organ music and singing drifted downstairs as the choir practiced once again their rendition of *Day By Day*, especially requested by Father Cullen.

The women in the kitchen arranged and rearranged the potluck contributions along the buffet table. Plastic-covered dishes had been arriving all afternoon and were still coming. The buffet was almost covered with the cold things; the hot things—staying hot in the two ovens—were yet to be added. Coffee had been put in the coffee urn and tea in the tea urn, with appropriate amounts of water in each. But not plugged in yet—it wasn't time.

And supposing eleven tables weren't enough? Two folded tables leaned, at the ready, against the back wall, with a stack of two more cloths, twenty napkins and two more flower arrangements waiting on the windowsill.

Andrew celebrated the Eucharist with Father Leffingwell assisting. He had preached a short sermon, telling the people some of the things he hoped to accomplish at Saint Polycarp's in the years to come. There was a sense of anticipation and hopefulness. It had been a long and often untidy search and everybody was glad it was over—having found the new Rector in their own backyard, as it were. Was there a lesson here, perhaps? When the last prayer had been prayed and the last blessing said, the people began to stream out of the church past the two priests, and on down both stairways to the dinner below.

By the time Fathers Cullen and Leffingwell had put their vestments in the sacristy and gone downstairs, both extra tables had been set up for the overflow. Many people had already filled their plates and sat down. The coffee and tea servers were beginning to circulate among the tables.

Father Leffingwell, as speaker of the evening, was at the head table. He looked around him, seeing all the now-familiar faces. What a long way he had come in half a year. And what had he done here as God's vicar?

Amid the rising sounds around him of talk and laughter, he tried to think back on his work in this place. There was a shadow of sadness at his failures, but there had been successes. He had brought back into the church some people who had turned away. The Blalock baby would be born. The Griswolds, mother and son, were learning to love each other again. And he and Andrew had salvaged Mark. He felt a wellspring of gratitude that his own day-by-day work—sometimes when he least wanted to do it—had dragged him up out of his own sin of despair, so that his calling had come alive again. He had, after all, done His Father's work to the best of his small abilities—and no more than that had been asked of him. He was filled with a peaceful joy.

The room was crowded with beautiful people. The food was fantastic. The coffee smelled wonderful. It was indeed a time of celebration. This little church—this small portion of the Body of Christ—had stood here for sixty-one years doing its work, and it would stand for many more. He looked across the room at Andrew and they both smiled.

It was like an explosion of happiness—everybody was having a wonderful time. Gloria was seated on his right and he turned to her. She had a new dress and had done her hair differently. Someone was standing behind her, offering her more food.

"No thanks. I've had my limit. I'm a recovering glutton, don't forget." She was laughing.

The next table over was filled with Sunday school children with Mrs. Burris at its head. Father Leffingwell looked for, and found, Lucy Pruitt. She was animated and eager. Peter Pruitt's wheelchair was drawn up at the next table. He was smiling politely, but his eyes still held sorrow. Coming to terms sometimes took a long time, but he was trying.

Irma Blalock, looking serene and very pregnant, was seated at the fourth table down. Her daughter, Diane, had substituted for her mother in helping the women serving. Her job seemed to be coffee cup refills. She hurried among the tables looking for empty cups. She squatted down beside Father Leffingwell's chair for a moment.

"Dad got a promotion at work," she said. "I thought you'd like to know."

"Indeed, yes. That's wonderful news. Is he pleased?"

Diane gave her abrupt laugh. "Yes and no. He says he should have gotten the promotion three years ago but didn't. Musgrave—that's his boss—thought he was over-the-hill. Then Musgrave got the word that Mom's expecting and all of a sudden Daddy's not over-the-hill any more. Daddy says he wished he had got his promotion for the quality of his work and not his sperm count." She bounded up with another bark of laughter. "Glad you're over your heart attack," and hurried off. He had to laugh with her. That odd, funny, graceless girl, with all her rough edges. God's children were all so different.

When the meal was finished, and the clatter of dishes being removed died down, Father Leffingwell rose to make his speech.

Andrew, across the room, watched him. *That dear, wise old man.* Father Leffingwell was frailer now than when he had come. The shining silver hair might be a bit thinner. His patrician face looked a little more tired. His blue-gray eyes moved slowly over the lifted expectant faces, and he began to speak.

"Dearly beloved . . ."

And without even realizing he had said it, Andrew murmured, "*Amen.*"

# About the Author

Virginia Myers has written ten novels for the general market, historical and contemporary, published by Pinnacle, Dell, Fawcett and Harlequin. Several of her books have been translated into other languages. She teaches writing workshops and participates in panel discussions at several writers' conferences. She is an active member of her Episcopalian parish. This is her first Christian novel.